By Gloria Getman
Deena Powers Mystery Series
Lottie's Legacy
Birds of a Feather
A Calculated Risk

Happy Birthday
Barb —

I hope you enjoy
the book

Love
Gloria

Della's Destiny

A coming of age novel

Della's Destiny
Published by Squirrel Creek Books
786 Meadow Ave., Exeter, CA 93221

Copyright © 2022 Gloria Getman

Dedication
To
Marvel Johnson Bennett Boardman
A woman I met only once but whose
picture inspired this book

Acknowledgments

Many thanks to the writers in my critique group:

Arthur Neeson, Judith and Roger Boling, Irene Morse, Carolyn Barbre, Ronn Couillard, Mona Self, Shirley Keller, and Grace Dolton. It is people like these who stick with you when the writing isn't going well, offer encouragement and help you celebrate when the work is done.

A special thanks to Arthur Neeson who managed to keep our group going for over twenty years, who always found a good place for us to meet, and whose talent for finding punctuation errors was first rate.

Chapter One

June 1904
Arizona Territory

Della McCrea listened to the clickity-clack of the train's wheels on the track and stared out the window at the vast Arizona landscape. It stretched for miles in all directions, a baked expanse broken only by clumps of gray-green brush. She'd heard that Indians still lived in this part of the country, so she half-expected to see an encampment out there somewhere with teepees and campfires, and maybe a brave, stripped to the waist, riding a wild horse. But all she'd seen since the train had left Ashe Fork was emptiness.

Shimmering heat danced in the distance outside the window, a withering kind of heat. She leaned her head against the vibrating glass, closed her eyes to the glare of the sun, and dabbed her damp forehead with a handkerchief. Despite the fact that she'd chosen a shirtwaist made of the thinnest fabric, the sleeves still stuck to her skin. How in the world could her father think a place like this would improve her mother's health? He'd told the family the doctor recommended a dry climate. Well, this was dry all right.

The fact that Jerome, where she'd soon be living, had the richest deposit of copper ore in the country, worth millions of dollars, was of little interest to her. Her thoughts returned again and again to her home in Ohio, her music lessons, and the deep blue eyes of Johnny Archer.

She glanced across the aisle at her parents. Her mother's eyes were closed, her head bobbing with the movement of the train. Her father was staring out the window. She wondered what he was thinking. Did he ever have second thoughts about his decisions? It didn't seem so, or if he did, he never expressed them out loud.

She returned her gaze to the landscape and a moment later sensed the train was slowing down. Soon wooden buildings came into view. Della straightened in her seat. Glancing from one side of the train to the other, she saw a depot just ahead. The building was hardly more than a short barn with a wooden boardwalk on either side of it. A collection of smaller wooden structures stood nearby.

The passenger coach groaned and the grinding sound of steel on steel could be heard as the train's engine belched to a stop. Yellow lettering above the depot entrance read *Junction*.

In the past week, she and her parents had changed trains so many times she'd almost lost count, but now it seemed the journey had come to an end.

The other travelers, a dozen men and women, rose from their seats and made their way out of the passenger car, the women raising their parasols against the afternoon sun.

Della stood, put her hand on the seat back as she stepped into the aisle, and bent forward to scan the other buildings. Her pulse surged when she noticed that besides a post office, there was what appeared to be a hotel within walking distance. She envisioned a bathtub, a place to rid herself of the sooty grime she'd acquired during the trip. Even though she and her parents had stopped overnight during the journey, the wash basin gave little relief. The next day brought another dose of soot from coal-burning locomotives that left a quarter-inch of the abominable stuff on every windowsill.

Though anxious to stretch her legs and get a better idea of what the town was like, she hesitated until her parents stood. With a nod from her father, she moved toward the exit. No sooner had she descended the steps from the train when the wind, mixed with sand and dirt, caught her skirt and twisted it around her ankles. She put her hand on top of her straw hat for fear she'd lose it with the next gust and turned in time to see her parents navigate the steps. She didn't wait for them but wormed a path through the milling passengers to the wooden platform.

Looking around, she was amazed to see such a town in the middle of the desert. Besides a complex of sidings, switching yards, and railroad buildings, there were live-stock pens, water tanks, and storage buildings, plus homes, a hotel, two saloons, and what looked like a school.

Noise from a flurry of clanking activity erupting along the railway siding and drew her attention. Men wearing overalls and light blue shirts emerged from adjacent buildings and pulled empty handcarts next to the train's boxcars as the doors rolled open. Crates and wooden barrels from within were hustled onto the waiting carts and wheeled away, while others of similar design hastened to move into position.

As her parents approached, her father pointed to a wooden bench positioned against the outer wall of the depot. "You can wait over there," he said. "I must see that our luggage is unloaded before this train heads back to Prescott." He marched off toward the baggage car, his coattails flapping in the wind.

"Where is the mine where Father will be working?" Della asked, taking her mother's arm as they neared the bench.

Anna McCrea patted her daughter's hand before sinking onto the seat. "Not here, thank goodness. We have another short train ride up the mountain to Jerome. I understand it's a growing community."

Her mother pulled a handkerchief from the draw-string bag she always carried, covered her mouth, and coughed several times. The fact that her cough occasionally brought up a tinge of blood had not gone unnoticed by Della. She made a silent plea to God that this drastic change in their lives would prove worthwhile.

Her mother had become so thin in the last year that all of her clothes had to be altered, a task that had fallen to Della. And now, even her gloves didn't fit her hands as they should.

Her father soon returned with a dark-skinned man who was pushing a cart that held their steamer trunks, suitcases and satchels, parked it, and when he had received a few coins for his trouble, moved off to help another passenger.

"Look. There's local produce," Della's mother remarked when two horse-drawn wagons loaded with boxes of fruit and vegables began to arrive from an adjacent roadway.

Della's father removed his hat, wiped his brow with his coat sleeve, and replaced it. "Everything entering or leaving Jerome is hauled by United Verde's narrow-gauge railway," he said. "There is no adequate road. It's the only means to get people and goods to the town. All the supplies for the mines come from up north and have to be loaded onto the company railroad to reach the town."

Della barely heard her father's explanation. Her attention had been drawn to a man with a rifle as he came into view in the doorway of one of the rear train cars. He wore a broad-brimmed hat and a plain gray shirt with a blue kerchief around his neck. Stepping down onto the roadbed, he squinted and gazed up the track. She wondered what was in the car that needed to be guarded.

A shrill whistle made heads turn as a smaller locomotive appeared coming from the opposite direction. It chugged to a stop on the opposite side of the depot and people started moving in that direction. Della and her mother followed.

It had barely halted when the workmen tending the carts and wagons moved into position to transfer their loads onto the smaller train's flatcars.

A man wearing dark gray trousers and a vest swung down from between the passenger cars onto the railroad bed of the smaller train.

Her father approached him. "I say there, my family and I are headed for Jerome," he said, motioning toward Della and Anna who'd followed him to the other side of the depot platform. "Is there someone to help me transfer our luggage?"

"Sure," the conductor said. "Tote your cart on over to the door of the rear coach. There's room in there." He removed his slouch hat and used it to attract the attention of a stocky fellow in tan coveralls. When the man responded, he said. "Give this here fellow a hand, will you, Joe."

Della and her mother watched as her father and the other man pushed the cart into place and struggled to transfer their steamer trunks from the cart to get the steamer trunk hoisted through the doorway of the baggage car. The smaller pieces took less effort, and when the transfer eas complete her father passed the man a few coins.

By then Della's attention had shifted again to where the guard held his rifle ready for action. He didn't look at the two men who passed four metal boxes and several canvas bags from the mail car into the smaller train's rear car. With his back to them, his narrowed eyes surveyed the gathering of passengers on the platform. As soon as the men who had loaded the boxes finished, the guard hoisted himself inside and closed the door.

"Seems like it might be payday at the mine," Joshua said as he rejoined his family.

After a bit, the engine of the Santa Fe, Prescott and Phoenix train in which they'd arrived, groaned and puffed. The wheels strained to turn, and soon the cars clanked into motion and started moving on down the track. Della watched it as chugged off and finally disappeared behind a distant ramshackle building. She sighed, knowing it was headed back to what she considered civilization.

Shaded her eyes, she gazed across the desert floor to where mountains rose like huge lumps of blue-gray coal. "Is that our destination?" Della asked.

"They're called the Black Hills," Joshua McCrea said, taking his wife's arm. "Come on. Let's get ourselves on board,"

They followed as people clustered and waited for a turn. Della followed her parents and lifted her skirt to negotiate the steps into the open vestibule and followed her parents into the coach.

The narrow wooden seats filled quickly as people filed down the aisle ahead. Her father indicated a place in the middle and took the seat next to the window, removed his brown derby hat and placed it on his knee. Her mother gathered her skirt and settled beside him.

Della considered the long narrow bench that took up much of the left side of the coach. It looked very uncomfortable, so she slid onto the empty seat across the aisle from her parents.

She turned her gaze to watch other passengers find places to sit. Among them were two burly men who moved into a rear-facing seat near the entrance. One in particular caught her notice. He was of ordinary height and had immense shoulders covered by a dull brown shirt. His bushy mustache only partially hid a scar on his left cheek. The sight of him gave her the shivers, especially when he glanced in her direction. She thought his scowl was probably a permanent part of his dark features. His companion wasn't as tall or as broad-shouldered but had the same swarthy complexion.

Della leaned out the window. "Excuse me, sir," she called to the conductor who turned at the sound of her voice. "There aren't any outlaws around here, are there?"

He removed his trilby hat and wiped the back of his hand across his brow. "Sometimes, Miss. Sometimes."

Chapter 2

The thought of outlaws brought an image of flashing guns to mind, like those she'd seen on the covers of dime novels her brother, Lon, was so fond of. Surely her father wouldn't risk their safety by bringing them to a place that harbored such people.

With a quick glance to the rear of the train where the last of the crates and boxes of produce were being loaded, Della returned her attention to the interior of the car in time to see a young lady pause in the doorway. The pale green dress the girl wore engendered a mixture of envy and admiration in Della as she noted the matching parasol in her gloved hand and the hat box that dangled from her other hand. A green straw hat topped her honey-colored curls with a feather attached to the crown. It bobbed as she stepped forward.

It wasn't just the girl's attire that Della thought striking. She'd seen fashionably dressed women back home many times. It was the way the girl ambled along, stopping to greet two older women, delaying another passenger as if she owned the railroad.

After swishing past, Della heard her speaking to the

conductor.

"Tom, would you please find a place for these?"

"Certainly, Miss Blocker," he replied.

Presently, Della felt a tap on her shoulder. "May I join you?"

Della turned in surprise. "Of course." She scooted over to make room for the newcomer.

Once seated, the girl smiled and extended her hand. "I'm Vesta Blocker," she said. With a little giggle, she continued. "Actually, my name is Victoria, but when I was a baby, my brother called me something that sounded like Vesta and it stuck."

Della thought the girl was unusually friendly with a stranger, but smiled and took her hand. "I'm Della McCrea."

"My father is William Blocker," the newcomer said with a note of pride.

The name meant nothing to Della.

"He's the manager of this railroad," she continued as if to jog Della's memory.

Della twisted in her seat to introduce her parents. Her father obliged by nodding in Vesta's direction. Her mother raised her head and gave the young woman a nod and weak smile.

Turning back around, Della suddenly felt dowdy next to Vesta's elegance and self-assured manner. Her much-washed blue skirt was two shades lighter than her gloves. She also wished she'd followed her mother's advice to attach a lace collar to her striped shirtwaist. Her white straw hat was fashionable enough but was embedded with soot.

"I hope I'm not being too forward," Vesta said, interrupting Della's thoughts, "but your mother looks weary. May I have Tom find a cushion for her? It's a twenty-six-mile run to Jerome, and she might be more comfortable. These seats soon feel like stone."

"That's very kind of you. This trip has been very hard on her."

Vesta rose and spoke quietly to the round-faced conductor. No sooner had he passed a cushion to Della's mother than a whistle blasted and the train lurched forward.

Settled again, Vesta said, "I'm just returning from my aunt and uncle's ranch in Green Valley. It's on the other side of the river. They treated me to a shopping trip to Prescott. That's where I found this hat." She touched her fingertips to the brim.

"It's very attractive," Della said, thinking it must have cost a considerable amount.

"May I ask? Are you and your parents visiting Jerome or planning to stay?"

"We're just arriving from Ohio. My father is to be one of the foremen at the mine. But mainly, we're here because of my mother's health."

Vesta nodded her understanding. "I just know you are going

to love living here."

As the train picked up speed across the flat valley floor toward the mountains ahead, Della glanced at the arid landscape and wondered how anyone could love it. The heat must have affected the girl's mind.

"I'll bet right now you think you've come to the worst place on earth," Vesta said as if reading Della's thoughts. "You're going to be surprised. For instance, this train is special. Mr. Clark, the owner of United Verde Mines, bought the equipment from the Baldwin Locomotive Works. It came all the way from Philadelphia. And then last year, he had the engines switched to use fuel oil. No soot," she said with pride. "And in Jerome, we have all the up-to-date conveniences, running water, electric lights and telephones. There are two churches, live theater, and we even have opera performances." She paused for a breath. "Do you know where you'll be living?"

"I believe we're to stay in a boarding house until our furniture arrives. Even after we're settled, it's not likely I'll have much time for social activities, what with household duties and my mother's illness."

"Surely, you'll have hired help." Vesta's blue eyes widened. "There's plenty available."

"Perhaps," Della said. "However, I'm well-schooled in the domestic arts. Mother felt it was important for all young women to understand how a household should be run." Della didn't want to admit that her father thought that with three daughters under his roof, there was no need to pay for extra help.

"Unfortunately, there aren't many folks our age in town," Vesta said. "The younger ones are in school. And the older, well, my brother Percy and his friends are great fun, but they are off at college. Percy is studying to be a mining engineer. He won't be home until July. Everyone is very nice, but most are much older or married. There are the miners, of course, but Father won't let me associate with them."

Vesta continued to chatter, pointing out the window to draw Della's attention to the local flora, naming the cottonwood, sycamore, and later, the mesquite. As she did, Della realized that Vesta really wasn't snobbish, as she'd first assumed. Perhaps they could be friends.

"Do you have brothers and sisters in Ohio?" Vesta inquired.

Della nodded. "I have two brothers and two sisters, all older than me."

"You're lucky. I have only Percy. Will they be joining you?"

"No. My oldest sister is married, has three boys and a baby girl. Lizzie, the next youngest, is a teacher in Portland, Indiana. My brothers, Lon and Richard, are at home in Dayton and have employment there. Aunt Gertrude, my father's sister, is keeping house for them. She's a widow."

Vesta gazed at her with interest while Della described at length the Victorian home she loved so much, her piano, and the school she had attended.

Della glanced in her father's direction to see if he was listening and lowered her voice. "My ambition is to be a concert pianist and travel around the country. But Mother thinks that I should get married or be a teacher like Lizzie. I begged Father to let me stay behind. I thought my aunt could travel with them and look after Mama. But Father wouldn't hear of it, said it wouldn't be proper." Della's voice wavered. "I hated leaving home and all my friends."

Vesta laid her gloved hand over Della's. "I'll introduce you around. You'll soon have new friends. There're many things to do in town. The Fourth of July is the greatest celebration all year. And during August, our church sometimes gets a group together to go for a picnic in the gulch or at Peck's Lake."

Vesta's description of local events served to distract Della while the train began the steady climb. It soon negotiated the first of the 180 or more curves and switchbacks. The dizzying heights, however, could not be ignored. She closed her eyes when the train passed over a trestle above a canyon, or alongside one of the ragged drop-offs that made her head swim. As they neared the upper reaches of Woodchute Mountain, she stole a glance at her parents. Her mother had her father's arm in a death grip, and her father's face was fixed in grim determination.

"Do people make this journey very often?" Della asked through gritted teeth.

"Many do." Vesta smiled a knowing smile. "The train runs six times a day."

After a while, the train track leveled out. "This is the top," Vesta pointed out. "It's all downhill from here."

And indeed, it was. While the incline had been slow and steady, the descent was swift. Della couldn't help but grip the edge of her seat as the train rattled and jolted down and around the curves. Finally, it slowed and made sounds of an exhausted effort as it pulled the final grade and heaved to a stop on a level area next to a wooden building.

Della sucked in a breath. "Is this it? Is this Jerome?"

"Yes," Vesta replied, "but we must transfer to a coach now." She indicated the two horse-drawn wagons up ahead. "It's just a short ride down to town."

Della gave the wagons a quick glance, but then noticed a row of buildings in the distance at a lower level with towering metal stacks that were billowing gray smoke.

She pointed to them. "What's that?"

"The smelter," Vesta responded. "A hot, disagreeable place."

"And that smoking strip on the hillside lower down?"

"That's the roasting levels," Vesta explained as they rose

from their seats. "The rock has to be cooked before it goes to the smelter to separate the copper from the other metals. We studied all about it in school."

They stepped into the aisle behind Della's parents and followed them toward the exit. As they approached the doorway, Vesta retrieved her hat box and parasol from a coat hook.

While waiting their turn, a low rumble was heard, and the ground shook beneath the train. Della grabbed the handrail beside the door. Her mother gasped and Della reached out to steady her. When the shaking subsided, she turned to Vesta, wide-eyed. "What was that? An earthquake?"

Vesta smiled. "No. It's just the blasting down in the mine. It happens all the time. You'll soon get used to it."

Della blinked and shook her head. "I don't think so."

Chapter 3

The idea that the earth could shake at any time was a bit unnerving to Della. She felt an urge to escape the train but forced herself to stand behind her mother and watch as her father exited the passenger car, donned his hat and offered a hand to assist his wife.

As soon as Della set foot on the ground, she glanced at the faces of the other passengers. None of them acted upset by the incident. These people must have nerves of steel, she thought. Indeed, they seemed unfazed and rushed off as if their only focus was the final leg of their journey.

The travelers hurried to the first of two coaches lined up in front of the small depot, a wooden building a third the size of the one at the Junction.

Della viewed the conveyances with a critical eye. Except for a canopy on the first one, they looked like ordinary buckboards with thin wooden wheels and shallow beds, not much different from the ones her Uncle Herman still used on his farm to haul pumpkins to market.

"It's cooler here," Della's mother remarked. She lifted her skirt and picked her way over uneven ground.

"Yes, ma'am," Vesta said as she followed along toward the first coach in line. "It's rarely very hot, except in August."

The coach driver on the bench behind the first team of horses was a short fellow in a wide-brimmed hat. He held a tight grip on the reins. The passengers chattered and climbed on board, filling the bench seats in the rear first.

Della and Vesta waited again while Joshua navigated the narrow wooden step, turned and took his wife's hand to assist her. He chose a bench at the front of the coach, and as soon as they were settled, leaned forward to speak to the driver.

Della lifted her skirt, climbed in and scooted over on the second bench to make room for Vesta. When Vesta was seated, she said, "I'd be very happy to give you a tour of the city tomorrow if you think your parents would allow it. I could ask my mother for the use of her buggy."

What Della really wanted to do was to get back on the train and leave Jerome, but since that wasn't an option, she decided it would be rude to decline the invitation. "I'd like that. I'll ask Father, but it will depend on how Mother is feeling in the morning."

Vesta nodded. "I do pray she makes a quick recovery from the trip."

The coach driver twisted around in his seat and looked past Della to the rear of the coach. Della followed his gaze, noting that everyone was seated.

Turning back around, the driver released the brake and flicked his whip. The leather harness on the two horses creaked as the big animals tugged the conveyance into motion. As the coach pulled closer to the point of descent, Della got her first look at what was ahead. It made her gasp. She clutched the edge of the seat beneath her.

The swift, bone-jarring ride down the three-hundred feet of steep dirt road made her teeth rattle. A shriek came from a woman in one of the rear seats.

"People say it's like a carnival ride," Vesta said, her voice vibrating.

Halfway down the slope, the stench of sulfur caught Della by surprise. She held her breath and looked at her mother who made a vain effort to suppress a strangled cough. But within seconds the coach passed to a lower level and the noxious odor was left behind, much to Della's relief.

At the bottom of the hill, the wagon made a turn onto a slag-covered street, and the wheels then rolled along with ease. After a brief interval, the second wagon came clattering down the hill.

It held the trunks, bags and boxes, all piled high and tightly secured with ropes.

Soon, what appeared to be the business district soon came into view. Awning-shaded store fronts lined the street. Boardwalks on either side were crowded with men and women, and all of them gave the appearance of being in a hurry. Some of the buildings looked as modern as those in her hometown, while others tilted on the hillside.

Two slow-moving, mule-drawn wagons obstructed traffic, compelling the coach driver to maneuver around them. And then the tinkling music and laughter could be heard coming from a saloon.

The wagons rumbled along until they came to a halt in front of a tall brick building. Two-foot-high lettering across the front announced the T.F. Miller Co. Two men emerged from inside. The driver of the second wagon secured the reins and hopped to the ground. The three men unloaded several boxes and readjusted the ropes.

The delivery complete, the driver regained his seat, and the horses of both coaches were urged forward on down the sloping street. Several minutes later, the first coach driver pulled back on the reins and brought the coach to a stop in front of a building labeled Hanover House, an unpainted, two-story frame structure with a gallery over the entrance.

Joshua shifted in his seat. "This is where we will be staying."

Della glanced at her mother's expression as she shaded her eyes and squinted at the rustic building. Compared to hotels in Dayton, this was a dismal place. It probably had bed bugs too.

But, so be it. Della was tired of traveling and her mother was obviously worn out. She turned, took Vesta's hand, and forced a smile. "I'm so glad we met."

"Indeed, the pleasure is all mine," Vesta said. "And I'll be delighted to show you around. Perhaps your mother would like to join us."

"That would be really nice if she is sufficiently rested."

Vesta nodded her agreement. "Till tomorrow then."

Joshua slipped past his wife, exited the coach, and hurried back to the rear wagon to point out their baggage.

Della stood, navigated the steps to the surface, then turned in time to see her mother, on the brink of exhaustion, waver. She offered her hand for support and assisted her mother to the boardwalk at the entrance of the building.

Della opened the door and just as they entered, a woman of ample size appeared. Joshua stepped in through the doorway behind them and removed his hat. "Mrs. Sayers?"

"Yes, Mr. McCrea. I've been expecting you. And this must be your wife and daughter." She nodded to them with a welcoming smile. "I hope your journey wasn't too difficult."

Della sensed that the woman's sharp eyes had caught her mother's fatigue.

Mrs. Sayers turned her attention to Joshua. "I received your letter and bank draft. Your room is on the second floor just at the top of the stairs. My sons will bring up your trunk." She handed him a key.

Joshua cleared his throat.

Della figured he was about to protest the second-floor room knowing climbing the stairs would be a trial for her mother. But Anna put her hand on her husband's arm, a signal that silenced him before he spoke, a gesture Della had observed before. Her parents had been married so long, it seemed, that sometimes no words were needed to communicate.

Curious about their temporary lodging, Della looked both left and right. A dining room could be seen through a doorway on one side of the entrance hallway. It held a banquet-sized table with seating for at least twelve. On her right was a small, but surprisingly well-furnished parlor with an elegant dark green settee, several cushioned chairs, a table with a lamp, plus a bookcase.

"Don't gawk," her father said, motioning her to follow them up the narrow stairway. Halfway up the flight, her mother paused and took a deep breath. Della wondered if she would be able to climb the full length. However, her father took her arm and she managed.

They paused at the top for Joshua to open the door to their room. Once inside, Anna all but collapsed into the nearest chair. Della rushed to her side, but her mother waved her off. "I'll be all right in a minute."

Della's father looked around the room and nodded. "This will do," he said.

Della took in their surroundings in one sweeping glance. The room appeared to be clean and the rugs relatively new, though the furnishings were sparse. Three lounge chairs were positioned around a reading table with an electric lamp. The fact that the drab-looking building had electricity was something Della hadn't expected.

She stepped to the doorway of a second room. Two brass beds crowded the smaller space, each with a colorful but thin coverlet. An electric fan sat on top of a highboy chest, with a three-drawer dresser nearby, plus two straight-backed chairs located against the wall. A washstand with a basin and large pitcher stood next to one of two windows which had been left open to freshen the air.

The sound of thumping and grumbling came from out in the hall, followed by a knock at the door. Her father stepped over to open it. Two young men in plain shirts and dark pants supported by suspenders commenced to wrestle the McCrea's belongings inside the room. When all of it, the trunks and several bags, were stacked inside next to the door, Joshua gave them a few coins and they hustled off down the stairs.

He turned to Della. "See to your mother's comfort. I have some errands to take care of." He stepped out into the hall and closed the door.

With some effort, Anna rose from the chair. "I suppose we should unpack."

"I'll do that," Della said. "You need to rest before dinner. Let me help you undress."

Anna gave a weary nod. "I confess, I *am* tired."

Della took a tan satchel from the stack of baggage, followed her mother into the bedroom, and set it on one of the straight-backed chairs.

Her mother removed her hat and placed it on the dresser along with her drawstring bag and her gloves. Della removed her gloves, placing them and her bag beside her mother's. She pulled a loose gown from the satchel and laid it on the bed.

Anna gave her daughter a weak smile as she helped her out of the dress. She untied and loosened the laces of the corset back and watched her mother fumble with the front fasteners. How uncomfortable it appeared to Della, especially the way it made her mother's back curve unnaturally. Her sisters thought such garments were necessary to look fashionable, so she expected it wouldn't be long before her mother would take her shopping for one.

Della picked up the dress and draped it over the back of the chair, then took up the gown and held it out for her mother. Anna gladly slipped it on and stretched out on one of the beds. She closed her eyes and within a minute, the pattern of her breathing indicated she was asleep.

Della gazed at the woman who had once been strong enough to manage a huge house and five children. Her dearest hope was that the change of climate would prove worth the exhausting trip.

Chapter 4

Della pulled the hairpins from her hat, removed it and laid it on one of the chairs. She pushed up the sleeves of her shirtwaist, went to the washstand and poured water from the large pitcher into the washbowl. As she washed her face and hands, she wondered if there was a water closet in the building or if they would be forced to use an outside privy. Surely her father wouldn't put them in a boarding house without proper facilities. Maybe it was behind that door she'd noticed at the end of the hallway. If it was, she suspected that it wouldn't be anything like the accommodations at home where she'd availed herself of the big white claw-foot tub.

After drying her face and hands, she proceeded to unpack her valise, placing her clothing in the dresser, and continued with the other bags. She hoped they wouldn't be staying in the boarding house long enough to need the contents of the trunks. But what sort of house would her father find in a town like this? From the train, she'd seen, lower on the hillside, some canvas-sided structures that looked like they were being lived in.

A sudden loud braying startled her. The noise brought her to the closest open window. She looked out and below she saw the broad back of a burro wandering along an embankment. She shook her head. A very curious town indeed.

Lingering at the window, the muted sound of music came to her ear. She looked off to the distant valley where the tops of green trees could be seen. But why were there no trees along the roads or next to houses in town? Another curiosity, she decided.

The light of her first day in Jerome was fading. Shadows were beginning to form. Della felt like her life was in shadows as well. Her thoughts drifted to what evenings at home had been like not so long ago when her family would gather on the broad front porch of their home to relax in a comfortable chair or rocker. A breeze would often come up from the river to drive away the humidity of the day. Murmured conversations recounted the day's events. And sometimes, before dusk, she and her brothers might play a game of croquet.

And later, if she stood in the dark on the porch with her father, she'd see the lights in houses around the neighborhood, one by one, begin to come on. It was a comfortable neighborhood, where people were more or less alike, orderly and sincere. Her father would soon tap the ashes from his pipe against the porch post, a signal that it was time for them to go inside.

Della heaved a sigh. Tears clouded her vision. Her mother's illness had changed everything. For reasons she didn't understand, her mother had developed a nagging cough. Soon, she barely touched her food. The result was a gloom that hung over every family meal.

A change had come over her father too. He'd always been a man with a ready smile and quick to relate a humorous story. He'd grown more serious, his smiles gone. And then, in less than a year, both her sisters left home. She supposed that was normal, but the house fairly echoed without them.

Her father's announcement that they were going to Arizona and that Aunt Gertrude would be coming to stay and keep house for her brothers, stunned Della. Her heart ached, remembering his stern pronouncement when she pleaded to stay behind. "Now, Della, don't whine. Your mother needs you and it's your duty."

A tear trickled down her cheek. If only she could have stayed at home, she just knew Johnny Archer would have come to call. Maybe he'd have taken her to the church social. Maybe he would have kissed her too.

The burro brayed again. Della shook her head. This town will *never* feel like home. Mother just *has* to get well. But how long will it take; weeks, months, years? The thought of years in this strange place sickened her. She lifted her chin and wiped away the tears with her fingertips.

Footsteps on the stairs outside the room echoed in the hall. The sound jarred her out of her meandering thoughts. It was suppertime, she realized. Anticipating her father, she moved to meet him.

"Mother is sleeping," she whispered as he entered. "Should I wake her? She's hardly eaten anything all day."

Joshua McCrea nodded and hung his hat on the rack by the door. "She'll feel like eating when she's rested. Let's go to the dining room. I'll ask Mrs. Sayers to prepare a tray for your mother."

They moved out into the hall, their steps echoing as Della followed her father down the pine staircase.

"I've located a house for us," he said to her. "We can move as soon as the furniture arrives. Things will be better when we're settled in our own place. I've also located a doctor. If your mother feels up to it, he will see her tomorrow."

Chapter 5

Sunlight reflecting off the bedroom walls woke Della the next morning. She turned over, raised herself on one elbow, and squinted at her parent's empty bed. They were already up and dressed. How had they slept through the racket she'd heard in the streets below during the night?

"About time you woke up, young lady," Anna said through the doorway to the sitting room. Her father was seated in a cushioned chair, his glasses perched on his nose, studying a sheaf of papers. He laid the papers on the marble-topped table at his elbow and rose. "I'll wait for the two of you downstairs." Glancing in her direction, he pulled his watch out of his vest pocket, scowled at it, and returned it to its place. "Be quick about dressing, Della. Your mother and I have an appointment with a doctor." He disappeared from view, and she heard the door to the hall open and close.

Grateful her father was sensitive about her privacy, Della slid from under the light coverlet and went to the wash bowl, poured out some water, and washed her face. After drying on the linen towel left for that purpose, she slipped out of her nightgown and into her undergarments. She took her blue skirt from the hook where she'd hung it the night before and pulled it over her head. It was the same skirt she'd worn the day before and the day before that. Her dresses were in one of the trunks along with the rest of her belongings.

Her mother entered the room, withdrew a shirtwaist from the bureau, and handed it to her. Della hurried to put it on and buttoned the shirt as fast as she could, tucking it into her skirt. Her father might respect her modesty, but he was not a patient man. She fetched her hair brush from the dresser top and began brushing her dark brown hair.

Her mother watched. "You're growing up so fast," she said, taking a ribbon from the dresser and holding it out for Della to use.

Della pulled her hair back and tied it with the ribbon. "When am I going to be allowed to put my hair up?"

"Don't be in such a hurry, dear. You'll be a grown woman long enough. I like your hair that way. You can wait until your birthday. Come along. We mustn't keep the other guests waiting."

Della forced herself not to scowl, thinking her mother wanted her to remain a child, while her father couldn't wait for her to be grown and assume a woman's work.

As soon as they stepped out into the hall, the aroma of breakfast was detected. Della made a motion toward the doorway at the far end of the hall. Her mother nodded and followed her.

Having relieved themselves, the two descended the stairs to the dining room.

The table Della had seen the day before was covered with a white linen tablecloth and set with a handsome blue China service similar to her grandmother's dishes.

Her father, along with four men and three women were already seated. Della and her mother took their places and Joshua introduced them to the other boarders. Each one in turn smiled and nodded in greeting and introduced themselves.

Conversations already in progress when Della and her mother entered, resumed. Della spread a linen napkin across her lap and glanced at the faces. The men looked older than her father, the women at least as old as her mother. No one there was her age.

Surveying the table, she saw a bowl of hard-boiled eggs and a jar of jam. A cube of butter the size of a brick waited on a plate for guests to help themselves.

Mrs. Sayers came bustling through a swinging door from the kitchen. She wore a white baker's apron over a light blue dress and carried a large coffee urn.

"Good morning, everyone," she said in a cheery voice.

Circling the table, she poured strong-smelling coffee into the cups in front of each person.

A woman, much younger than Mrs. Sayers, entered from the kitchen. She carried a platter heaped with sausages in one hand and a plate of biscuits in the other. As soon as she'd set both down on the table, she hurried back through the door and returned with a bowl of steaming gravy.

A bald man at the end of the table reached for the biscuits, put a couple on his plate, and passed the dish to the woman next to him. "Mr. McCrea. What brings you to Jerome?" he asked in a voice deep.

While Joshua related his new foreman's position in the mine, the guests helped themselves to the biscuits. The large bowl of gravy went from hand to hand, followed by the one filled with hard-boiled eggs. Additional dishes were added to the fare: fried potatoes, fresh peaches, and a plate of cinnamon-scented sweet rolls.

Paying little attention to the others, Della stabbed a sausage with her fork and placed it on her plate, then plucked a biscuit from the platter as it passed. She sliced the biscuit and topped it with gravy. The first bite fairly melted in her mouth and brought back memories of her grandmother's buttermilk biscuits. How did Mrs. Sayers get her grandmother's recipe?

The woman seated on Della's right spoke. "Miss McCrea.

Will you be attending school here?"

Della shook her head, swallowing the piece of biscuit in her mouth. "No," she said, keeping her voice in a low confidential tone. "My mother's health is poor. I'll be taking care of the household."

"A pity," the woman said. "I understand there's a very fine school."

The urn of coffee was brought around the table a second time and cups refilled. Everyone at the table was quietly enjoying the meal, including Della, though she noticed her mother had cut her biscuit into quarters, took a single bite, and pushed the remaining pieces around on her plate, the usual sign of her poor appetite.

Her father, on the other hand, had second helpings of everything and ate with gusto until at last, he laid his napkin on the table and heaved a satisfied sigh. He pulled his watch from his pocket, glanced at it, then nodded to his wife.

"It's time we must leave." He pushed back his chair and rose. "Please excuse us. We have an appointment. Mrs. Sayers, the breakfast was excellent."

Murmurs of agreement came from the other boarders.

Joshua assisted his wife with her chair, and after bidding everyone goodbye, Anna and Della followed Joshua to the front door.

"We'll need our hats and gloves," Anna said, looking at Della. "Run up and get them, would you dear?"

Della dashed up the stairs to the room, snatched the items off the dresser, and returned within moments.

"I've made arrangements for a buggy," Joshua said as they stepped out onto the boardwalk. "Wait here. It'll only take a few minutes to walk to the stable and return." He stalked off down the sloping street.

Anna positioned her hat, removed a pair of gloves from her bag and pulled them on. Della gazed at the cloudless sky and wished she'd had time to avail herself of a second juicy sausage.

A moment later, a two-seated buggy pulled up in front of the building, the driver in a dark suit and bowler hat. Vesta bounded out of the rear seat, her eyes shining with excitement. She was attired in a dark blue skirt and striped shirt, plus a plain straw hat with a small white feather tucked into the band.

"Good morning, Mrs. McCrea. Good morning, Della. I talked my mother into letting me have her buggy and driver today. I'd be ever so happy to give you both a tour of our fair city."

"That's very sweet of you, Vesta," Anna said. "But I'm afraid I am previously engaged. However, I believe Della would be grateful for the opportunity."

"Are you sure it will be all right?" Della asked her mother. The mere thought of a little freedom lifted her spirits.

When Joshua pulled the rented buggy in behind the first, Anna approached him. "This young lady has offered to show Della around town if that meets with your approval."

A crease formed in Joshua's brow, but he nodded. "Be back here by noon," he said to Della.

Della plunked the hat on her head and gave her mother a peck on the cheek. "Thank you."

Chapter 6

The two girls scrambled into the back seat as if someone might change their mind. Once settled, Della smoothed her skirt, pulled on her gloves, and held her purse in her lap.

The driver clucked to the dappled horse, and the buggy started toward the center of town.

"I can't show you everything today," Vesta said, "but I can acquaint you with a few places I think will interest you." Vesta leaned forward and spoke to the driver. "Thomas, please take us along Main Street." She turned to Della. "We'll go through the business district first. I want to introduce you to our dressmaker. After that, we'll go to Millie Swanson's house. She's a swell girl and a first-rate friend."

"Thank you. I guess I'll have to learn my way around." As the buggy rolled along, Della took note that the streets wound back and forth down the mountainside. It seemed like a curious way to lay out a town, but she decided not to mention it. Some of the houses sat on flat spots carved out in between the streets, while others, perched on the hillside above were held in place by heavy wooden stilts. Those required a steep stairway to gain entrance. She wondered what sort of house her father would find for them to live in, unable to imagine her mother coping with anything she'd seen so far.

"Where do you live?" Della asked.

"Up there." Vesta pointed in the general direction of a string of houses sitting on terraces above the town. "I don't think you can see our home from here. It has a green roof."

Continuing along, they passed a park with a bandstand and approached the T.F. Miller building where their coach had stopped the day before.

Vesta motioned to it. "The bank and the post office are on the ground floor. The second floor is the mercantile and the third, the opera house. We have a musical or a play in the opera house every month. Year before last, I was an angel in the Christmas pageant. It was so much fun until one of my wings came loose and fell off." She covered her mouth and giggled.

"It sounds entertaining, but it must be quite a climb for the audience." Della was thinking of her mother again.

"Not at all. We have a very nice elevator."

Vesta pointed to a three-story white building on the hill above the town. "That's the hospital. I've heard it has all the up-to-date equipment."

"Father secured an appointment for my mother with the

doctor."

"How fortunate," Vesta enthused. "Dr. Woods is the very best. A few years ago, there was an outbreak of smallpox here, and he developed a cure. I am certain he can help your mother."

"I sure hope so. What is that tall building just ahead?" Della indicated a huge edifice. "It looks like a courthouse."

"Oh no. That's the Montana Hotel. Mr. Clark, the owner of the mine, had it built for the miners. I've heard it's incredibly elegant inside." She leaned forward and spoke to the driver again. "Now to Mrs. Whipple's shop, please."

Vesta squirmed on the seat. "Mother said I could have a new dress for the Independence Day Celebration. I'd like your opinion. That day is the highlight of the summer. There'll be a parade and all kinds of contests. The workmen from the mines have a mucking contest and the firemen race with hose carts. It's just the most fun to watch!"

Della had to admit Vesta's enthusiasm was catching, but she was sure it couldn't possibly come close to the festivities her brothers would be enjoying back home.

Reversing course, the buggy driver deftly maneuvered the buggy around a high-sided mule-drawn wagon before pulling over in front of one of the awning-shaded shops that populated the main business district.

Della glanced around the busy street front and was struck by the mixture of skin tones of people going in and out of the various businesses. Unlike her hometown, many of this population appeared to be from other parts of the world.

"Please wait," Vesta said to the driver. "We won't be long."

Vesta climbed out of the buggy and motioned for Della to follow. She pushed open the shop door, triggering a jingling bell. The two entered a long narrow building where electric light bulbs hung from the ceiling. Wallpaper covering the adjacent walls displayed dark green leaves and sprays of yellow daisies. Pictures of the latest fashions were pinned to the wall along with paper dress patterns. At the rear of the room, three women sat at sewing machines, their feet working the treadles below. Dress forms stood nearby, each covered with garments in different stages of completion.

A plump woman leaning over the table in the center of it all, straightened, removed a couple of pins from between her lips, and stuck them into a rounded pin cushion positioned within easy reach. Strands of the woman's dark hair had worked loose from a tight bun and curled at the nape of her neck.

"Vesta, I'm so glad you stopped in." Her round face broke into a smile. "I received the yard goods for your dress just yesterday." She approached the girls and gave Della an appraising once-over before asking, "Who is this pretty young lady?"

"Mrs. Whipple, I want you to meet Della McCrea. She and her family arrived here from Ohio this week. Her father's going to be one of the foremen at the mine."

"I'm mighty pleased to meet you, Della. I hope you'll soon feel right at home here in Jerome."

As Della took Mrs. Whipple's hand, she noticed the woman's rough fingertips, no doubt due to many needle pricks, an affliction Della was familiar with. Her own fingers had sometimes felt the same when she sewed for her family, especially her brothers' trousers. She smiled. "And I'm pleased to meet you."

Mrs. Whipple motioned to Vesta. "Come and see what I have for you." She turned and led the way to a closet shelf in the back of the room, where she ran her hand down a stack of folded yardage and lifted out a piece. It had wide red, white and blue stripes with little flags printed at intervals.

Vesta reached out to touch it, then turned to Della. "This will be my skirt. My shirtwaist will be white with a blue collar and cuffs, and I'll wear a long red ribbon in my hair. Don't you think it will be elegant?"

"I do, indeed," Della said. "Very patriotic."

"I think so, too," Mrs. Whipple said as she extracted a two-inch roll of red satin ribbon and unrolled a length. "Here's the ribbon." She tilted her head toward Della and lifted her eyebrows. "Perhaps I could make you a dress for the festivities too."

"I packed all my dresses. I'm sure I have one that will be appropriate." A bit of discomfort touched Della. It was a fib. She hadn't had a new dress in over a year, not since the extra expense of her mother's illness.

The bell over the door jingled and drew their attention as a slender woman in a long-sleeved green dress walked in.

Della stared. Her dress wasn't so remarkable. Gibson Girl sleeves and lace collars were common back home. Her black hair, piled high in a pompadour under her hat, wasn't unusual either. It was the woman's dark-rimmed eyes and red lips that drew attention.

"You girls come back tomorrow," Mrs. Whipple said. "I know you have many things to show your new friend." The dressmaker's tone invited them to leave in a hurry.

Vesta took the hint, grabbed Della's arm, and guided her toward the door, giving the new visitor a wide berth.

Once outside Della asked, "What was that all about?"

"That woman is from one of *those* houses near the Connor Hotel."

"What do you mean, *those* houses?"

"You know, where painted ladies lean in doorways and lure men into their establishments."

Della's eyebrows lifted. "Oh, you mean she's a whore."

Vesta gasped.

"Dayton has a section of brothels too. I've heard my brothers talk about it, how it's a very dangerous place."

"It's no different here. There's a stabbing or shooting almost every night."

"Do you know that woman's name?"

"No. And I don't care to. Mrs. Whipple is such a skilled dressmaker that those women want her to make all their clothes."

Della shrugged, glancing down the street to where a man in a brown shirt and dungarees leaned against a power pole. She tugged at Vesta's sleeve. "That's one of the men I saw on the train yesterday. He and his friend didn't get on the coach. I wondered why."

"Where?"

"Over there. The one with the thick eyebrows and mustache."

Vesta gave a sideways glance in that direction, then brusquely grabbed Della's arm, pulling her toward the buggy. "For heaven's sake, don't look at him. Never look at people like that."

"Is he an outlaw?"

"I don't know, but it's not good to draw his attention. Two years ago, a man like him attempted to court the daughter of a hotel owner. The girl's father disapproved and the Mexican ended up getting shot."

Chapter 7

The girls scrambled into the buggy, and Vesta gave Thomas
directions to Millie Swanson's house. He clucked to the horse
and guided the conveyance around to head in the direction
residential part of town.

As they passed the stranger, Della tilted her head and peeked
out from under her hat to get a good look at him. "Is he a
Mexican?" she whispered. "I've never seen a Mexican before. We
have colored in Dayton, but no Mexicans."

"It's hard to tell sometimes," Vesta said. "I've heard my
father say the miners come here from all parts of the world."

The buggy soon made a hairpin turn and rolled along a street
that angled up the hillside. "Millie's father travels a lot," Vesta
said. "He works for Mr. Clark in the big office building. Her
mother is in charge of the Ladies Aide Society at the Methodist
Church. Millie's older brother is a friend of my brother, Percy's.
He's ever so handsome. She also has two little brothers who are
pests."

Della smiled. "I know how that is. I have a friend whose little brother put a frog down the back of my dress."

"Oh, how awful!"

"I had a terrible time getting it out, and it left a streak of mud down my back. But I got even. I pushed him into the fish pond."

Vesta put her hand over her mouth and they both giggled.

"Did you get in trouble?"

"No. His mother said he had it coming."

A few minutes later, the buggy came to a stop next to a wooden staircase. Della glanced at the steps that led to the house on a level area above. A girl with hair the color of molasses stood at the top. She was waving a white handkerchief. "Vesta, hurry. I have lemonade with ice."

Vesta waved back as she fairly jumped out of the buggy and turned to Thomas. "You don't have to wait, but come back for us. We must be sure Della returns to her parents by noon."

The girls lifted their skirts and began the climb. Della thought such an entrance would be an awful chore every day. Any deliveries from the grocer would be rather inconvenient. She hoped her father would find better accommodations for her and her mother.

When Vesta reached the top, she gave Millie a quick hug before introducing her to Della. Millie took Della's hand in a welcoming gesture. "I'm ever so glad to have you visit my home."

It was clear to Della that Millie had dressed up for the occasion. Her puffed-sleeved blue dress looked new, and her hair had been carefully styled in long curls. She escorted the girls along a stone path to the front door, opening it with a sweeping gesture, inviting her guests inside. Light from the two front windows illuminated a parlor with chairs and lamp tables similar to the ones at Mrs. Sayers.

Millie motioned them through a doorway into a dining room where it appeared the table had been set for tea. "Please take a seat," she said. "Would you prefer tea or lemonade? I have both ready."

The girls agreed on lemonade. Millie took a place at the head of the table, filled glasses, ready to pass them to the others. Vesta pulled out a chair and gathered her skirt before sitting. "Della came all the way from Ohio on the train. Isn't that exciting?"

"I'd like to make such a trip," Millie said as she offered a plate of flakey cookies. "I imagine the cities would be very interesting,"

It was evident to Della that Millie was trying to sound very grown up, likely mimicking her mother's manners. She looked at Della expectantly, as if waiting for her to report her adventure.

Della felt hard-pressed to say anything flattering about the cities she'd passed through. About the only things she'd seen were train stations and one or two ordinary hotels.

"Our train passed over a number of rivers," Della said, "the Mississippi being the most impressive all the boats carrying logs from up north." She took a sip of the lemonade and found it somewhat tart than she expected. While trying not to make a face, she decided sugar must be scarce in this part of the country.

"We stopped at Mrs. Whipple's shop," Vesta said. "I wanted Della to meet her. The yard goods for my new dress arrived. I can hardly wait for Independence Day."

"Me neither," Millie chimed in. "And Melvin will be coming home this weekend." She focused on Della. "Mel's my big brother. He's been at college in Phoenix."

A slender woman appeared in the doorway from another room. She wore her blonde hair gathered into a knot on the crown of her head. Her plain dark skirt and white shirt were partially covered with a white apron.

Della rose to her feet thinking she must be Millie's mother.

Millie turned in her chair. "Mother, this is a new friend, Della ... er, ah ..."

"McCrea," Della said with a slight curtsy.

"Pleased to meet you, Mrs. Swanson said. "It's always nice to meet new people when they arrive. Perhaps I'll have a chance to call on your mother soon."

"I hope so—once we are settled in a permanent place and she's feeling stronger." Della was reluctant to mention her mother's illness but felt she had no choice. "We are hoping the dry climate will bring her to good health soon."

Without warning, a boy of about six years landed on his belly in the doorway next to his mother's feet. Above him, peeking around the door frame was the freckled face of an older boy. It was easy to conclude that the younger one had been pushed.

"Mother, you promised," Millie complained.

Mrs. Swanson scowled. "Arthur, get to your feet and properly greet Miss McCrea. You too, William."

After a bit of clumsiness and tucking their shirts into their pants, each boy presented himself at his mother's side and gave a slight bow. "Pleased to meet you, Miss McCrea," they said in unison. Both were on the verge of a snicker, knowing they'd embarrassed their sister. Their sister glared daggers at them.

Though Della kept a straight face, she wanted to laugh. The scene reminded her of her own brothers' antics when her oldest sister had tried to entertain a suitor.

Millie's mother put her hand on the back of each boy's neck, turned them around, and marched them from the room. "Your sister has guests. Behave."

A clatter of footsteps indicated the boys had run off to another part of the house, probably very pleased with their accomplishment, Della thought.

Millie's face was still a bright pink, and Vesta was staring at her half-empty lemonade glass, equally embarrassed.

Della felt sorry for them. "I have brothers too. I understand how troublesome they can be," she said, smiling at her new friends.

Relief flooded Millie's face, but she'd lost the demeanor of the proper hostess. Her brothers had spoiled her party, and it was likely she would exact retribution.

Recovering some of her composure, Millie asked about the boarding house where Della was living. Della described a little of the building but stated that it was only temporary.

The conversation soon fizzled and Vesta rose from her chair. "I think I just heard the tinkle of our driver's bell. I'm sorry, but we must leave. I don't want to make Della's parents wait for her."

Millie walked Vesta and Della to the front door. She followed them to the steps and waved as they descended to the waiting buggy.

All during the drive back to the boarding house, Vesta chattered on about how horrible it was to have little brothers like Millie and how glad she was that her brother was older and had handsome friends. She enthused over the upcoming Independence Day Celebration, promising to introduce Della to Percy. "I do hope your father locates a home for your family soon. I've never lived in a boarding house, but I think living among strangers would feel odd."

"I've never been in one until now. It's much like a hotel, but with family meals."

When the buggy pulled up in front of Hanover House, Della climbed out and turned toward Vesta. "Thank you for showing me around and introducing me to your friend."

"I'll send an invitation. We can make plans for the holiday."

As soon as the buggy and Vesta's waving hand disappeared from sight, Della entered the building and climbed the stairs to the room. She found her mother and father seated in the sitting room. Her father was inspecting his watch again.

"Am I late?" Della asked.

"Not at all," her mother replied.

Della walked to where her mother sat and bent to kiss her on the cheek. "I hope the doctor had good news."

"He did. He's going to give me a series of injections he says will make me stronger."

Della felt relief at the thought of such an improvement. She took her mother's hand and squeezed it. "I'm so glad."

"I imagine Mrs. Sayers has the noon-day meal on the table," her father said. "Let's go down."

Chapter 8

By the time their furniture had arrived seven days later, Della had read every book in Mrs. Sayers' library, written a letter to each of her sisters, and reorganized the clothing in the bureau at least twice. She hadn't heard from Vesta, and boredom was making her restless. She was eager to move into a place where she wouldn't have to be careful not to disturb other guests.

Her mother had visited her doctor for a second time and received her first shot. Della couldn't detect any improvement in her energy level, although her coughing did seem to be less forceful after her afternoon nap. Her father, dressed in his best suit, went out on business he never explained. Sometimes when he returned for supper, she noticed the scent of spirits on his breath. It disturbed her a little because it had not been his habit back home. The one break in her doldrums was a letter her father brought from her sister, Etta. She didn't wait for her mother to awaken to open it.

Alexandria, Ohio – June 17, 1904

Dear Mother and all,

I pray you are feeling better and will soon recover your health. I must report that late spring rains made it impossible to plant hay at the usual time making it a sparse crop. Gus has had to buy hay from another farmer for the horse and cow. The baby has a bad cold, and her teeth have been bothering her a great deal. She has been fussy all week. The cold seems to have collected in her lungs and she coughs so much that nursing is a problem. The boys have been well, but the rainy weather keeps us all inside and restless.

I was hoping to make a trip home to see Aunt Gertie last Saturday. But the horse was ill and we didn't dare drive her. Aunt Gertie gave me 5 pounds of carpet rags the last time I was there. So you see I have plenty for a rug if only the baby would get well enough to give me the time to work on it. I must quit. She is fussing now.

Your loving daughter

Etta

July first was Della's seventeenth birthday, though no one took notice. She had in mind to write to her sisters, but in the middle of the afternoon, she heard the tread of feet on the stairs out in the hall. Joshua came into the room with two workmen who, from the overalls they were wearing, looked like common railway men.

"The furniture arrived this morning," he announced. "Pack our bags. The house is ready to be occupied." He directed the men to take the trunks. They each grabbed a leather handle and lifted the first one out through the doorway, soon returning for the second.

After feeling like a caged animal for days, excitement gave Della a burst of energy. She hurried to open one of the luggage cases on her bed and began transferring clothes from the bureau.

Anna, who'd been awakened by her husband's booming announcement, swung her legs around to sit on the edge of the bed. "Oh, Della. Help me dress. Can you manage the packing too? I'm afraid I have no energy."

When fully clothed, she watched Della fill the valise and soon proceeded to give directions on proper packing technique.

The packed bags were lined up by the hall door when Joshua returned. He had one of Mrs. Sayer's sons in tow, a scrawny lad with a missing front tooth. Joshua told him to take the bags down to a waiting carriage. "Come on, ladies. We need to get everything settled before dark. I've ordered a box of groceries to be delivered. You can prepare supper for us, Della."

Though Della had been taught the basics of cooking by her mother and her sister, the realization that she was going to be responsible for food preparation every day was jolting. It was a cinch her mother wasn't capable of doing it. Since arriving in Jerome, she'd barely managed to get dressed and walk to the dining room. Della put on her hat, helped her mother with her shawl, and assisted her down the steep staircase. Mrs. Sayers met them at the door and they lingered a moment to say goodbye.

The carriage was a two-seater. Her father helped his wife into the front seat and then hoisted himself into the driver's place. With their baggage crammed into the back seat, there hardly seemed room for another thing.

"You'll just have to squeeze in, Della," her father said. "Come on, now. Be a good girl."

Della moved one of the bags up on top of another and held it there, wedging herself into the narrow space.

Her father gave the reins a snap, and the horse tugged the vehicle into motion, turning into the street at Joshua's direction. The carriage clattered along on the cobblestones until they reached the south end of the little city where he then maneuvered a hairpin turn that brought the conveyance onto a slag-covered road some distance below the main part of town.

As the carriage moved along the rough surface, Della was relieved to see that the entrance of the houses stood closer to street level, and not the kind that required a stair to gain entrance. On the negative side of the scale, there was barely enough space between buildings to toss a stone.

Joshua stopped the carriage in front of a house that stood rather close to its neighbor with only a shallow ditch running in between. Neither place was much to look at, white clapboard with matching covered porches on the front. The screen door hung somewhat askew on one of them. Gauging the size, she supposed there might be four or five rooms inside. Thinking of interior accommodations, she sent a quick prayer heavenward. Please, God, let there be indoor plumbing.

Della slid off the carriage seat, took the bag she'd been balancing with her and followed a stone path to the front porch. The screen door gave a squawk when she opened it and pushed through the main door. Stepping in, she paused and glanced around, immediately recognizing the sideboard that once stood in the dining room at home and the narrow sofa that had been in the upstairs hall near the landing. She felt a tight clinch in her stomach as the remembrance came to her. Somehow the pieces lost their appeal in these plain surroundings.

The furniture had been placed rather haphazardly with little thought to comfort or convenience. The cushioned chairs, lamp, and table, plus the small writing desk that had been her grandmother's, had come from the attic.

"You and your mother can decide how you'd like the furniture arranged," she heard her father say when he'd helped her mother gain entrance.

Della set the bag she'd carried in on one of the chairs and went to look at the other rooms. The bed chambers held spare beds from the attic at home, plus familiar bureaus and another trunk containing winter clothes they wouldn't need for months. Much to her relief, there was an indoor water closet.

In the kitchen she saw a faucet over a kitchen sink, but no icebox. She turned completely around in the eight-by-twelve kitchen, small compared to the one at home. Open shelves lined one wall and a wood cook stove stood adjacent to a rear door. No pantry. Her head whirled with thoughts of housekeeping in such rustic accommodations but knew she should feel fortunate. Some of the homes she'd seen from the train had been primitive board structures, a few with only simple canvas walls.

She moved to the back door and stepped out onto a rear porch that ran the length of the back of the house, and seeing the steep slope below, realized that the back part of the house was supported by posts of some sort to keep it from sliding down the hill. Leaning over the railing, she didn't see a washing machine; only wash tubs and a clothesline. She hurried back inside to help her mother.

Over the next hour, she and her father unloaded the bags from the carriage and moved furniture around until her mother was satisfied with the arrangement. Della hurriedly unpacked their belongings and the groceries, as soon as they were delivered by a young man on horseback.

She was leaning over the stove, arranging pieces of kindling she'd found on the back stoop when she felt a tug on her skirt. She scowled and turned, thinking her skirt had somehow caught on the kitchen chair. To her surprise, a curly-haired child was grinning up at her. Barefoot and wearing a loose dark-blue dress, she guessed the toddler was about the same age as her oldest sister's little guy.

"Well, hello. Where'd you come from?" she asked.

The screen door banged and a woman in a gray dress rushed forward and snatched the child off the floor. "I'm so sorry," she said. "This boy has learned to untie his tether. I have to watch him every second."

Della stood, smiled, and tweaked one of the boy's bare toes. "No harm done. He reminds me of my nephew. Same age, I believe. What's his name?"

"Georgie. He's a scamp, faster than greased lightning when he gets loose." The woman shifted the boy to her hip and stuck out her hand. "I'm Cora Hovey. We live just next door."

Della accepted her neighbor's welcoming hand and introduced herself. As she explained her family's recent arrival and reported that her father would be working at the mine, she noted that Cora was quite thin under her tan dress, and though her face was unlined, a bit of gray could be seen in her dark brown hair.

Georgie tugged at the front of his mother's dress, and she patted his hand away. "I'll be glad to have a neighbor again," she said. "The last people weren't very friendly."

"Mama?"

Della looked through the kitchen doorway to see a girl of about eight standing just outside the front screen door.

"I finished peeling the potatoes," the girl said.

"That's my daughter, Nellie. I must go get supper cooking. The six o'clock whistle will be blowing soon. Will expects a hot meal when he gets home."

Della motioned to the wood stove. "I was just trying to figure out how this oven is regulated."

"Oh, that's simple. The one I use is identical." Cora shifted the boy's weight. "Let me show you."

She hastily gave Della some pointers on how to control the heat before hurrying away to her own kitchen. Della smiled to herself. Cora seemed like someone who would be a good friend to have.

Chapter 9

While Della and her mother continued to unpack, Joshua returned to the boarding house to settle affairs with Mrs. Sayers, and to make certain that none of their belongings had been left behind.

It wasn't long before her mother was worn out. She fairly dropped onto the cushioned chair beside the bed. "Don't bother with the rest of my clothing in the trunk, Della. I won't be needed those things very soon. They can wait for another day."

Della had just finished hanging her dresses when her father returned. He held out an envelope to her. "Mrs. Sayers said this was left for you."

Della glanced at her name on the envelope and lifted the flap. To her delight, it held a note from Vesta. It was an invitation. Her pulse raced. It was hard to keep the excitement out of her voice. "Vesta has invited me to view the Independence Day parade and games with her and her brother at the park."

Her father scowled but said nothing.

"My favorite holiday, next to Christmas," her mother said from the bedroom. She came to stand in the doorway. "We should all go to watch. The entertainment would be good for us."

Della was surprised by her mother's enthusiasm. She glanced at her father. The look in his eyes reflected his doubts. "If you're feeling strong enough, I could hire a buggy." He glanced at the nearby table. "What happened to the newspaper? General Minty is giving a speech in the opera hall that I'd like to hear."

The thought of sitting through a boring speech by a moldering old man made Della's spirits tumble. She'd heard her father speak about the general's exploits at some important Civil War battle. And when he learned the man lived in Jerome, he'd seemed very impressed. The speech, if it were anything like other orations she'd heard, would likely be long and rambling. In her opinion, watching the games in the park with Vesta would be a much more patriotic thing to do. The hitch would be to convince her father to give his permission. She'd have to think of a way to persuade him but first, there was the issue of what to wear.

The celebration was three days hence, not enough time to fashion anything new. With the invitation clutched in her hand, she went to the armoire in her bed chamber, glad she'd hung up her dresses right away. Maybe the wrinkles would shake out by then. Which one would best express the theme of the holiday? Rummaging through her box of ribbons, she pulled out one of each color, red, white and blue. If she wore the blue dress that had once belonged to Lizzie, she could create a red and white bow for the neck, and then wear the blue one in her hair. Or maybe the white batiste would be better with red and blue ribbons for a bow.

One thing was certain. She'd style her hair in a more grown-up way like her sisters. Brushing up the back of her hair with her hand, she turned to look at her image in the mirror on the bureau. The reflection of the clock in the parlor halted all speculation. She'd have to decide later. It was time to begin preparations for supper.

The old wood stove proved to be a challenge Della hadn't expected. An hour later, with little help from her mother, she had shelled peas cooked and pan-fried chicken ready, but she'd scorched the biscuits. She filled their plates and carried them to the table, which her mother had covered with a linen cloth from one of the trunks. Her father asked a blessing on the meal and they were seated.

Anna ate only the smallest portion, though she said the food was tasty. Her lack of appetite was no surprise, but when her father eyed the biscuits with suspicion and laid aside his napkin after consuming only a modest portion, she was crushed. Cooking a simple meal shouldn't have been that difficult. Her mother said she was dreadfully tired, excused herself, and retired to the bed chamber. Her father took up his usual after-dinner routine of sitting in his easy chair and reading the newspaper. It was a habit he'd brought with him from home.

Della sat alone and tried to eat, but soon gave up and carried the dishes to the kitchen sink. As she passed the wood stove, she gave it a kick, vowing to master the beast. The stove was still hot from cooking, so she filled a kettle with water and set it to heating for the next task.

Later, after she had finished washing the supper dishes, she hung the dish towel on a hook by the sink and wiped her face with her apron. Hoping to find a breeze, she walked out onto the front porch.

Dusk approached and shadows crept between the houses along the street. Voices coming from next door drew her attention. Glancing over in that direction, she saw Cora and her family on the porch. Cora was seated in a wooden rocker with little Georgie on her lap, while two boys on their knees in the dirt near the steps argued over a game of marbles. The girl Cora had identified as Nellie was sitting on the top step watching her brothers and cuddling a small rag doll. A man Della assumed was Mr. Hovey occupied another chair facing Cora. He spoke in a tone Della couldn't make out.

Her father stepped out behind her. "Listen, Della..." He moved over to the far end of the porch where the hill slanted down to the roadway. "Come here. I don't want to be overheard."

Della felt a sinking feeling in her stomach, certain her father was going to say she couldn't attend the celebration with Vesta. She followed and stood by his side.

Joshua rubbed his chin with the palm of his hand. He didn't look at her but stared at some distant point across the road for a moment. "I know these recent changes have not been to your liking." He cleared his throat and turned to face her. "I start work at the smelter tomorrow. The shifts are twelve hours, not like my job in Dayton where I came home at noon. I'll need a full dinner pail to take with me in the morning. It will be up to you to take charge of managing the household and all the meals. Be sure your mother gets her rest and takes her medicine. The doctor says it's our only hope for her to get better."

Della felt tears start to form. Her father had never spoken to her in such a frank way before. He put his hand on her shoulder. "You're a grown-up girl now, and I know you are capable." He turned and took a couple of steps toward the door.

Della's thoughts raced. "How will I obtain groceries? What about the laundry?" Back home she'd never had to think about things like that.

He paused with a half-turn. "I made arrangements for groceries to be delivered every second day. If you need anything else, give the boy a note. And I ordered an ice box from the mercantile. It will be delivered tomorrow and ice every other day. Ask the neighbor woman where to get the laundry done."

Della blinked. "What...what about the holiday?" she blurted.

Her father turned and stared at her for a moment. "I'll have Sunday and the holiday off. We'll be able to attend General Minty's speech."

Her father's hand on her shoulder woke her before dawn the next morning. "Get up, girl. I need a full breakfast and my dinner pail prepared."

Della bolted upright. As he left the room she scurried to dress. The next hour was a blur for her. She rushed to stoke the stove, get a pot of coffee brewing, boil eggs, fry potatoes and bacon, and wrap leftover chicken in oilcloth for the dinner pail.

By the time her father left for work, the sky had barely begun to lighten. She stood in the doorway at the back of the house, leaned against the brown doorframe and yawned. Her future looked rather dreary to her. She had hoped that once her family got settled, she'd have a chance to meet some of Vesta's other friends, but it appeared there would be little time for anything more than household duties and taking care of her mother. Her earlier prediction was coming true.

She didn't consider her mother a burden, but the prospect of managing *all* the meals and the laundry made her stomach sour. She'd lied to her father when she begged him to let her stay behind in Ohio, told him she was perfectly capable of keeping house for her brothers. The fact was, even before their mother became ill, her sisters had done the bulk of the housework. She'd wormed her way out of the hardest chores, things like making soap, gardening, and cleaning the chicken coop. Instead, she'd chosen the mending and sewing that her sisters hated.

Della heaved a sigh and let her gaze wander around her new neighborhood. Looking to her right, she observed that the only thing that kept houses from sliding down the mountainside was the use of terraced land, or by making the buildings fit the slope with posts to prevent slippage. In most cases, the backyards faced one another with no trees to obstruct the view of whatever activity was occurring.

Not far away, Della noticed a woman fling a rug over a clothesline, hustle back inside the house, and return a moment later with a wire rug beater. She began smacking the rug like it was an errant child. The plume of dust released by her effort made Della turn her head aside as though the dust might blow her way.

Another chore she'd soon be doing since her mother's carpet sweeper had been left at home for her aunt to use. No matter, she thought. The most important thing was her mother's health. It was the key to her future.

That afternoon, with the household chores completed, and her mother napping, Della focused on her plans for the Independence Day holiday. The white batiste dress was the best choice, she decided. A red, white and blue bow at the neck would be perfect.

Her hairstyle was next. Now that she'd passed her seventeenth birthday, it was time to master putting her hair up. She stood in front of the mirror on the bureau, loosened her braid, and took her hair brush and comb out of the top drawer. She knew exactly the look she wanted. She'd watched her oldest sister fix her hair like the Gibson Girl pictures often enough.

After brushing out the tangles, she parted her hair from front to back on either side of her head to separate the sides from the crown. Next, she drew her comb across the back and gathered the top section in her left hand. She let it fall forward over her eyes, then rolled sections of it, making little tunnels to lay atop her forehead, and anchored each with several hairpins. Della felt fortunate to have hair thick enough so, unlike her mother, she didn't need to use a hair rat.

After rolling the sides and back in the same manner and securing each part, she placed her straw hat on top. Taking a hand mirror from the drawer, she held it up and turned slowly. What she saw wasn't the picture she had in mind. Somehow it didn't look the same on her as it did on her sister.

What she really needed was a new hat, but she was sure her father would never give consent to such a purchase. To him, one hat was as good as another. Laying the mirror aside, she removed the hat, and loosened the old black and white ribbon, thinking to replace it with a red one. She opened the cover on her sewing basket, feeling glad to finally have it, threaded a needle, and tacked the ribbon in place to keep it from slipping. Much better, she thought, holding it out to admire her handiwork. She laid it on the bureau and returned her attention to her hairstyle.

After loosening the back section of her hair, she brushed it upward, twisted it several times, then pinned it to the crown, leaving a few stragglers at the nape of her neck. Turning her head from side to side, it still didn't suit her. She scowled at the mirror, pulled out all of the hairpins, and tried again, determined to master the process. An hour later, after more attempts, though still not really satisfied, she heaved a sigh. It would have to do.

Removing the hairpins, she plaited her hair into one braid, went to the kitchen, and put on her apron. Her mother had set out a pan of potatoes to be peeled for supper. She picked up the paring knife. When it came time to choose a husband, she'd choose a rich one, not a poor farmer like her sister's, but someone who'd hire a kitchen girl to peel potatoes.

Chapter 10

Sunlight streamed through the kitchen window the morning of Independence Day, but Della didn't have much time to notice. For her, the early hours were a flurry of activity, first preparing the morning meal for her family, cleaning up, and then helping her mother dress for the planned outing. The fact that she was going to be able to join her friends for the festivities lifted her spirits and made the tasks less burdensome.

With her mother's help, Della had cajoled her father into allowing her to spend the day with Vesta rather than accompanying her parents to hear General Minty's speech. The availability of the elevator at the opera hall was a strong point in her favor. Her mother would need minimal help gaining entrance. Plus, she had assured him that Vesta would give her a ride home after the celebration. Though disgusted with his daughter's lack of civic interest, he relented and gave his consent.

By mid-morning Joshua was dressed in his best suit and hat. He was a striking figure as he left to acquire the buggy he'd rented for the day at the Fashion Livery Stable. He was not a tall man, but quite muscular with a broad Irish forehead and a square jaw. It was evident to Della, by the look in her mother's eyes, that she thought he was handsome, despite the lines in his forehead and gray hair at his temples that made him look older than his forty-five years.

After final preparations, Della and her mother went out on the porch to wait for Joshua to return with the buggy. Next door Will Hovey held a tight rein on a gray horse while his two sons pushed and shoved one another as they scrambled into the backseat of a large buggy. Nellie waited at a safe distance until her father's gruff words made her brothers settle down, after which, she climbed in to sit next to them.

Cora came out of the house and waved when she saw her neighbors. "Good morning," she called. "You ladies look mighty pretty." Little Georgie squirmed in her arms as she descended the steps and hurried to the vehicle. She'd chosen a blue skirt and white shirtwaist for the day. Her hair had been wound into a tight bun on the back of her head, and she'd pinned a broad straw hat on top.

"Thank you," Della said, smiling. She raised her gloved hand toward the sky. "Looks like a fine day for a parade."

"Certainly does." Cora hoisted her little son up onto the seat next to her husband and climbed in herself. "Be sure to watch the sack races. The boys are planning to win this year."

Mr. Hovey urged the horse into the roadway, and the whole family waved as the vehicle moved up the incline in the direction of the town center.

"Those boys remind me of your brothers when they were that age," Anna said, smiling at the remembrance.

The Hovey family was barely out of sight when Joshua approached with the horse and buggy and halted it in front of the house. He pulled his pocket watch out, gave it a quick glance. and put it back. "We had better hurry. There's a good deal of traffic in town."

Della was almost giddy with excitement as she assisted her mother into the conveyance before clambering into the back seat. Styling her hair had been easier than she anticipated, and she was sure the white batiste dress was the most appropriate for a summer day. Plus, her blue purse and parasol added just the right contrast. She smoothed her skirt and settled back for the short ride.

Though their house was no more than a mile from the business district, a walk of that distance would have been too much for her mother. It would have been no trouble for Della. Back home, it was over a mile to her school and two miles to Mrs.

Cathcart's house where she had taken piano lessons. Of course, the streets in Dayton were level. In Jerome, it seemed that nothing was level. All the streets and roads sloped in one way or another.

As they came closer to the center of town, it was evident that Main Street had been blocked off to accommodate the upcoming races. The local newspaper had featured the planned agenda: sack races for younger boys, a donkey race for older boys, a parade featuring the fire department band, and the high point—a fire hose cart race between the Jerome fire brigade and a team from Bisbee. Prizes would be awarded by the mayor.

Congestion was to be reckoned with as buggy drivers and autos maneuvered to stop and let out passengers. Band instruments could be heard warming up somewhere at the far end of Main street. A blond-headed boy in dungarees tossed a firecracker onto the road, scaring several of the horses to the point that one of them bolted, giving the people in the buggies a wild ride. Curses uttered by men could be heard as they strained to gain control of their animals, while the ladies held onto their broad-brimmed hats and howled their displeasure.

Joshua pulled his horse to a stop more than a block from the park. "I don't dare go any further, Della. You'll just have to walk the rest of the way. We'll take another route."

"I don't mind at all, Father. This is just fine." Holding her parasol and purse in one hand, Della gathered her skirt with the other and descended to the slag-covered roadway. Careful not to step in any horse leavings, she turned and blew her mother a kiss, then stepped up onto the boardwalk and raised her parasol.

Joshua's brow furrowed. "Be sure you are home in time to cook supper."

With her father's warning ringing in her ears, Della hurried past the shops that lined the street, intent on her destination, the bandstand in the park, where Vesta had indicated in her note that she would wait for her.

Along the way, she passed a hotel, a cigar store, and the millinery. Farther on, she picked up her pace as she came to one of the many saloons that were sandwiched between ordinary businesses. In the doorway to one such place stood the Mexican she recognized from the train. The man stroked his mustache with his thumb and forefinger, then tipped his hat and gave her a big grin. At his overture, Della felt an unpleasant surge in her stomach. He chuckled, taking a little pleasure in recognizing her apprehension.

The incident left her a bit unnerved, but she put it aside as soon as she spotted the bandstand. It had been wrapped in the red, white and blue bunting with a flag on the peak of the roof. Waiting on the street corner below it was Vesta. Determined that nothing would mar the day, Della fairly ran the short distance to greet her.

Vesta's face brightened when she saw Della approach. The girls lowered their parasols and a quick embrace followed.

"Isn't this exciting?" Vesta said. "The parade will start soon. Millie is going to join us. Her brother, Melvin arrived just last night." She gestured up the street. "Percy is helping organize the boys for the sack race. I may not be able to introduce you. Now that he's old enough, he joined the volunteer firemen department this summer. He told me this morning that he was going to take part in the hose cart race."

Della barely took notice of what Vesta was saying. She was admiring the dress Mrs. Whipple had designed for her. Della took Vesta's hand and twirled her around. "Your dress is perfect for today's celebration."

"Isn't it? And *you*. Your hair, so grown up. I can hardly wait, but my birthday isn't until November." She looked around. "Are your parents here somewhere?"

"No. They went to hear General Minty's speech."

Just then the sound of band music filtered their way, a bass drum pounding out the rhythm.

Vesta wrinkled her nose. "Mine too, and Millie's parents as well." Vesta motioned in the direction of two young people coming toward them. "Oh, look, here comes Millie and her brother."

Millie Swanson, wearing a blue and white gingham dress, rushed up to the two girls. "I thought I'd never get here in time," she said, nearly out of breath. "Melvin insisted we help my little brothers find out where they are forming up for the sack races." She turned and motioned to a lean young man who seemed to be in no hurry. "Come on, Mel. I want you to meet my new friend."

When he drew near, Millie shouted over the sound of the drum as she introduced him to Della. He nodded a greeting and pushed a lank of dark hair off his forehead revealing pale blue eyes. From his expression or lack thereof, he had little interest in his sister's young friends. He turned his attention to the approaching marching band.

Men removed their hats, and the crowd cheered as Old Glory passed by. A sudden breeze from the valley below made the flag flutter. It was a moving sight.

After a short space of time, the boys' sack race came next. The foursome stood together and cheered as each racer finished. Neither of the Hovey boys won. The youngest fell twice and the older one came in third. The winner strutted over to the mayor and grinned as he accepted the prize.

"Isn't that your little brother?" Della asked Millie.

Millie's lip curled. "Yes, it is. There's going to be no living with him now."

The donkey races followed and brought reels of laughter from the crowd as the bigger boys tugged and pushed the stubborn donkeys to get them to comply with directions.

The hose cart race was last with the local fire brigade pitted against another from a nearby town. Vesta pointed out Percy when the young men came into view. Each team strained to move the wheel that carried the heavy hose, pulling it along the cobbled street. In the end, Jerome's fire brigade won. Cheers went up and Percy grinned while the leader sprinted up the slope to accept the prize from the mayor. Watching Percy, Della had to confess he was quite handsome even though his body was streaked with sweat.

With the races over, the mayor gave a rousing speech, and the band members entered the bandstand to play patriotic music for the crowd. A vendor selling a fizzy drink came by. At Millie's request, her brother dug a few coins out of his pocket and treated the girls.

Time slipped by as they chattered and giggled while they sipped the beverage. They hardly noticed when Millie's brother left their company. And when Della did note his absence, the sun had drifted to the west. It seemed to her that the day's events had flown by all too quickly. She was reminded of her suppertime chores and what she'd told her father. But Vesta actually hadn't promised her a ride home. Should she ask for a ride? Would that be too bold?

Millie's brother came toward them, having elbowed his way through the crowd. "Come on, girls. Dad says we're to meet him by the post office. He's going to take all of us to visit the newest section of the smelter."

Vesta's face registered surprise. "I didn't know they ever let ladies in, even on holidays."

"It's not routine," he said. "You're the lucky ones. The equipment is the best available."

Della bit her lip, her disappointment acute. "I'm afraid I won't be able to accompany you. I have duties at home I must attend to."

Vesta turned to her. "I'm so sorry." She hugged Della. "It's been such a treat to have you with us, I almost forgot about your mother's illness."

Della gave Millie a quick hug and told Melvin she was happy to have met him. "I've enjoyed a wonderful day, but I must go."

The heat of the afternoon radiated off the buildings as Della hurried along the boardwalk. It pained her to think of what she was missing by having to leave her friends. She hoped the outing hadn't been too exhausting for her mother, so there might be other similar opportunities to spend time with her new friends.

Intent on arriving with time to spare before starting supper, she paid little attention to the two men loitering at the corner of a saloon up ahead. She cast them a surreptitious glance as she passed by and heard one of them say something to his companion in a language she didn't understand. The other laughed.

As she approached the corner of the next building, she hesitated. To her left, she could see the street below through a passageway wide enough for a pack mule to move between the buildings. A shortcut would save time. So rather than follow the long road and the switchback to the house, she closed her parasol and turned the corner.

The surface of the crude alleyway was uneven. She'd have to watch her step or risk twisting an ankle. Her descent had hardly begun when she heard footsteps on the stone surface behind her. She hurried her downward pace. The person behind her did the same, and she heard snatches of a foreign language. A sense of danger surged, making her heart pound. If she could reach the next street, there'd be other people. But abruptly, her heel caught on something. She stumbled, tried to right herself, and gasped when in a flash, a strong hand gripped her arm.

Chapter 11

Her breath caught in her chest. She tried to jerk from his grasp, but he held her arm tight, still speaking in that strange tongue she couldn't understand. Panicked, she twisted, hitting at him with her parasol. "Let go of me, you beast!"

Her blows had little effect; his grip was unyielding. As she struggled, to her horror, the shoulder seam of her sleeve gave way, leaving her upper arm exposed. She screamed, certain she was fighting for her life. But he was undeterred and commenced to pull her along the narrow sloping street. She stumbled, causing her hat to slide to one side and her hairpins to loosen.

So focused on escape, she didn't notice when a door in the adjacent building opened. A woman's husky voice uttered a curse and began banging the assailant with her handbag. "Emelio! You dirty rotten pig! What's the matter? Aren't my girls good enough for you? Let her go!"

When the heavy blows landed on his head, the man expelled a stream of oaths, released Della's arm, then hoofed it around the corner and disappeared from view.

Della collapsed to the brick surface, tears streaming down her face. She pushed her hat back on her head and raised her eyes to discover the identity of her rescuer. Though her vision was blurred, she looked into the face of one of those "painted ladies" she'd heard about. Her green dress appeared shiny in the afternoon sun as she leaned over Della.

"There, there now," the woman said. "You're going to be all right. He's gone."

Della sobbed out the only thing she could utter. "Thank you. Oh, thank you."

The woman held out her hand. "Come on. Up on your feet."

Della gathered her skirt and stood. She tugged at her sleeve, picked up her purse and parasol, and attempted to brush off her white skirt. "My dress is ruined," she sobbed noticing a soiled spot.

"It's nothing that can't be mended. Come with me. I have a small sewing box." The woman moved to a weathered door in the brick building that stood on the east side of the narrow street. She opened it and motioned for Della to enter.

Though uncertain about the invitation, Della felt she couldn't go home in the state she was in. Her father would never let her out on her own again. She followed the woman, stepped through the doorway, and found herself at the bottom of a stair. The door closed behind her.

Through a haze of smoke, she saw an open barroom about twice the width of a standard train car. A dark polished-oak bar on the left stretched the length of the room with a line of stools in front of it. From the street entrance to the rear of the building, a single string of dim lamps hung from the pressed-tin ceiling. Afternoon light filtering through windows at the front revealed several men leaning lazily against the bar. A balding man stationed behind it took a bottle from a shelf and poured amber liquid into several glasses arranged on a round tray. Laughter of men came from a room somewhere behind the stairway.

Though still somewhat shaken by what had just happened, she could hardly help but gawk. She'd never entered such an establishment before. She'd only heard about them from her oldest brother. Would she dare write to her sister about this place? She was sure neither of her sisters had ever been in a barroom. When one of the men turned and looked her way, she averted her gaze and tugged at her sleeve to cover her arm.

The woman, now halfway up the steep staircase, paused and turned, looking down on her. "Come on. My room is up here. Let's see what we can do about your dress."

Della lifted her skirt and followed, arriving at a landing and a dim gallery with a railing on the right. On the left, five doors were spaced at intervals. Her rescuer opened the first and motioned for Della to enter.

The room, though crowded with furniture, was anything but plain. Directly ahead, a pair of tall casement windows were draped with wine-colored fabric. A bed on the right was covered with a woven spread, also wine-colored. A chaise lounge was positioned with its back to the windows with a low table in front of it. On the left, not far from the door, a pine armoire occupied the corner along with a decorated screen that Della assumed was used as a place to dress. The woman opened the armoire and took a cigar box out of a drawer, then sat on the chaise. "Take off your dress."

Della hesitated.

The woman smiled. "What is your name?"

When Della told her, a look of surprise flitted across the woman's face. "The same as my little sister," she remarked.

"What may I call you?" Della asked.

"If you must know, I go by Lena Larson. You may call me Lena."

"I don't know how to thank you. You saved me from ..."

Lena gave a dismissive gesture and opened the cigar box. "I can't fix your sleeve while you're wearing it."

Della worked the buttons, shimmied out of her dress, and handed it to Lena. She felt awkward and exposed standing in front of a stranger in her chemise and petticoat. She crossed her arms over her bosom. The corset she was wearing was one her sister had discarded. She'd laced it as tight as she could, but it was not the right fit for her.

Lena turned the bodice and sleeve inside out, laid the dress across her lap, and proceeded to thread a needle.

"Come sit," Lena said without looking at her. She drew the sleeve and bodice together, ready to begin the repair.

When Della had seated herself, Lena began stitching. Calmer now, Della observed Lena's makeup, her hair, a deep henna shade, her earbobs, and her crimson lips and nails.

"I doubt you realize that there are three men for every woman in this town," Lena said. "A pretty face like yours can be a strong temptation for some. It'd be best if you stick to the main streets if you must be out unaccompanied."

It wasn't like she'd been out there looking to be assaulted, Della thought. "I've been here less than two months," she said, the heat of embarrassment rising in her cheeks.

"I figured," Lena said.

Della nearly started crying again. She didn't know why, but she soon found herself pouring out her troubles and her longing for home to this woman she'd barely met.

Lena listened while she sewed, nodding every so often. "It's called homesickness. The people here are from all over the world, and I'll bet they've all felt homesick on arrival. Get acquainted with your neighbors. It will soon pass."

With an over-and-over stitch, the sleeve was soon repaired. Lena stood and shook out the dress. "There," she said. "It's none the worse for wear." She handed it to Della. "I imagine that spot on your skirt will wash out. Fix your hair and you'll be good as new."

Twenty minutes later Della slipped through the door of her house. She peeked into her parent's bed chamber. Anna was lying on the bed, asleep. She paused, struck by how small her mother looked, hardly making a bulge under the sheet. The fact made her decide she would not burden her mother by telling her of her harrowing experience. She proceeded to her room, rushed to change into her everyday dress, put on a clean apron, and hung her soiled dress in the armoire behind her coat to deal with later.

Noting her father wasn't in any of the other rooms, she went through the kitchen to the rear door. Looking out, she saw him standing with his back to her, talking to the neighbor, Will Hovey. He was leaning on a shovel. A nanny goat, tethered in the neighbor's yard, was busy chewing on a stubble of green.

Good, she thought, knowing Joshua liked discussing the news of the day with other men. She took kindling from the wood box and busied herself arranging it in the cook stove's firebox. While the fire was getting started, she took the roast beef, leftover from Sunday supper, out of the icebox, put it onto a cutting board, and began slicing it.

When her father came into the house, he glanced at her, but said nothing, and passed through to the living room. When she heard the creaking of his favorite chair, she knew he'd be reading until she had supper ready.

Della moved the big cast iron skillet over to heat and poured in gravy from the roast. As soon as it started to bubble, she added the sliced beef, cooked turnips, chunks of boiled carrots and potatoes. Summer vegetables from the valley were at the peak of harvest and plentiful. Fresh peaches from Saturday's delivery were still good, so she put some in a bowl to serve.

She was slicing bread and cheese when Anna appeared in the kitchen doorway.

"Did you enjoy the speech?" Della asked, looking up at her mother, gauging her rested appearance.

"General Minty is rather long-winded," Anna said, "but it was nice to be out among people. I had the opportunity to be introduced to one of the ladies from the Methodist church, a Mrs. Samples. She told me the church is sponsoring a picnic trip to some place called Deception Gulch in August. Everyone is welcome."

Anna went to the shelf above the sink, removed plates, silverware and napkins, and took them to the table. As she arranged the settings, she said, "I'm sure I'll be feeling better by then. Perhaps we can attend." After a return trip to the shelf for cups, she asked, "Did you enjoy your day?"

"I did indeed," Della replied. "But I'm sorry to report that the boys next door did not win any of the races this year." She described the marching band, the music, and the fire brigade.

The meal was soon hot and ready to serve. The family gathered, and after a blessing, filled their plates while Joshua recounted the highlights of the speech Della had missed. She suspected his intent was a subtle chastisement.

That night as Della lay staring at the ceiling of her bed-chamber, moonlight filtered through the thin curtain on the open window. She revisited the day's events. It had been a delight, up until that awful creature had tried to abduct her. Were all the men in this town like him? She'd never had to think about such things back home. Resentment toward her father began to take root. Why pick such a wicked place for her and her mother to live in? There had to be better places in Arizona.

She thought about Lena, her hair, her makeup, and the men in the smoke-filled barroom. Questions flitted around in her brain like gnats on a hot night. Why did Lena know that awful man's name? And what had Lena meant by her "girls?" Where were they? Lena had been so kind to her, she hated to think of it, but from everything she'd seen, Lena was a prostitute.

Chapter 12

The following week it rained for hours every day, torrents of water rushing down the mountainside. The railroad was blocked with rocks and debris which halted the delivery of supplies to the community. The smelter closed down for several days due to water invading the ore roasting beds. That slowed work down in the mine too, so Joshua was out of work causing him to pace the floor, worried about his pay.

He'd walk from window to window in the living room, then out onto the front porch and glared at the sky. His restlessness and short temper kept Anna and Della on edge. Della stayed busy with household chores. The pots and pans received an extra scrubbing, the kitchen shelves a second and third rearranging. Anna occupied herself mending her husband's socks, or writing letters to distant relatives.

So it was a relief when after the mid-day meal on the third day there was a let-up in the storm, and Joshua announced he was going to walk uptown to learn of any news about the situation at the smelter. He put on his hat and coat and left the house with a measure of purpose in his step.

Shortly after he left, there was a knock on the door. When Della opened it, she saw Cora Hovey holding little Georgie wrapped up in a light blanket. She was wearing a brown checkered dress under a flowered apron. "I'm afraid I haven't been very neighborly," she said. "I'd be pleased if you and your mother would join me for coffee. I made fresh scones this morning."

Anna pushed herself out of the wingback chair and smiled. "Oh my, that is so kind of you." She moved toward the doorway. "But I'm afraid I am not well, and my energy fades by afternoon. I must take my rest. However, I'm sure Della would enjoy your good company."

Cora's brow creased. "I'm sorry to hear that. Perhaps another time when you are better."

"Of course. But you go, Della." Anna nodded encouragement.

Although Della rarely drank coffee, fresh scones sounded like a real treat. "Are you sure, Mother? I should help you undress."

"Not today. Go, go. Enjoy yourself."

Della removed her apron and handed it to her mother, then followed her neighbor across the narrow path between the houses. Wiping her feet on the door mat, she stepped inside Cora's home.

The interior layout of the two houses appeared to be identical. However, the Hovey house was crowded with furniture. A rather worn, dark green sofa stood against one wall, and nearby, a table held a lamp with a tilting shade. Several well-used upholstered chairs and a sideboard were positioned at one end of a braided rug that covered the floor in the middle of the room. A narrow table, sandwiched between two other chairs, held a stack of papers, pencils and a few books.

The older Hovey children were sprawled on the living room rug, the boys playing marbles, and eight-year-old Nellie pretending to feed her doll with a spoon.

"This wet weather keeps the children inside," Cora said as she stepped around the legs of her two sons. "Let's sit in the kitchen. I'll put this young'un down for a nap and we can enjoy ourselves."

Maneuvering around the game of marbles, Della noticed Nellie lay the spoon aside, pull up her dress and press her doll's face against her chest, obviously mimicking her mother.

Moving on into the kitchen, Della settled herself on a chair at the table while Cora went to put her infant son to bed. The delicious aroma of simmering beef stew emanating from a cast iron pot on the stove couldn't be missed. She noticed a smattering of crumbs on the tablecloth. By the arrangement of the scones on the platter, it appeared that someone, the children, no doubt, had helped themselves to a treat in their mother's absence. It reminded her of her brother's ferocious appetites, and how they always found a way to snitch cookies, in spite of their mother's warnings.

"The rain sure has made a mess of things at the smelter," Della commented as Cora rejoined her.

"In the mine and with the railroad, too." Cora took cups, small plates, and a sugar bowl from a kitchen shelf and put them on the table, followed by a creamer from an ice box. She then brought the blue speckled coffee pot from the stove to fill the cups.

"What happens if they don't get it cleared?" Della asked.

Returning the coffee pot to the stove, Cora seated herself and dipped a spoon into the sugar bowl. "Don't worry. We've been here three years and haven't starved yet." Indicating the platter, Cora said, "Help yourself."

Della put a scone on one of the plates, broke the pastry in two pieces and took a bite. The sweet raisin-filled scone fairly melted in her mouth. "Golly, these are good."

"My grandmother's recipe," Cora said, dumping a heaping spoonful of sugar into her cup.

Della took another bite and followed it with a sip of coffee. The aroma, she discovered, didn't match its bitter flavor. "Where did you live before you came here?" Della asked as she followed her hostess's example by adding sugar to her cup.

"Montana. Will and his father worked for Marcus Daly in the copper mines there. But Will heard the pay was better down here, so here we are." Cora stirred her coffee, put the spoon aside and took a swallow. "I'm glad. The winters were so cold and dark. And not healthy for the children."

As they chatted about their respective backgrounds over the next hour, Della observed Cora's easy smile and how she hugged her daughter when Nellie came into the kitchen and leaned against her. She broke off a piece of scone and handed it to the girl. "Go along now," she said. "Let us grownups visit."

By all appearances, Cora didn't seem to be much older than Della's oldest sister. Her light brown hair had been wound into a bun and fastened in back. Her dress was common to most homebound women, her sleeves rolled up to keep them from getting wet during cooking and cleaning.

"Does rain like this often affect your husband's work?" Della asked, taking another bite of the scone.

"Only if water seeps down into the mine. That can be very dangerous. They rarely stop working unless there's a cave-in like two days ago when a man got buried, and then it's too late. The only thing I can do is pray, and I do a lot of that."

Della listened while Cora explained that the United Verde paid better than any of the other mines in the region, plus the hospital was provided for everyone who worked for the owner.

"But not the storekeepers," Della said, "or other people, like the ... uh, ladies in the, uh, cribs."

Cora gave Della a quizzical look. "Well, I wouldn't know about that." She stood, went to the stove, and brought the coffee pot to refill the cups. "There are several doctors in town." After returning the pot to the stove, she sat again. "Most people give those women a wide berth, but I'd guess someone would take care of them if they were sick." Cora added more sugar to her cup and gave it a stir. "What made you think of them?"

The incident on Independence Day had given Della nightmares almost every night since. She didn't dare tell her father about it. He wasn't normally a violent man, but she wasn't certain how he would react, and she didn't want him to get in trouble with the law. Talking to her mother about it was out of the question. Did she dare risk confiding in Cora? She took a swallow from her cup before speaking. "I, uh, happened to meet one of those ladies the other day."

With the first words out of her mouth, a flood soon followed. She poured out the details of the whole episode. When she finished, her eyes were full of tears, not sure what Cora's reaction would be.

Cora rubbed the side of her neck, then reached across the table and patted Della's hand. "It's just one of those hard lessons a woman's gotta learn in life. In a town like this, you gotta be on the lookout for men like that. Especially on holidays when they've been drinking. They get downright bold after a few drinks more than usual." Cora leaned her elbow on the table and rested her chin on the back of her hand. "The thing about the kind of woman you met is that, in spite of how nice she treated you, they're always looking to recruit girls your age for their business. It's another thing you gotta be aware of."

Della gasped, her eyes wide as she looked at Cora. "I would never ..."

"I know." Cora cut her off. "But you're going to learn that towns in the west are not like where you came from. I've heard that back east they call Jerome the wickedest town out here."

Babbling coming from another room in the house indicated Georgie's nap was over. Cora smiled and stood. "I'll bet he needs changing. Excuse me." She headed in the direction of the noise.

Della nibbled the remainder of her scone and pondered what Cora had said. She wondered about her young friends, Vesta and Millie. Did they know about such things? She glanced out the window and noticed it was late afternoon now. She'd have to start supper soon.

Minutes later, Cora came back into the kitchen with a happy and smiling Georgie in her arms. She sat at the table with the baby on her lap, Georgie patting the tabletop with his fat little hands.

"I best be going," Della said. "My father will be back from town soon. Thank you so much for the coffee and your delicious scones ... and the advice."

The sound of loud singing and the rattling of a vehicle of some kind coming down the road outside drew the attention and curiosity of both women. Cora stood, propped her son on her hip, and went to open the front door. Della followed and they went out onto the porch.

A farm wagon pulled by a mule stopped in front of the McCrea home. Seated on the wagon were two men. One was Joshua McCrea, his face an unnatural shade of pink. The other man, Della didn't recognize. Both of them were singing a raucous old Irish drinking song Della had heard her grandfather sing when he'd been out with his friends. She felt her cheeks flush. Not looking at Cora, she closed her eyes and wished she could make herself vanish like a genie in a bottle.

Chapter 13

"I think I heard my mother calling me," Della said. She lifted her skirt and dashed across the space between the two houses and through the front door. Just inside, out of sight, she watched Joshua descend from the wagon, still singing along with his new friend. Her embarrassment gave way to anger when she saw the paper sack in his hand. It was another thing that reminded her of her grandfather McCrea. At the sight of it, her thoughts swirled with memories.

Even though she had been only seven when the old man came to live with them, and then when he died, her recollection of him swaggering into the house was vivid. She remembered her sister, Etta, crying, telling her mother how he trifled with her like he was not an old man at all. She'd overheard her mother trying to console Etta, telling her to avoid him and barricade her door at night.

Later when she'd overheard heated words between her parents, though she didn't quite understand, she knew whatever the trouble, it was bad. It had made in her stomach churn. She'd slipped out of the house and hid in the woodshed. After she'd crept into bed, she heard shouting, her father's voice, and her grandfather's response.

It wasn't until the old man's funeral that she'd learned from an aunt about her mother's fear that her father would follow Grandpa McCrea's path to drunkenness.

Joshua looked up at Della and grinned, his steps unsteady as he approached the porch. She whirled around, went directly to the hall by her parents' room, and quietly closed the bedroom door. Her thought was to protect her mother from the knowledge that he'd broken his promise of sobriety.

Her best course of action, she decided, was to make coffee and prepare supper for him. It was what her mother had done when her grandfather had arrived in such a state. She hurried to the kitchen, stirred the coals in the stove's firebox with the poker, and tossed in several sticks of kindling. Closing the firebox door, she reached for the coffee pot, filled it with water, and put it on the stove.

Joshua let the front door shut with no effort to be quiet and soon leaned against the frame of the kitchen doorway.

"I brought you somethin'," he said with a faint slur. "You been so good takin' care of your mama." He stepped forward and held out the paper bag.

She faced him and seeing his glassy-eyed gaze, stiffened. Her hands trembled as she took the bag from him and extracted a small box. Doscher Brother's Confections, she read. It was a well-known and popular brand, but she had no stomach for it. All she could think of was how she'd seen her grandfather hand her mother a bag of candy each time he returned from an evening at a saloon. With effort, she choked out, "Thank you."

Anna appeared behind him in the doorway. "What is that I smell?" It was a rhetorical question. She wrinkled her nose. "Liquor. You reek of it, husband." She pulled on his sleeve. "Come," she said, let her hand drop and left the room. Joshua followed his wife like a puppy following his master, and seconds later, Della heard the door to their bedroom close with a bang.

She didn't hear what was said between them. She put the box of candy on a shelf, resentment filling her chest. How could he come home like that with her mother so sick? With her jaw set tight, she pushed the thoughts aside and busied herself putting together the evening meal.

By the end of the week, the rainy spell had broken. Joshua returned to work to help with the cleanup at the smelter and peace settled in at home. The primary result of Joshua's indiscretion was that the family attended church services the following Sunday. Jerome had a fine Methodist Church, and

Anna insisted that her illness should not prevent her husband and daughter from attending, even if she were unable to accompany them.

Her mother's family had been Methodists for generations, something Della had learned at the funeral of Grandpa Chrisman, her mother's father. They'd thoroughly agreed with the Methodist stance on temperance, she'd heard her Aunt Beatrice remark to a friend after the services. The fact that her mother had married into the McCrea family had caused no end of consternation for her mother's parents.

On that first Sunday at church Della found herself almost glad her father had broken his promise to her mother. Everyone she encountered seemed so friendly and welcoming. The pastor's wife made an effort to introduce herself. She was a slender woman, dressed in a modest blue dress with a white lace collar. Her smile was genuine and her blue eyes reflected an inner sweetness. "Please, call me Ruby," she said as she grasped Anna's gloved hand in her own.

Vesta was there with her family, as well as the Hoveys from next door. And when Vesta linked arms with Della and introduced her to a few of her other friends, Della determined that, with luck, life might not have to be so monotonous.

However, as Anna had predicted, her attendance at Sunday service was rare, the amount of energy it took to dress for church being more than she could manage. Some nights she coughed so much, she barely slept at all. When that happened, and it seemed to Della that those nights were becoming more frequent, Joshua was forced to sleep on the sofa in order to get enough rest to be able to work the next day. But he never complained. He only inquired about her supply of medicine and if she were taking it properly.

The weeks peeled away and August arrived with the days so hot an egg could have been cooked on the sidewalk, if there had been sidewalk in town. Frequent fast-moving rain storms from the southwest lent little relief.

Once again, Della accompanied her mother to the doctor for another injection, and once again, the doctor cautioned them both about cleanliness and how to avoid spreading the illness in the family.

He handed Della a sheet of printed instructions. Nourishing food, fresh air and exercise were at the top of the list. Promoting general good health was key to overcoming the devastating disease of consumption, he had told them. The bedroom windows were to be kept open both day and night, no matter the weather. And Anna was to get as much exercise as her lungs would tolerate.

And she *did* try, though it made her chest hurt. Every morning, she would dress and sit in her rocking chair on the front porch, or walk along the road in front of the house. She never ventured very far. After a few hundred feet, her energy would be spent. It was evident to anyone watching that the effort made her struggle for air. But she'd smile and try to make light of her difficulty.

"I'll walk a little farther tomorrow," she'd say to Della. And Della would nod, though they both knew it wouldn't happen. It was part of the game they played—the "getting well" game. Despite their effort to follow the doctor's orders, Anna's condition didn't seem to change.

As Della and her father entered the church the following Sunday, a girl of about ten years handed her a handbill announcing an upcoming picnic. Della studied the information. It was to take place three weeks hence on Sunday afternoon in a location called Deception Gulch. She had no notion of where that was, but the thought of a picnic sounded enticing. Back home, family picnics had always been a lot of fun.

Cora Hovey saw Della reading the bulletin and moved to stand next to her. "I hope you and your parents will come along on the picnic trip. Mrs. Samples is head of the committee. She asked me to extend a special invitation to you folks. Deception Gulch is wonderful this time of year. The children can play in the creek.

With luck, the weather should be perfect, and we'll be home before dark. It's our best summertime event."

Della shook her head. "The name Deception Gulch sounds rugged. I doubt my mother would be up to it, and my father wouldn't go without her. But thanks, anyway."

What Della had said wasn't the whole truth. Since the flood in the mine, her father had come home from work utterly exhausted and gone to bed right after supper. She was sure neither of her parents would be interested in such an outing.

Cora pursed her lips and frowned. "Now wait. Perhaps your parents would allow you to go along with us in our buggy."

Joshua stared at the church's handbill that evening after supper. The three of them were still seated at the kitchen table. He laid it aside and took the piece of pie Della was offering him. A familiar scowl formed on his face.

Della was sure it meant he would reject any idea of her attending without him being present.

Anna caught his reaction too. "You know, my dear, it's important for a young lady Della's age to meet eligible young men. It's time suitors were knocking on our door. As soon as my health returns, she'll be able to marry and start a family of her own."

Joshua looked up at his wife's smiling face, and then let his gaze slide over to his daughter's limpid brown eyes. His expression changed, thoughtful, as he forked a mouthful of pie.

Anxiety nibbled at Della. Was there a message in that look? Did he think she wouldn't find a good husband? Or was it that he didn't want her to marry? She couldn't discern the answer.

Anna broke the moment of silence. "You wouldn't mind keeping me company on a Sunday afternoon, would you, my dear?"

Joshua gave her a weak smile. "Of course not. All right Della, you have my permission to attend. I'll have a word with Will Hovey."

Chapter 14

So it was that on the last Sunday afternoon in August Della climbed into the Hovey's buggy with her straw hat snuggly anchored to her hair and her blue parasol under her arm. All week she'd dithered about what to wear. She liked the way her brown dress matched her hair color, but it had a high collar and it might be too warm for the day. Besides, it was a hand-me-down from her sister, Lizzie. The white batiste was out of the question. She finally settled on the blue skirt and white shirtwaist. The skirt would have ample room for hiking if there were that opportunity.

She settled herself on a thick pile of blankets that would soon be spread out on the ground. Cora handed Georgie to her. He jabbered as if he were telling her something important. She nodded and smiled at him. "Sure thing, little guy. We're going on a ride." They had become well acquainted during afternoon coffee klatches she'd been having with his mother. The two older boys needed no help. They stepped on her feet as they shoved and elbowed one another for a favorite spot. Their father gave them a stern look and their pushing halted.

With everyone settled in their places, Will Hovey clucked to the horse and maneuvered the buggy up the road to School Street. Before long, they arrived at the church where a gathering of vehicles were parked. Four large buggies filled with adults and squirming children, a horse-drawn wagon, and an automobile waited there.

A woman walked alongside each waiting vehicle, greeting people and shaking hands. She wore a grass-green dress with a broad collar trimmed in white lace and a matching wide-brimmed green hat.

Della leaned toward Cora, who was sitting in the front seat. "Who is that?"

"That's Mrs. Samples.

"Isn't she one of the opera company group?"

"She is, and a very fine family too. Her brother just arrived from Chicago. I think she said he's some sort of mining executive."

The woman approached the Hovey's buggy. As Cora introduced them, she offered her hand to Della. "Miss McCrea. I'm pleased to meet you. Mrs. Hovey told me about your mother's illness. I'm so sorry to hear of it."

Della nodded and thanked her for her concern. "And thank you for inviting me to the picnic. I've never been to Deception Gulch."

"I'm glad you were able to come along. There'll be a good view of the valley along the way. When we get there, I'll introduce you to my brother. We better be on our way before everyone dies of hunger."

The heavy rain in July had left ruts in the road causing a good deal of careful maneuvering on Will Hovey's part. The buggy tilted this way and that, along with the occupants. Della didn't mind, just going somewhere outside of Jerome was exhilarating. The absence of sulfur fumes was such a relief. She took a deep breath and gazed at the clear blue sky. It was going to be a wonderful day.

Two hours later everyone was climbing out of the conveyances. The Hovey boys jumped from the buggy and scampered down the rocky hillside to a shady level area in a small group of trees. Della handed Georgie to his mother and stepped to the ground. She gathered the blankets to carry and took the picnic basket Will Hovey handed her. He hobbled the horse, took a second basket and a large umbrella out of the buggy, and followed his family.

When everyone had managed to descend the uneven path to the chosen spot, the umbrellas were situated, and women spread out blankets on the ground. Soon picnic baskets were opened and everyone was talking and eating.

Georgie toddled around the blanket, stumbled and fell. Cora pulled him to her and cuddled the sobbing baby. He quieted and in a few minutes was happy again. His brothers gobbled their food, took cookies from a shoe box, and hurried further down the hill to the creek. The slow-moving stream was rocky, hardly deep enough for fishing or swimming, but it drew the children like a magnet.

It appeared that several people had arrived ahead of the main group and had scrapped a clearing for croquet. Boxes of the equipment were soon opened. The space wasn't nearly adequate for a good game, but still, Della, reminded of times she'd played with her brothers and sisters, hoped to be invited to join in.

She felt a tap on her shoulder, and Vesta's voice jarred her from her reverie. "Miss McCrea, I want to introduce you to my brother."

Della sprung to her feet. A young man with a handlebar mustache removed his straw hat and gave a slight bow.

"This is my brother, Percy Blocker." Della didn't hear the rest of the introduction. She had seen him on Independence Day and thought he was quite handsome, but now as she looked at his intense blue eyes, she felt an unfamiliar flutter in her chest. Playing croquet with him would be a delight.

Vesta tugged on her sleeve, pulling her attention away from the young man. "I have news," Vesta said.

Della turned to look at her friend. Vesta was grinning and her eyes sparkled."I'm going to school in Phoenix for the fall term. It's the best finishing school in all of the west. I'm so excited." As if she'd suddenly realized she'd be leaving her friend, her expression changed. "But I'm going to miss you."

Although Vesta had hinted at the possibility when they'd first met, Della was still shocked. She blinked. "You're leaving? When?"

"Next week. My aunt lives there. I'll be staying with her until the day I enter. It's what I've been hoping for all year. I have so much to do." Vesta babbled on with her usual enthusiasm about packing, the upcoming train trip, and the beauty of her aunt's house, but Della didn't hear half of it.

She forced a smile and offered congratulations, but her words were hollow. Even though Vesta was a year younger, she was the only friend she'd acquired since settling in Jerome and now she was leaving. Della fought back tears. In a matter of seconds, the day that had been full of fun and laughter had changed to one of disappointment.

Chapter 15

"Come on, Della. They're choosing up sides for croquet." Vesta hurried off down to the leveled area where stakes were being driven into the ground. Percy gave Della a quick smile and a nod before following his sister.

Vesta's announcement had dampened Della's enthusiasm for the game. She sank down onto the picnic blanket, her shoulders slumping and gnawed on a fingernail.

Cora, who was in the process of returning silverware to the picnic basket, noticed the change in Della's mood. "What's the matter?"

"Vesta's going off to school in Phoenix."

"I see." Cora closed the lid on the basket. "You'll miss her, but don't begrudge her the opportunity. It's what's best for her right now."

In her heart, Della knew Cora was right. Opportunity is what *she* wanted too, the opportunity to go home and go to the music school in Cincinnati. She took a deep breath. Everything depended on her mother's health. That's what she had to concentrate on.

"Will you look after my little one?"Cora said, holding little Georgie out to her. "Even though the water isn't deep, I think I better keep watch on those boys." She motioned to the creek where Billy and Buster Hovey were pushing each other and splashing about.

As soon as Della took Georgie onto her lap, he began to fuss, reaching for his mother. Cora paid him no attention. She lifted her skirt and made her way down to the stream.

Della tweaked his cheek, rolled him onto his back, and tickled his tummy. In no time, she had him giggling. To her surprise, a pair of small feet appeared at the edge of the blanket. She looked up to find a brown-eyed boy of about four years standing in front of her. He held out his shoes. "Hold these, please."

She didn't have a chance to refuse. He dropped the shoes on the blanket and scurried off to join the other children. She watched him run. Children are so trusting, she mused. With Georgie happy again, Della let her gaze wander down to the croquet game and then farther up the stream to where Nellie was climbing over the rocks. She reached out to pick a wildflower, abruptly jumped back and shrieked, the sound echoing off the hillside.

All heads turned. Will Hovey bolted in the direction of his daughter. Three other men were right behind him. The others in the party stood silent as if holding their collective breath.

Nellie pointed. "A s-s-snake." Will grabbed her around the waist and pulled her back away. With the girl at a safe distance, Will turned his attention to the pile of rocks. One of the men who'd followed handed him a croquet mallet. Will approached the spot Nellie had pointed out. He poked the scrub brush in several places for a full minute but found no snake. Satisfied it had slithered away, Will straightened and lifted his arms in an "all clear" gesture.

With a communal sigh of relief, everyone returned to their former activities, and Nellie was sent to join her mother by the creek. Several parents were heard warning children to not wander off, as there could be other snakes in the area.

"Where there's one, you're likely to find its mate," Della heard a man behind her say.

She looked over her shoulder to see who was speaking. A man, attired in a black suit and tie and wearing a bowler hat, was standing next to Mrs. Samples who was holding a white parasol for shade. "Snakes are uncommon in town," she said, "but we've learned to be cautious."

Noticing Della looking at them, Mrs. Samples moved in her direction. "Let me introduce you to another newcomer, Hiram."

Understanding her intention, Della placed Georgie on his feet next to her and rose, though knowing how quick he was to run off, she kept a grip on his little hand.

With a broad smile, Mrs. Samples said, "Miss McCrea, may I present my brother, Hiram Bennett."

The man approached, gave a little bow, and removed his hat. "Pleased to meet you, Miss."

Della returned the greeting, but it struck her that the man's attire looked out of place. The other men had chosen dungarees and wide-brimmed hats for the afternoon.

"Hiram arrived just last week from Chicago," Mrs. Samples continued. "He plans to make his home here. His company has invested in one of the local mines."

"I see my son presumed upon your kindness," he said, pointing to the pair of brown shoes on the blanket.

"Oh, I don't mind," Della replied, while at the same time trying to keep Georgie, who was tugging on her hand, from escaping her grasp.

The boy who'd left his shoes in her care came running up the hill and stood in front of Mr. Bennett. He was shivering. His father chuckled. "That water's cold, I see." Turning to Della, he said, "My son, Davie." Looking at his sister, he said, "I hope there are towels available."

"Right over in that black satchel," she responded.

Mr. Bennett picked up the shoes, excused himself, and led the boy away to be dried off.

"My brother is a widower," Mrs. Samples said. "His dear wife, Florence, died in childbirth almost four years ago. So sad. She was such a sweet girl, and so young, barely thirty. It's been such a trial for him and the boy."

Della gave a little nod in an expected sympathetic gesture, now cued into recognizing that the woman was trying to play matchmaker. She felt herself bristle. She'd never consider marriage to someone so much older than herself.

Georgie was whining and continuing to pull on her hand. Responding to him, she lifted the boy into her arms.

"I can see you get on well with children," Mrs. Samples said with the smile of a snake charmer.

But Della didn't have a chance to answer. A sudden gust of wind blew the beach umbrella down the slope. She set Georgie on his feet and rushed to catch it. The little boy squealed and ran after her. When she'd retrieved it, she was quick to take Georgie's hand and returned to the picnic blanket. While she secured the umbrella with extra rocks, she noticed Mrs. Samples had wandered off to talk to someone else.

Settling herself and the boy, she heard a shout come from the croquet game. Apparently, there was a winner. Soon Georgie leaned against her, his eyelids heavy and nearly closed. She looked down at his sweet face and sighed. Any chance of playing croquet had passed. The heat of the afternoon had reached its peak, and despite the shade of the umbrella, she was beginning to feel uncomfortable. She snatched one of the picnic napkins and dabbed her forehead.

Cora Hovey came up the hill with Billy. He'd fallen and a large blue spot was forming on his forehead. She sat him down on the blanket. "Stay put," she said to him. Handing Della the towel she'd brought from the creek, she began gathering the family's belongings. "I don't know if you've noticed, but dark clouds forming over in the west. We'll have to leave soon or we could get caught in a thunderstorm."

Della picked up the water jug and the bag containing Georgie's clothing. "Mrs. Samples introduced me to her brother.

"That's nice. He's from Chicago."

"I think she's hoping to find a new wife for him. I don't know why she introduced him to me."

Cora chuckled. "You could do worse. I hear he's rich."

"People always say that, but I don't care if he's gold-plated. I'm not interested."

The rain began just as Will Hovey pulled the buggy to a stop in front of their house. Everyone scrambled out as big raindrops began to fall. Della helped unload the buggy, thanked both Cora and Will, and made her way home.

She found Anna sitting in her rocking chair in the living room. Della glanced around. "Where's Father?"

"He went uptown for a bit. Did you have a good time at the picnic?"

Della perched on her father's footstool and recounted the events of the afternoon, describing the gulch, the snake incident, and the fact that Vesta was leaving for school.

"I'm sure you'll miss her, but you have to be glad she'll be getting a wonderful education."

Della heaved a deep sigh. "Of course. And I *am* happy for her." She stood. "I should fix supper."

Anna made a dismissive gesture with her hand. "Your father stoked the stove, and I warmed the roast and potatoes from last night." She motioned to the library table. "There's a letter from your Aunt Gertrude over there. Your brother just got a raise in salary."

Della picked up the letter and went into the kitchen. She made a sandwich out of cold roast beef and sat at the kitchen table to read the news from home.

Chapter 16

One hot month slid into another with brief rain storms and windy days until October arrived. But Della hardly had time to take notice. Her days revolved around household chores and the care of her mother. She often reviewed the printed sheet of instructions the doctor had given them during the earlier visit to his office.

Often in the evening, Anna's cheeks would flush, signaling a fever. A weakness would overtake her, and she'd ask Della to help her to bed. The only thing Della knew to do for the fever was to put ice chips into a pan of water and use a washcloth to cool her.

One evening as Della wiped Anna's feverish brow, her mother reached out and laid her hand on Della's arm. "My sweet daughter. I've made life so hard for you."

"Don't be silly," Della protested. "You're my mother. I wouldn't have it any other way." It wasn't entirely true. If she'd had a magic wand to wave over her mother and make the awful disease go away, she'd have done it in an instant.

"This is all my fault," Anna said. "I'm such a burden. Other girls your age are enjoying parties and dances with a new beau every week. And you should be too."

"Being sick is not your fault, Mama. No one chooses it. It's the sort of thing that just happens."

Anna sighed. "You're wrong. If I hadn't gone to Chicago to help Cousin Harriet after little Elizabeth was born, I wouldn't have caught her sickness. I had no idea she'd developed consumption till after I got to her apartment, and then it was too late. There was no one else to take care of her and that poor baby."

Della remembered her mother's absence, but couldn't recall any mention of her cousin's situation. "Did she get better? I don't think you ever spoke of a baby."

"I stayed two weeks until Aunt Grace arrived from New York. A letter came the following Christmas. Both Harriet and the baby died." Anna's eyes filled with tears. She started to cough and reached for the small jar, the receptacle she coughed into.

At night Della lay in bed and listened to her mother cough, knowing the homemade handkerchiefs her mother placed in her bedside basket would be streaked with bloody phlegm. In the morning, Della carefully gathered the cloth items and burned them in the fire pit behind the house. Everything that touched her mother's lips had to be either burned or boiled, according to the instruction sheet.

In November when they visited the doctor, he gently thumped Anna's rail-thin chest and back, and listened to her lungs. As he applied the stethoscope to her back, he looked at Della, who stood nearby, and shook his head, acknowledging what Della had suspected. Her mother was not getting any better.

By the end of the month, Anna had almost given up on leaving her bed. Della brought her meals to her bedside, though she never ate more than a few mouthfuls. Her night chills and fever became more frequent, and her coughing made sleep impossible for anyone in the house.

Joshua gave up trying to sleep on the sofa. He came home for supper, and then, after inquiring about his wife, would walk off toward town before dark. He'd return in the morning in time to dress for work and collect his dinner pail. He never said where he spent the night. Della convinced herself that he was staying in a hotel so that he could get needed rest.

One morning Anna asked her daughter to write a letter for her. Della took a piece of lined paper from her notebook and wrote what her mother dictated. It was a short note to the family in Ohio and had the ring of a goodbye missive. By the time Della finished, she could hardly see the ink on the page for the tears in her eyes. But Anna seemed satisfied as if it was something she needed to do. She asked Della to make a copy and send it to her sister in Indiana.

Other than the fact that the days and nights had cooled considerably, it was hard to tell it was autumn as far as Della was concerned. There were no trees to turn color. The sulfurous fumes from the smelter had killed them years earlier. Though she hardly had time to notice the landscape outside the house, when she did, the desolate mountains and chain of brown hills grated on her. She longed for the sight of the colorful maple and ginkgo foliage that made Ohio so beautiful in the fall.

Even if there had been something of beauty to look at, she could never venture far from the house. She feared being out of earshot of her mother's call.

It didn't help that she could hear sounds from nearby houses: voices of children coming home from school, a baby crying, or the bleating of nanny goats pastured a stone's throw away. The whistle at the mine reverberated all over the town. And, of course, there was the rumble from the underground blasting which she'd never gotten used to, as Vesta had suggested. She missed the time when she'd been able to have afternoon coffee with Cora next door, but that was out of the question.

The boy who delivered the groceries couldn't leave fast

enough. It was clear that he'd been warned about Anna's disease. He'd leave the basket on the rear steps, snatch the new list from Della's hand, and be gone.

She did have occasion to speak to the "goat lady," who lived catty-corner across the fence. She was a buxom woman who dressed like a farmer in overalls and a man's shirt. A few coins would buy a jar of milk and a few minutes talk about the weather, the price of potatoes, or other such foodstuffs.

From the time they'd settled in the house, though a neighbor might wave in passing, no one came to call as was the custom back in Ohio. Della knew why. Word of Anna's illness had passed among the families, and soon it was like their house had a skull and crossbones painted on their front door.

However, one afternoon Della was startled by a knock on the front door. When she opened it, she was surprised to see Cora Hovey.

"Georgie is taking a nap, so I thought I could get away for a few minutes. How is your mother?" she asked, peeking around the door frame. "I miss seeing her sitting on the porch."

"She's sleeping," Della responded. "Her cough gives her little rest."

Della stepped out onto the porch and motioned to the chairs located there. "I wish I could invite you in, but you know ...." She left the door open lest her mother might call, and moved to sit in the wooden rocker chair, while Cora settled on the chair next to her. "I fear she'll never have the strength to sit out here again."

"How are you getting on? I see you out in back of the house washing clothes with those tubs and boiler."

Della pressed her lips together for a second. "I have no choice. I can't send anything to the Chinese laundry. All the bedding, towels, our clothing, the dishes, everything that comes in contact with Mother, has to be boiled. Most of my dresses are ruined from it." She lifted the skirt of the one she was wearing. "The sun has faded the colors of every one of them. But I have kept one dress set aside for when ..." Della bit her lower lip, her eyes glistened with tears.

Cora plucked a handkerchief out of her apron pocket and passed it to her.

Della thanked her, wiped an eye, and rested her hands in her lap. "I don't even bother putting up my hair anymore." She touched the edge of the tan night bonnet covering her hair. "I just braid it and wear this."

Cora noticed Della's hands were red and raw. "Your hands ..."

Della gave a sniff. "Yes, aren't they lovely? It's because I wash them twenty times a day aside from doing the dishes and washing clothes. And still I'm fearful I will have the disease too."

"Is there no chance at all of her improving?" Cora asked.

"It's hopeless. The doctor wanted her to go to a sanatorium when we first arrived here, but she refused. Now it's too late." Agitated, she twisted the handkerchief in her hand. "There are days when I wish all this would be over." The second the words were out of her mouth, she regretted them. Cora couldn't possibly understand. She was so calm and satisfied with her life.

Cora blinked, her eyes filled with astonishment. "You don't mean that."

"She's suffering. We all are. When I get letters from my sisters, I sit and cry. I miss them so much, my brothers too. I long to be home by Christmas."

Chapter 17

Cora reached out and took one of Della's work-worn hands in hers. "You're carrying too big a burden for someone your age. I'm sorry to say it, but the only thing I can do is to pray for you."

Della pulled her hand away, aware of the risk in Cora's impulsive gesture. "It's good of you to listen to my troubles." She clasped her hands in her lap. "My father isn't around much to listen, and even if he were, I doubt he'd put up with my whining. He'd remind me that it's my duty."

"Mama ... mama," a small child's voice called from next door.

"Georgie's awake." Cora glanced toward her house and stood. "The other children will be home from school soon. I must go." As she turned to leave, her little son, barefoot and in his nightshirt, pushed open their screen door, stepped out onto the porch, and rubbed one eye with his fist.

Della watched Cora cross the space between the houses, pick the child up and go inside. After the door quietly closed, Della remained seated for a few minutes and thought about her neighbor. There was nothing remarkable about Cora except her good heart, Della observed. She wasn't homely, but she wasn't pretty either. Her thick brown hair was always pulled back in a practical bun. She guessed plain would be the right word. Her everyday dress was made from flour sacks as was her apron, but she didn't seem to mind.

Della pressed her lips together. I'm not going to end up like her, stuck in this town and wearing flour-sack dresses. I'd lose my mind.

Suddenly struck by a pang of guilt for her critical thoughts, Della had to admit that Cora knew many things that she did not, things about the town, the mine, the people, and even more. She'd concocted a medicine that cured a sick goat belonging to the neighbor over the fence.

Della pushed out of the chair and went to the door. She paused at the doorway and looked up the road toward the center of town and the undulating slopes above. The mountain was starting to cast a shadow over the houses perched at the highest elevation. In a window here or there, a light came on. She had to admit when all the lights of the city twinkled, it was sort of pretty. It was about the only time she could say that because the landscape was hard to admire. Other than in a gully where determined cottonwood might take hold, there wasn't a sprig of green anywhere.

The sound of coughing came from the bedroom and pulled

Della from her musing. She stepped inside, closed the door, and hurried to the kitchen where a pan of tepid water sat on the drainboard. She wrung the clean cloth she'd left there and went to her mother's room.

"Della?" Anna whispered, her voice raspy.

"Yes, Mama. I'm here." Della settled on the side of the bed. The pallid face she gazed upon barely resembled the picture of her mother embedded in her memory. Her skin was tightly pulled over her facial bones, her eyes dull, sunken and tired. Della folded the cloth which had been torn from her mother's second-best petticoat and wiped her mother's parched mouth, then folded it again, and placed it on her feverish brow.

"Your papa ... supper," Anna said with a gasp. "Fix it nice." Her lips formed a cracked smile.

Della grimaced. "If he comes." In the last week, Joshua had twice failed to arrive at all, and Della ate the cold supper alone.

The sick woman made an effort to raise her head and gave her daughter a sharp look. "Don't think ... bad ...'bout your papa." Her head dropped back on the pillow. She sucked air as if the exertion had taken her last ounce of energy.

Della laid her hand on her mother's boney shoulder. "I don't, Mama. He'll be coming along soon, I'm sure." But she wasn't sure at all. In fact, she thought it was likely he'd stopped at one of the saloons in town.

"Listen." Anna paused to take in a breath. "He just ...can't abide." She gasped before continuing. "Tears him up inside ... to see ... me laying here..." She closed her eyes, grimaced, and shook her head. "After I'm gone..." A coughing spasm gripped her, causing her face to turn a dusky shade. She placed her hand over her mouth, revealing dried blood under her fingernails. When the spasm subsided, a trickle of dark blood showed at the corner of her mouth. Della took the cloth from her forehead and wiped it away.

"Oh, Mama, don't say that. I'll make some potato soup. It'll give you some strength."

Anna gripped her daughter's wrist, her voice rasping. "Won't help." She pursed her lips and sucked in air. "If you," another breath, "Papa all right ... I ... can die in peace." With each inhaled breath, the skin beneath her collar bones pulled inward. "Tell me ... take care ... him."

"Of course, I will, Mama." Della stood. "Let me just rinse this cloth."

Her thoughts jammed together as she hurried to the kitchen. Where is he? She's worse off today. She dipped the blood-tinged rag and wrung it. The sound of another coughing spell came from the bedroom.

When Della returned to the bedside, a smattering of crimson stained her mother's gown. In former days, that sort of thing would have horrified her mother. Now she seemed unaware. Della sat again and rubbed the spots in an effort to remove them.

Anna reached up and touched her daughter's cheek with boney fingers. "So precious." Her chest heaved as she sucked in a breath. "I pray ... a good man ... babies." A forceful cough followed, and blood spattered on her cheeks, gown and pillow.

Fearful now, Della's heartbeat quickened as she leaned forward to wipe her mother's face. With the next spasm, blood seeped from the corner of Anna's mouth.

"Oh, Mama." Della jumped up and hurried to the kitchen, threw the cloth on the floor, and grabbed the dish towel. She tore it in two, dipped it in the pan, squeezed it, and ran back to the bedroom where she saw blood oozing from her mother's mouth. Sitting again, she said, "It's all right, Mama. I'll wipe it away."

Frantic, she slid her arm under her mother's shoulders and lifted her as she tried to clean her mother's face. But the blood wasn't to be contained. It ran freely over Anna's chin and onto her neck, soaking into her gown.

Anna gave out a strangled cough, then slowly turned her head as though she'd heard someone call. Her glassy gaze drifted to the open window next to the bed, and she nodded. A blue-gray pallor crept over her face, and her brown eyes became a vacant stare.

"Mama. You can't. Not now!" In disbelief, Della stared at her mother. As realization sank in, tears blurred her vision. She lifted her face heavenward and wailed.

Seconds later, the front door slammed and Cora was at her side.

"Do something," Della pleaded, still cradling her mother.

"Lay her down, child. There's nothing anyone can do. Your mama's gone."

Della gently eased her mother down on the blood-stained pillow, turned to Cora, buried her face in her apron and sobbed. "I didn't mean it, Cora. I didn't want her to die."

Cora's voice quavered. "You had nothin' to do with it, girl. It was time for your mama to go, that's all."

Della rose, stumbled from the room and into the kitchen. She dropped onto the chair at the table and leaned her head on her folded arms. Her body shook as she sobbed, "Oh, Mama, I didn't mean it. I didn't mean it. I'm so sorry."

Chapter 18

Joshua McCrea arrived home a short while after his wife's passing. When Della heard the front door close, she thought it was Cora, but then saw it was her father. She ran to him and still sobbing, buried her face against his chest. He dropped his lunch bucket and folded his arms around her. "I hurried, Della. Something told me ..."

They stood wrapped in each other's misery for some time. Finally, Joshua took a deep breath and stiffened his back. He pulled away from his daughter and put his hands on her shoulders. "There are some things we must do," he said.

Confused by his words, she looked up at him, her eyes liquid.

Grim-faced, he gazed at her, then raised his chin and pressed his eyes closed for a second. "You must prepare your mother for burial."

"Oh no. Papa, I can't."

"You must, the consumption—no one else can or would do it."

She stepped back and looked around for Cora, but Cora was

gone. "I can't. I just can't."

Joshua walked out the back door and sat down on the steps. He braced his elbows on his knees and held his head in his hands, shutting out the world.

Della stared after him, then stumbled to her room and pushed the door closed. She pulled off her apron, threw it aside, and clawed at the buttons on her dress. She let the dress drop to the floor, crawled up onto her bed, and curled herself into a ball.

Della carefully prepared the message for her family, directing it to her oldest sister. She handed it through the window to the telegraph operator. The wizened old man read it and muttered the required fee.

> To: Mrs. Henrietta Hill
> Peach Lane
> Alexandria, Ohio
>
> From: Della McCrea
> Jerome, Arizona
> December 1, 1904
> Brothers and Sisters. Mama passed at
> 6 P.M. yesterday.
> Burial here. Letter follows.
> Della

The following afternoon a small gathering of people trudged along behind the hearse to the cemetery for Anna McCrea's funeral. The slag-covered road led to a rocky hogback less than a mile east of town where the graves of many of the townspeople were located, including those who died in less than peaceful circumstances.

It took every ounce of determination Della could muster to force herself to move forward. She had a sickish feeling in her stomach. Her hands trembled. The last few days had been the worst of her young life.

She'd fumbled her way through washing and dressing her mother's body. The hardest part was combing her hair and sliding the mother-of-pearl combs, Anna's favorite, into place. She wasn't sure why she did it. No one was likely to view her, aside from her father and herself, but it seemed like the right thing to do. The only reason she knew what to do at all was because she'd seen her mother prepare her grandfather. The difference was that back then they didn't burn his clothing.

This time, Joshua had built a bonfire in back of the house, and Della had carried out Anna's bedding, nightgowns, dresses, hats and shoes, even her Bible. Everything she'd used, except what could be boiled. The mattress and the bedroom rug took the longest to burn and smoldered for hours.

The only exception was her mother's best Sunday dress.

Della had saved it, the brown one with a white lace collar. Anna, so thin Della had to fold the excess material beneath her, wasn't much more than a skeleton with skin stretched over her bones. But it hardly mattered. As Della had expected, no one came to view her. The house was considered a place of pestilence. Cora and the goat-lady brought dishes of food as was the custom, but neither came in. The minister from church came and stood on the porch to talk to her father, sharing a few words of consolation.

As the grave markers came into view, Della glanced around and was appalled at the dismal location. Unlike the park-like cemetery where her grandparents had been laid to rest, this was beyond imagination, no grass, no trees, not even a decent-sized bush. The graves were arranged in a haphazard fashion. Looking at the rocky terrain, Della reasoned that it was due to the difficulty of penetrating the surface. The tops of the coffins were barely beneath the ground. Many had a cement slab covering them, or a metal fence for protection. Some had both. Most had some sort of wooden marker. She strained to read names she didn't recognize as she walked along. A few had no marker at all and only a pile of rocks covering the coffin. She shuddered at the thought of some wild animal defiling her mother's grave.

With the exception of her father, Reverend Smith, the Methodist minister, and the undertaker, all who attended were women, neighbors who felt a duty. Cora stood among them, holding little Georgie. The work at the mine prevented men from attending, even if they felt like it.

Della barely heard the words spoken over her mother's grave. A numbness permeated her being. She watched the plain wooden box being lowered a mere three feet into the ground, and absently pondered about how long it had taken the mortician's men to dig even that far. A pile of stones nearby told a tale of how hard it had been.

As the neighbors departed, each nodded to Joshua and a few touched Della's shoulder in an act of condolence. They hurried off, returning to their daily lives. After all the women had left, Della stared at her mother's grave, hoping the ache in her chest would soon pass. Who would finish covering the coffin, she wondered. But then she supposed her father had made arrangements for that to happen.

She turned away and walked back down the road to where the rented horse and buggy were waiting. When she climbed in, the horse swung his head around to glance at her.

As she waited for her father to finish his business with the undertaker, she tried to recall what the minister had said. She'd found herself distracted by thoughts of finding the empty coffin setting on the porch that morning. She'd known one would be necessary, but still, the sight of it startled her. Her father had pulled the coffin inside, then laid a clean bed sheet on the floor, and they'd moved her mother's body from the bed to the sheet. It took little effort to place her in the box since she weighed no more than a child.

It wasn't until then that she realized that having deluded herself into thinking her mother would get well, she hadn't thought of needing mourning apparel. With the press of time, her only recourse was to remove the blue and white lace trim on her gray dress to give it a more subdued appearance. It hardly mattered, anyway, as she wore her winter coat.

She twisted in the seat and looked back to where her father was standing and studied him. Was he really more stooped now, or had she simply not looked at him lately? That morning she'd noticed that he had more gray hair and that his face was more lined and weary-looking.

A rush of apprehension passed over her, but she pushed it aside and turned back in her seat. How old is he? Etta would be twenty-five, she calculated, and Lizzie twenty-three. That would make Richard twenty-one and Lon nineteen. Then the twins who'd died at birth. Father must be forty-six and Mama, forty-five. Della pulled a handkerchief out of her drawstring bag and wiped her eyes. That's not old, she thought, not like Grandpa Chrisman. He was all bent over and almost blind.

Her reflections were interrupted when she heard her father

approach. He climbed into the buggy, untied the reins, and gave them a snap to urge the horse forward. They rode in silence with only the clap of the horse's hooves on the road to mark the miles returning to town.

Chapter 19

During the week following her mother's funeral, Della scrubbed every surface of the sick room and the bathroom. With her loss heavy on her heart, she often found herself crying while she worked. And even after the work was complete, little things caused a torrent of tears, like the absence of Anna's Bible. She'd read passages from it every morning all her life until the last month. Or the sight of her jewelry box, a gift from her daughters the previous Christmas. Remembering those happier times made her weep.

She didn't sleep well either. The last hours of her mother's life replayed in her dreams. And when she'd wake in the night, her thoughts wandered to the grave on the rocky hilltop where she imagined some animal sniffing around.

Though she prepared meals as usual and sat to eat with her father, he was poor company since he had little to say. He didn't finish his supper that first night and left the house shortly after, only muttering the name of a man he intended to see.

When he returned many hours later, the smell of alcohol was

evident. It was understandable, she decided. He'd just buried his wife of more than twenty-five years.

In the morning, he rose from the sofa where he'd slept and barely spoke to her. He rushed through his breakfast, grabbed his dinner pail, and left for work.

When the same thing happened the rest of that week and into the next, she wrested herself from her melancholy and began to worry, fearful the new pattern would become permanent. And then one night he didn't come home at all. She sat in the dark soaking up the emptiness of the house and racked her brain trying to think of some way to influence him. She couldn't just sit by and do nothing.

The following Sunday turned out to be bright and sunny. There'd been a couple of days of rain during the week. While Della prepared breakfast, she settled on an idea. She scooped bacon, eggs, and potatoes onto one of the plates and set it in front of her father. When she'd served herself and took her seat across from him, she picked up her fork. "I think it would please Mother if we were to go to church."

Joshua's head jerked up, his fork poised before his mouth, and looked at her. He didn't respond and continued his meal. Several minutes passed before he finished eating. He drank the last mouthful of coffee, wiped his mouth with the napkin and stood. "I think you're right," he said, turned and left the kitchen.

Over the next half hour, while Della finished her breakfast and began cleaning the dishes, she heard doors in the house open and close. His words had puzzled her, but she supposed he was dressing to go into town, as it was his new habit. She was leaning over, putting the skillet in the oven to dry, when Joshua appeared in the doorway.

"You better hustle," he said, "if we are going to make it to church before the doors close. It's no short walk, you know."

A stiff wind off the upper peaks of Mingus Mountain made Della pull her shawl tighter around herself as she and her father walked up the long incline. By taking shortcuts between buildings, they were able to shorten the time it took to arrive at the corner of Center Avenue and School Street where Haven Methodist Church stood. The silver-gray building, with its art-glass windows, fairly shone in the morning light as they approached along the slag-covered road to the entrance.

Once inside, Joshua chose one of the back pews and they settled into their seats. The church was nearly full, and there was a buzz of conversation as people greeted one another. She looked around for Cora and her family, caught sight of them in one of the front pews, and when Nellie spotted her and waved, Della responded with a smile and a nod.

A hush soon fell over the congregation as Pastor Smith,

dressed in his black robe, stepped up to the pulpit. He was a short man, middle-aged, with thinning gray hair and a gray beard. He had shepherded the small congregation since its inception in 1900, according to what Cora had told Della, and had actually helped build the church building. After the first hymn, he grasped the edge of the lectern and launched into his sermon, reminding his flock of the true meaning of repentance.

When the service was over, Joshua stood and moved into the aisle. He was greeted by two or three other men and followed them out of the building to smoke and continue talking. Della supposed that they might be men he worked with in the mine. She draped her shawl over her arm and waited at the back of the church near the door in hopes of speaking to Cora.

To her surprise, Mrs. Samples stopped on her way out to offer condolence. Several other women followed suit, remarking that they'd heard the tragic news about her mother and understood how much she must miss her. A few commented on their own losses. The pastor's wife, Ruby Smith, told Della her sister had died from the same disease and she still grieved for her though it had been several years.

She was much relieved that no one seemed to have noticed she was wearing a gray dress rather than the traditional black. Maybe the shawl made up for it.

Immersed in her own thoughts, she barely noticed Millie

Swanson worm her way through the gathering until Millie reached to clutch her hand. "I'm so very glad to see you," Millie said. "And I'm so sorry to hear about your mother." Her brow furrowed, doing her best to convey sincerity. "I do hope you'll be able to come more often now." Millie moved aside to allow others to pass. "We're planning a Christmas pageant. I don't imagine you would feel like taking part," she said, raising her eyebrows.

Della shook her head. "It wouldn't be seemly. And I think we may be leaving for home soon."

"Oh. I'm sorry to hear that. I had a note from Vesta to say her school will close next week for the holidays. I so look forward to seeing her. I know she will be crushed when she hears you have left. She is hoping to get together a group to go caroling."

Just then, Millie's family came along the aisle, and her mother motioned to her, anxious to leave. Millie shrugged and smiled. "I better not keep my parents waiting." She fell in behind one of her brothers and passed through the doorway.

The Hovey boys startled Della, rushing ahead of their parents, bounding through the narthex and out of sight. Not far behind, was Will, carrying Georgie. Cora, holding Nellie's hand paused, reached out, and squeezed Della's forearm. "Good to see you out and about. Come over for coffee tomorrow."

"Thank you. I will." Della pulled her shawl around her shoulders and moved to follow them.

Just outside, Reverend Smith was shaking hands with people, and Della took her turn before scanning the lingering crowd for her father. She saw Joshua was engrossed in a conversation with two men. One of them, she recognized was Mrs. Samples' brother, Mr. Bennett. He was wearing the same suit and bowler hat he'd worn at the church picnic. The other man, a thin-faced fellow with a hook nose, seemed to disagree with whatever was being said. He shook his head, stepped away a few paces, and ground out his cigarette on the slag roadway before he hurried off to join his family.

Mr. Bennett put his hand on her father's shoulder and continued talking. Della hesitated, not wanting to interrupt. By Joshua's expression, the subject was a serious one. After a moment, they shook hands, and Mr. Bennett headed in the direction of a horse-drawn carriage where Mrs. Samples was waiting.

The assembly had thinned to a handful. Reverend Smith left his position at the church door, walked down the steps and over to Joshua. He put his hand on Joshua's coat sleeve.

Feeling impatient, Della took a deep breath and drew her shawl more tightly around her. She followed but stood at a polite distance while the two men talked, the pastor stroking his scraggly, eight-inch gray beard as she suspected, he often did when he was giving advice. After a couple of minutes, they shook hands, and the clergyman, retracing his steps, went inside the church.

Joshua turned to her. "Let's get on home." He adjusted his hat and started for the road in front of the church.

"Reverend Smith seems really nice," Della commented as she hurried to keep pace with him.

"Maybe. Too interested in other people's business, I think."

She didn't respond but wondered what the pastor had said to rankle him. They walked along in silence, passing between rooming houses and restaurants. Being Sunday, the businesses were closed and the town was relatively quiet.

Soon, they reached the switchbacks and entered the residential area. She began to rehearse the question that had been on her mind, and when they turned onto Holley Avenue which led to their house, she decided to wait no longer. "Papa? When can we pack the trunks and go home?"

He didn't answer and after a minute she began to think he hadn't heard her, perhaps distracted by his own thoughts of whatever Mr. Bennett had said.

Finally, he spoke. "Della, United Verde mine is one of the richest in the country. The pay here is better than anywhere I've worked. I've started to invest some. By next fall, I believe I should be able to send you to a good school, maybe in Prescott. You could become a teacher like your sister. No, Della, I don't intend to leave Jerome. Our future is here in Arizona Territory."

Della felt her pulse race. Next fall! That was practically a year away. And it wasn't going home. How could he possibly think she'd want to go to school in Prescott. It was only a dozen miles from Jerome—the same dry landscape, the same scorching summers. Her stomach turned sour. She couldn't speak, not even to argue with him. His decision was unimaginable. She blinked and tried to restrain tears that threatened. She fumbled to pull a handkerchief from her bag to wipe her runny nose.

Joshua glanced over at her. "Don't be a baby, Della. Arizona is thriving. Mining is expanding, especially around Jerome. There're a lot of opportunities. I've been thinking of writing to your brothers and advising them to come here to work. They could choose from any number of mines. You'd like that, wouldn't you?"

Her brothers? That meant she'd have three men to cook and clean up after instead of one. She loved her brothers and yearned to see them, but not in Jerome. She wanted to walk in the door of their home in Ohio and hug them both. Her father's plan made her heartsick.

Chapter 20

During the remainder of the walk to the house, Della focused her thoughts on how she could convince her father to change his mind, not only about recruiting her brothers to become mine workers but to reconsider remaining in Arizona. She was sure she'd have to appeal to some aspect of the financial part of his reasoning. However, she was out of her element when it came to such matters. She'd lived in frugal comfort in a nice home due to the fact that the house had been inherited, and her parents were careful about how they spent what her father earned.

For years her mother had made most of their clothing, at least all of the dresses that she and her sisters needed. She'd also taught her daughters how to sew, something Della, in particular, had become quite skilled at doing. She'd even learned how to do a little tailoring of her father's garments when needed.

However, recently, since her mother had become ill, the doctor bills seemed to have put a strain on her parents' budget. And now with the expense of her mother's funeral, perhaps her father was overly burdened.

All during the preparation for the noon meal, Della thought about the problem, hers and her father's. She placed a platter of fried chicken on the table, followed by a dish of mashed potatoes and a bowl of gravy. The season for fresh vegetables had long since passed, but Della had discovered that one of the grocers had jars of stewed tomatoes on his shelf. They were a bit more expensive, but she'd purchased one anyway. She heated the vegetable in a saucepan until the aroma had mixed with the fried chicken, then added the steaming dish to the meal.

While pouring coffee into Joshua's favorite mug, she said, "Father, what is the cost of renting this house?" She returned the coffee pot to the stove and took a seat at the table.

Joshua scowled. He scooped mashed potatoes onto his plate. "I don't think that is any concern of yours."

"I suppose not, but I got to thinking that if we were living in our own house, we wouldn't have to pay rent. And maybe the difference would make up for less money in your pay envelope." She watched his reaction and saw a flush of red creep up his neck.

"Daughter, you're getting into an area that is none of your business," he said, his tone hard. He stabbed a piece of chicken off the platter with such fierceness, that it almost frightened her. Clearly, she'd blundered into sensitive territory.

He looked across the table with a glare. "For your

information, I've given the matter a good deal of thought. There's more money to be made here than anywhere in the country. Even the youngest miner can make two dollars a day. I have no intention of going back to Ohio. And when your brothers come, you'll see that it was the best thing for all of us." He turned his attention to his dinner and poured a ladle of gravy over his potatoes.

Della's shoulders sagged. She'd lost her appetite. The meal was consumed in silence, and afterward, while Della cleaned up the supper dishes, Joshua composed a letter to his sons.

Della stepped into the post office the next day and noted a thirty-gallon waste container standing by the desk next to the door. Her father had asked her to post the letter to her brothers, and at that moment, she was sorely tempted to deposit it right there.

She hesitated next to the tall can, but then saw the jowly-faced young man behind the window at the counter was watching her. One of the irritating facts about living in a town of barely three thousand people was that everyone knew everyone's business. She bit her lip, stepped forward, and passed the envelope across the counter to him along with two pennies for a stamp.

He squinted at the envelope. "I believe there is some mail for you. Hold on, I'll get it." He disappeared behind a partition that separated the sorting room from the reception area. After a few minutes, he returned with two letters in his hand. "Here you go, Miss McCrea." He held them out across the counter and grinned, exposing the fact that he had several missing teeth.

She reached to take the letters from his hand, but then he didn't let go and leaned forward his grin widening. She could feel his eyes on the bodice of her dress.

Della's eyes narrowed. She gave the letters a quick tug and he released the pressure. "Thank you," she said through her teeth, spun around, and went out the door.

"What a wicked creature," she muttered. A man and woman passing by on the boardwalk gave her a quizzical look. She gathered her shawl around her with a jerk and proceeded down the boardwalk.

Later that afternoon when she'd settled on a chair in Cora Hovey's kitchen, she related the episode.

Her hostess laughed. "That fellow is Pete Collins," Cora said. She poured a cup of coffee for Della. "He lost those teeth when he made google eyes at Thelma Watson one time too many. Joe Watson popped him a good one."

"He's disgusting." Della picked up the cup and took a sip.

Cora set a plate of leftover breakfast biscuits on the table along with a dish of butter and a bowl of jam. "Keep in mind the men working here outnumber the women three to one. Some of those men have no manners at all. It's best to keep your parasol handy and give 'em a good whack when they get too friendly."

Cora poured herself a cup of coffee and sat down at the table. She broke one of the biscuits in two and spread a dab of butter on it, plus a spoonful of jam. "I see you need some curtains to replace the ones you had to discard. I have some yard goods you could use if you want to make curtains for that bedroom."

"Father said I can order from the Montgomery Ward catalog. I was hoping I wouldn't have to do that, since we'd be leaving for Ohio, but now he says he means to stay right here in Jerome. The pay is better, he says, than at home. I hardly slept last night for thinking about it."

Della went on to tell her friend about the letter to her brothers and the prospect of school the following fall. "But if Richard and Lon come here to work, I'll never be able to leave, even to attend school. I'm sure of it. I'll be cooking and washing clothes for them too."

Cora tilted her head a bit to one side. "Well, I just know God has a plan for you." She made a motion to the plate, an invitation for Della to help herself.

Della took a biscuit. "I suppose so, but I doubt I'm going to like it." She broke the biscuit, added butter and jam, and took a bite. Swallowing the morsel, she said, "I confess, you do make the best biscuits, Cora."

"It's the goat's milk. I let it sour before I use it." Cora finished her first biscuit and chose another one.

"Aunt Gertrude wrote to tell us how bad she felt that Mother had passed. She said she felt like my mother was her own sister. I guess they knew each other for a long time. She's anxious for us to return. She'll be shocked when she hears what my father plans for my brothers."

The noise of a wagon on the road in front of the house drew the attention of both women. They leaned to look through the kitchen window and saw a brown horse pull a wagon to a stop in front of the McCrea house. Among the boxes piled on the wagon was a huge crate tied to the side stakes.

"Father ordered a new mattress." Della stood and picked up the shawl she'd draped on the back of the chair. "Thanks for the coffee, Cora. And for listening to my complaints." She pulled the shawl over her shoulders. "I'd better get out there and make sure they uncrate it and put it into the right room. It looks like rain again."

Chapter 21

And rain it did, nearly every day that week. When it finally let up on Friday, Della donned the winter coat that had been in the trunk and made her way along the muddy roads to the boardwalk in the center of town. She knew it was a risk since the sky was still rather clouded, but she had her umbrella, and besides, she felt like she'd go mad if she had to stay indoors another day.

She had in mind stopping at the post office first, and then at the library to borrow a book. The two establishments were housed in the same building. Cora had warned that the previous winter the weather had kept many people indoors for weeks.

Traffic along the main street was minimal. A horse with its attached buggy was tied to a post near the bank. She saw only a scattering of people and concluded that the cold was keeping them indoors. As always, music came from the saloons. No amount of rain could deter miners from their major source of entertainment.

When she arrived at her destination, she stomped the mud off her shoes before entering. Much to her relief, she found a different man stationed behind the counter in the post office. Older and bespectacled, this one looked at her with a no-nonsense expression when she asked if there was any mail for her family. Though she always hoped for a letter from back home, she hadn't expected any. Her father's letter to her brothers had likely just arrived there.

So, when the postman handed her a letter from her sister, she blurted a cheery thank you and tucked it in her coat pocket. So anxious to read it, she decided to postpone the library visit until the next week and headed back toward the house instead. With Christmas only a few days away, the letter was like receiving a gift.

As she hurried along the boardwalk to 2nd Avenue, she couldn't help but think about past Christmases. Before her mother's illness and her sisters had left home, they'd always decorated the tree together and everyone made small homemade gifts to exchange. One year she'd received new sheet music from her father. What a thrill that had been. At the time, she hadn't known how expensive a gift it was, but now she understood what a sacrifice it had been. His pay at the haberdasher's had been a pittance compared to what he received working for United Verde.

A rumble from underground blasting in the mine jarred her into the present as the ground trembled and was accompanied by the sound of rocks crashing down a slope between two houses. A rock the size of a washtub rolled onto the road in front of her. Her breath caught as she realized she could have been injured by it. She resolved to stay alert, lest she end up with a broken leg. One of the town's newspapers had reported that a boulder three times that size had been loosened by the rain and had crashed into the back of one of the houses on Hill Street.

Once she reached the house, she left her muddy shoes on the porch. She'd deal with them later. She settled on the sofa and turned on the table lamp to read her sister's letter.

Alexandria, Ohio, December 14, 1904
Dear Father and Sister Della,

Your letter, dear Della, was received with great sorrow. We must take comfort in knowing our mother is with the Lord and keep our memories of her and her love close to our hearts.

Winter seems to have come early this year. We've had snow several times already. It is fortunate that Gus was able to put up a good amount of hay for the horse and cow and calf. The calf has grown very well since spring. My summer garden got a late start due to the rain, but

I was able to put up 4 dozen jars of tomatoes, also some beans and carrots. My chickens have laid enough eggs so that I have had some to sell, plus they have given me a brood of chicks.

I caught a cold last month and have been quite tired since, but am some better today. I started a rug with the rags Aunt Gertie gave me, but haven't had time to finish it. Little Sister, as Willie calls her, is walking all over the house now. I have to watch her like a hawk. She has nearly outgrown her little bed. I want Gus to make a bigger one for her before the new baby comes.

I must close as the light from the window is too dim now. I pray for both of you to be safe and well.

Your loving daughter and sister, Etta

Della read the letter a second time and drew in a deep breath. Her sister was expecting another baby, and it had been only five years since the wedding. Gus was likely hoping for another boy to grow up and help on the farm. She bit her lower lip as her thoughts spun a new web. Etta would need help.

Perhaps she could convince her father to let her go to stay with her sister during her confinement. It was the least a good sister could do.

After supper that evening while they were still sitting at the table, Della read the letter to her father. When she finished, Joshua shook his head. "That land Gus bought is in a low spot. He's always going to have trouble when there's a wet spring."

Della blinked. It appeared her father had little concern for his oldest daughter. "With three babies in less than five years, it's clear that Etta needs help. I think I should go stay with her until after the baby is born."

She held her breath waiting for Joshua's reaction.

He pushed back his chair and stood. He drew in a breath, let it out with a huff, and looked down at her. "Gus has family not ten miles down the road. They can help out if there's a need. You, young lady, are needed here."

"But ..."

Joshua dropped his napkin on the table. "Until you marry, or go away for teacher's training, you will remain here." He turned and went through the doorway to the living room.

She heard his weight register in his favorite chair. A rustle of paper indicated he was reading the Mining News. Her shoulders sagged and she stared at the empty dishes on the table.

Marriage? In a pig's eye. If she were back home, there might a chance for a good marriage, but not here in a mining camp populated by a bunch of ruffians.

Her thoughts drifted to Johnny Archer, his blue eyes, and the way his brown hair fell over his forehead. No. Like a homing pigeon, she'd find a way. She'd never resign herself to life on the side of a barren mountain where the ground shook every day. Not a chance.

Chapter 22

Though she had no reason to, Della had awakened early. It was Christmas, but word had gone out the day before that all planned festivities at church had been canceled due to inclement weather and road hazards.

She pushed her feet into slippers, grabbed a spare blanket to wrap around herself, and padded her way into the living room. It was raining again. She'd heard it start clattering on the roof during the night. At the front window, she pulled aside the curtain and looked out. Daylight was struggling to penetrate the thick layer of clouds, and water rushed down the hillside cutting a jagged furrow across the road in front of the house. She supposed she should be grateful that it had taken a path alongside their house instead of coming in the front door, but considering Christmas had been called off, at least in her part of the world, she couldn't manage to drum up any feeling of gratitude.

She'd spent her spare time during the last two weeks making

a new muffler for her father, an extra thick one, to keep him warm on his way to work. The material had been cut from one of her mother's woolen skirts that had been stored in the trunk. It was black and green plaid, colors she hoped he would like. Without the sewing machine that had been left back home, she had to sew it by hand, putting in extra stitches to make sure it would hold together.

Her thoughts drifted to her family in Ohio and wondered what they would be doing that day. Aunt Gertie was an excellent cook. Her brothers were lucky. She would likely prepare a goose or turkey for their dinner. In Etta's case, Gus had a big family, so she expected they would all get together for a hearty meal. And Lizzie, who was boarding with the Hendersons near the school where she taught in Indiana, would probably be invited to celebrate with them.

She sighed. It wasn't like she was alone, although sometimes it almost felt that way. Her father was still asleep. She'd heard his gentle snoring when she passed his bedroom. She wouldn't bother him. Each evening when he returned from the mine, his fatigue was visible. Whether due to hard labor, grief, or worry, Della couldn't discern, but she did recognize that the lines in his face had deepened since her mother's death. It had become his habit to eat his supper, sit in his favorite chair for a spell to read whatever newspaper he'd managed to acquire, and then go to bed.

Cold seeped through the blanket, making her shiver. She returned to her bedroom to dress, and then went into the kitchen to stir up the coals in the stove to get the fire going. She'd developed some concern about the amount of firewood it was taking to heat the house. A washout had delayed the train during the previous week, and since all the town's supplies, including firewood, came by train or pack animal, she'd been careful to conserve her fuel for cooking. During the hours between breakfast and supper, she allowed the fire to dwindle. If she kept busy with housework, the cold didn't bother her much, but in the late afternoon, she wrapped up in a blanket to keep warm and passed the time reading.

But it was Christmas day. Surely, they should be able to be warm on Christmas. She fed an extra piece of wood into the stove's fire box.

Despite the soggy roads, at Joshua's request, the following week Della took a chance of going to the post office. He was anxious to hear from his sons.

"Any mail?" Joshua asked that night at supper. And when she told him there wasn't, he scowled as if it were her fault. He huffed and scooped the last forkful of stew into his mouth.

Though she continued her vigilance with regular treks to the post office, washouts along the narrow-gauge railroad often delayed mail service.

Then late in January, a letter from her brothers arrived. She recognized the handwriting as that of her oldest brother, Richard. In it, he complained about the harsh weather they'd been having and said they were anxious to join their father and her. They looked forward to getting away from the snow and cold weather.

Della sniffed at their illusion and glanced out the window at the rain. The letter went on to relate that they would make plans for the trip south when they had saved enough money for train fare, perhaps in March or April, when the weather cleared. Her father seemed encouraged by the news when he read it.

Della didn't know it at that moment, but the residents who lived on the side of Cleopatra Hill were about to experience the worst winters in years with heavy snow on the highest peaks and storms that would dump an unprecedented amount of water on them. Work slowed to a crawl at the mine, school was canceled for the weeks, and supplies arrived intermittently. Della coped as best she could. Her grocery orders were often short due to problems with the railroad. One week she even skipped her noon meal in order to have enough food for her father's supper.

March was unusual with exceptionally heavy rains that turned the streets into bogs. The steeper sections became gullies and railway washouts were common. When that happened, all commerce between Jerome and the valley below came to a halt until repairs were made. At the mine, drainage into the upper levels caused a number of cave-ins, and several men ended up in the hospital with broken bones. Smelter production was slowed due to water seeping into the smelter buildings again. Some days work had to be suspended until the area could be cleared. And that affected pay envelopes.

One drizzly afternoon early in April, Della sat on one end of the sofa in Cora's living room. Nellie was positioned at the opposite end with her doll on her lap and a book in her hands. Her lips moved silently, seemingly reading to her doll. The two Hovey boys could be seen through the doorway to the kitchen. They were seated at the table playing checkers.

Della laid down her crocheting for a moment and watched Cora nurse Georgie. Cora occupied a padded rocking chair with the boy snuggled on her lap.

"How do you know when he's full?" Della asked.

Amusement registered in Cora's eyes. "He'll go to sleep or stop nursing and babble like he has a story to tell me."

"But what if he doesn't let go or go to sleep? What if he just hangs on? How do you know when to stop him?"

"A healthy baby can empty his mama's breast in less than half an hour. The rest is gravy, so to speak."

"But he has teeth. Doesn't that hurt?"

"Only if he bites, and he learned real quick that he'll get a smack on the leg for biting."

Della shook her head. "I've seen pictures of babies feeding from a bottle. Wouldn't that be easier?"

"Not really. Bottles have to be warmed, and cow's milk costs money. And besides, it's not as good for a baby." She patted her son's bottom as she looked down at him.

"But..." A low rumble interrupted, and the ground shook with unusual force. Della's forehead furrowed. Looking at Cora, she scrunched her face. "I swear, that blasting is going to turn my hair gray before my time."

Cora didn't respond. She blinked and tilted her head as if listening for an answer to a question.

Minutes passed, and then the steam whistle at the mine cut the air with three short blasts followed by a long wail. It meant only one thing—trouble.

Chapter 23

Nellie slid off the sofa and went to the front window. Della followed her and looked out. She saw women emerge from nearby houses, one or two wiping their hands on their aprons. Each stood and looked in the direction of the mine, their faces etched with worry. A sense of alarm surged through Della and she turned toward Cora.

Billy and Buster stood in the kitchen doorway, their eyes wide with concern. Cora's brow creased. "I'm going up there." She pulled her shirt front together, sat Georgie on the chair, and stood. She went into the bedroom, quickly returning with galoshes and raincoat.

"You children stay here," she commanded as she stuffed her feet into her overshoes. She looked up at Della. "Are you coming?" When she'd flung on the rain gear, she picked up her little boy and wrapped a blanket around him.

"Wait for me." Della bolted out the door and across to her house. She didn't have a raincoat, so she grabbed her wool coat and a scarf and met Cora on the road.

They started out at a good pace, trudging up the hill, and following the roads. When they reached Hull Street, Cora was out of breath.

"Here, let me carry Georgie for a spell." Della reached out to take him. As soon as Della had the boy in her arms, Cora leaned over, bracing her hands on her knees, taking in several deep breaths.

The rumble of a farm wagon drew their attention, and they stepped off the narrow road onto soggy ground as it came alongside. "Climb on board," a woman's voice said.

Cora climbed up to sit on the bench seat next to the goat lady. "Thanks, Ruth. You're a lifesaver."

Della handed Georgie to his mother and hoisted herself onto the rear of the wagon. She scooted forward to lean against the backboard. The wet wagon bed had an odor, a mixture of hay, manure, and maybe goat's milk.

Ruth flicked a short whip against the back of the mule and the wagon jostled along the road, finally reaching the western edge of town.

They weren't the only citizens bent on reaching the mine entrance. Several horse-drawn buggies slowed their progress, plus the people who rushed along the roadside.

The wagon had to be left some distance from the fence at the entrance of the mine works. Della hopped off the back and followed Cora and Ruth. With so many people, it was hard to learn what was going on.

As they reached the mine, it seemed like the entire town had gathered at the gate. Della glanced around and recognized the minister from their church, also Mrs. Samples, and some of the other women she'd met.

Worry caused agitation in some. One woman pushed through the crowd to be closest to the entrance. Others whispered to one another with questions about shifts and who would be below.

Pinched-faced children clung to their mothers. Tragedy was no stranger to these families. The mine killed numerous men every year. Grief for one family was grief for all. Each woman knew, if not this time, next time the injured might be one of her own.

A group of miners milled around at a distance inside the gate, their smudged faces drawn taut. At seeing them, seeds of apprehension germinated in Della's stomach.

While the gathering shuffled around, Cora and Della edged into a spot next to the fence. "I don't see Will," Cora said, her voice tense. Waiting in the misty drizzle felt like an eternity.

Finally, a miner dressed in work clothes and wearing a cap with a lamp attached trudged toward the crowd with an air of authority. His grim expression forewarned them. "There's been a blowout," he said. "Twelve men were hit with hot steam. The doctor's in there now with 'em. Let me through. I'm going to get wagons to move the injured to the hospital."

"I got my wagon here. You can use it," a bearded man yelled.

"All right, Joe. Bring it on in. Stand back folks."

The crowd cleared a space for the gate to swing, and the man drove his team and wagon through and beyond their view to where the lift would surface.

"I'll go after another wagon," a second man called out.

Soon several miners appeared, carrying two stretchers, and loaded them into the first wagon. Della recognized Dr. Woods, who climbed in with them.

Cora clung to the fence, white-knuckled.

As the wagon passed through the gate, people crowded around to identify the occupants.

"I have Harry Parker and Angus Baxter here," the doctor called out. "We'll take them up to the hospital." Mrs. Parker lunged toward the carrier. Baxter's sister, Bernice, hung over the wagon side, weeping.

Della turned away, unable to make herself look at the burned men.

Soon the wagon from the livery arrived, the squeaking wheels protesting the steep hill. The drizzle of rain had stopped. Three more injured were carried out to the conveyance. A woman in a striped dress gripped the side of the wagon, steadying herself. The color drained from her face.

"That's Dora Lendinski," Cora whispered to Della. "They live across the road."

"He must be badly burned," Della murmured as the transport moved away. She stretched to search the faces of the gathering miners, looking for her father.

A short man in a black suit and white shirt pushed back his hat as he came from within a nearby building. He had a sheaf of papers and pencil in his hand and started shouting orders to several of the men near the opening to the lift.

"That's Mr. Thompson," someone in the crowd said, his tone signifying respect. Another man who had been watching everything from horseback, dismounted. He elbowed his way through the crowd to the gate and called out to get the attention of the man in the black suit. He was allowed inside, and they conferred for several minutes, the newcomer scrawling notes on a small pad of paper in his hand. Della thought he might be someone from the newspaper.

Another wagon arrived at the mine entrance, was allowed through, and the hushed townsfolk watched as five bodies, wrapped in canvas, were hoisted onto the back of it. As it moved forward and stopped just inside the gate, the tension was palpable.

The man in black stood before the murmuring crowd. His expression was grave, and he held up his hand to quiet everyone. "Water seeped into the burning stopes at the 700-foot level," he said. "Steam built up behind the concrete bulkhead that separated the old fire from the rest of the mine. It caused the blowout." He paused. "I'll read this list, and then we'll take these poor men to the undertaker."

He raised the paper he was carrying. It trembled. All murmuring stopped and heads turned in his direction. He cleared his throat before speaking. "Joshua McCrea..."

Della heard nothing else. Her senses froze. The scene blurred and her knees gave way beneath her.

Chapter 24

The Jerome Mining News, April 7, 1905

ARIZONA MINE EXPLOSION. FIVE MEN DEAD AND FIVE OTHERS SERIOUSLY HURT.

Jerome, Ariz. As the result of an explosion in the United Verde mine at Jerome, Ariz., owned by Senator Clark, five men are dead and five others seriously if not fatally injured. The accident happened just as the shifts were being changed and all the men except twelve had been raised to the surface. On account of the recent heavy rains, surface water found its way to that portion of the mine where fire has been smoldering several years, and steam thus generated caused the explosion, blowing out the bulkheads erected to keep the fire from spreading. The men were suffocated by smoke and heated steam.

Della folded the newspaper clipping and slipped it into the envelope along with the accompanying letter. She knew it would pass from hand to hand among her family members, each receiving the details with immense grief.

In the week following the explosion, she'd felt like she was living in a strange dream. At times she'd cried uncontrollably. Other times she'd sat in disbelief on the living room sofa and stared into space, or would have if it hadn't been for Will and Cora Hovey.

Will had made arrangements for Joshua's burial with money Della gave him, while Cora had gone with her to the telegraph office and helped her notify her family. She also saw to it that Della ate something at mealtime and led her through the burial service, a simple ceremony at the grave site.

With a few words spoken by Reverend Smith, Joshua McCrea was laid to rest next to his wife. In addition to a few close neighbors, some of the men who had worked with him attended, but most were back underground in the mine.

"If only he'd listened to me months ago," Della lamented to Cora the following Sunday after church. "We'd be home now and he'd be alive. Why couldn't he see the danger?"

Cora had looked at her young friend with sadness in her eyes. "He did know the danger. They all do. They live with it every day. The wages are what keeps them going back."

And now, she sealed the envelope. Though it pained her, Della had added a request for money in the letter. The train ticket home would cost thirty-four dollars, money she didn't have. Surely, her brother, Richard, would help her. Though he was only twenty-two himself, he was the oldest son and her guardian now.

She slid the envelope across the counter at the post office, along with two cents for postage. Waiting for their reply would be agonizing, but the anticipation also lifted her spirits a bit.

And then, on the last day of the week, reality knocked. Della opened the door to a short, slender man dressed in a black suit and matching fedora. She recognized Henry Wilcox, the man who owned their rented house.

He removed his hat. "Excuse me, Miss McCrea. I've come to collect the overdue rent."

There was nothing unusual about the request. Della had been giving Mr. Wilcox the rent money her father left all along. That is, up until the previous two months when the mine work had been interrupted due to cave-ins. When she'd asked about it, her father had said he'd take care of it. And now she knew he hadn't, and she didn't have the money to pay any of it. She leaned against the door frame and began to cry, shaking her head, tears streaming down her face.

Her sobbing unnerved Mr. Wilcox. He took a backward step. "I...I...I'll come back at a better time, Miss McCrea. Maybe tomorrow."

Della closed the door and wiped her face with her apron. Tomorrow would be no better. The rent money had gone to pay for her father's burial expense. As the specter of being homeless loomed, she pictured herself begging at someone's back door like the hobos she'd seen in Ohio. She whirled around and gave her father's favorite chair a kick. "How could you do this to me?" she shouted, raising her fist to heaven.

By chance, Cora had just stepped onto the front porch to invite Della to afternoon coffee, and hearing her shout, she hurried to enter.

"I might as well be dead," Della said when she saw her friend in the doorway.

Cora scowled. "Don't say such a thing. You have a long life ahead of you."

Della gestured toward the road out front. "Mr. Wilcox wants the rent money owed him, over two months' worth. I haven't got it. Do you understand? I have none, and my brother hasn't replied to my letter."

Cora approached, putting her hands on Della's shoulders.

"Can't you see, Cora? I'm an orphan. I'm stuck in Jerome till hell freezes over. And I'll starve unless I become one of those prostitutes."

Della could hardly believe the words that had come out of her own mouth. And neither could Cora, from the expression on her face. Della leaned her head against Cora's shoulder and began to sob.

"Now wait." Cora pushed her back until they faced each other. "You told me months ago that your father was saving for your schooling."

Della fished a handkerchief out of her apron pocket. "But I don't know where it is," she said, her words muffled as she wiped her nose.

"I imagine it's in a bank. Go to the bank uptown and ask for the manager. Explain what has happened. He'll let you draw the money your father saved." Cora gave a nod and smiled. "Now wash your face and come on over to my kitchen. I have biscuits and coffee waiting."

Della dressed carefully for her visit to the bank, donning her gray dress and freshly polished button shoes. She stood in front of the mirrored dresser and brushed her hair, then combed it up into her usual style and secured it with several hairpins.

The incessant rain had stopped and the day was rather mild for a change, so she decided her blue shawl would be all she would need. It still held the faint smell of mothballs from being stored in the trunk, but it would suffice. She needed a hat. Her straw hat wouldn't do. After a search of the armoire and dresser for a substitute, she settled on a black handkerchief Cora had given her at the funeral and pinned it into place with a hat pin of her mother's.

When she finished, she practiced what she'd say in front of the mirror, watching to see if her expression looked sufficiently demure. "I suppose I don't need to *act* pitiful," she said to the mirror. "I'm at the banker's mercy. But if I can get the money Father left, I'll be packed and on my way home when the next train leaves."

By the time Della reached the boardwalk in the business district, it was late morning, the sky was clear, and the town was bustling with traffic, both people and vehicles of various sorts. Being unfamiliar with either bank in town, she was a little nervous. Her plan was to make her inquiries at Bank of Arizona first. If it turned out that her father was unknown to the manager, she'd try the Bank of Jerome. She dodged around a mule-drawn cart, using care not to step in animal waste, and sucked in a shuddering breath as she grasped the bank's brass door handle.

The interior was similar to the bank in Dayton where her uncle Clement worked, except that it was narrower, barely fifteen feet in width. Two teller's cages occupied the left-hand side of the room, but only one was open.

A tall young man with a thin mustache stood behind the first window. His high white collar and black tie looked as though they were tight enough to choke him. He leaned forward and with a brief nod, said, "May I help you?"

"I wish to speak to the bank manager, please."

The man drew himself up to his full height. "May I say who is calling?"

"Miss Della McCrea." She tipped her chin. "My father was the late Joshua McCrea."

"Yes. Well, please wait here." He closed the grille and walked to the door marked "Manager" at the back of the building. After a quick knock, he went inside.

While Della waited, she studied the room, watched the clock, and tried not to fidget. A few minutes passed before the teller returned to his post. "He'll be with you in a moment."

At ten minutes past eleven, a tall man with a square jaw and a handlebar mustache appeared from behind the rear door and approached. "Miss McCrea. I'm the bank manager. Let me offer my condolences. A terrible accident."

"Thank you."

"Now, Miss McCrea. How may I be of service to you?"

"Sir, my father told me that he was saving money for my education. I've come to withdraw it."

The manager's thick eyebrows lifted. "Why, yes. A moment please." He walked back behind the last teller's cage and over to a counter where two large, thick books lay. With his back to her, he opened one of them and turned several pages.

Della moved over to an empty teller's window and watched as he ran his finger down three pages of the ledger. At last, he appeared to study the page, then closed the book and turned to face her. "Miss McCrea. It is true that over the period of several months your father deposited nearly a hundred dollars."

Della gasped. "A hundred dollars?"

"But I'm sorry to report that a little more than a month ago, he came in and withdrew all of it. As I recall, he told me that he was investing in the Big Five Mining Company. Perhaps you can find the certificate and reclaim the investment."

Chapter 25

Crestfallen, Della left the bank. She had no idea how to redeem a stock certificate, even if she could find it. And if there was one, why didn't he keep it in the bank? Thoughts churned as she hurried along the sloping streets back to the house. She *would* find it, by golly. A hundred dollars was an immense sum. That amount of money would pay the rent *and* buy a train ticket, plus food and a hotel room during the trip.

Upon entering the house, she went straight to her father's room and searched his dresser, plus every pocket in his clothing. She even lifted the mattress on his bed but found no certificate.

Feeling agitated, she walked from room to room, unable to think of anywhere else to look. She'd always thought she knew her father quite well, but now she wasn't so sure. The fact that he'd invested in some obscure mining operation was a puzzle. Was he a gambler? She was aware that his sobriety was fragile, but if he'd had other weaknesses, they hadn't come to her notice. And if gambling had been an issue between her parents, they'd kept it private.

At last, she stood in front of her mother's mirrored dresser, pressed her lips together, and ran the tip of her index finger across her chin. Though it pained her, without finding the certificate, and in the absence of a response from her family, she would have to sell the furniture. It would cost too much to transport it back to Ohio anyway.

Since she had no experience with such dealings, she wasn't sure how to go about doing so, or even how much to ask. Her father had never shared what things cost.

She returned to the living room and looked around. The couch. That would be what she'd sell. It was in good condition. The colors in the woven fabric were still bright and pleasing to the eye. She nodded to herself. A good decision. She would tell Cora the bad news regarding the stock certificate and ask her advice about how to proceed with the sale of the furnishings.

Cora was standing at the cook stove with a sizzling skillet of beef, browning it for stew. She listened while Della explained her experience at the bank, her search for the elusive stock certificate, and her decision to sell the furniture in the house.

"If I can find a buyer, the money will pay the rent and give me some time to wait for a reply to my letter to my family."

Cora had listened without comment until the beef was ready to simmer. She put a cover on the Dutch Oven. "Let's sit at the table." She took a tin of tea from the shelf, and prepared her teapot at the table, filling it with hot water from an aluminum kettle on the stove.

Della settled herself, eager to hear what Cora would advise.

"Mrs. Granger across the road just had a baby two weeks ago and probably could use another chest of drawers. It's her sixth child," Cora said as she went to fetch mugs from the shelf.

"I'm afraid I've been a very poor neighbor," Della said. "I've been so wrapped up in my own troubles, I hardly notice what is going on around me. What news have you heard about the injured miners?"

"Very little, except that Will told me that those who were burned are still in the hospital."

When the tea was ready, Cora poured a cup for each of them and they discussed what Della might expect to derive from each piece of furniture. When her teacup was empty, Della knew what she needed to do next.

Later that afternoon, Della wrapped her shawl around her shoulders and walked across the road to the two-story Granger home. Her rap on the door was answered by a thin, dark-haired girl who was holding a toddler with curls that matched his sister's. Della guessed the girl to be no older than twelve or thirteen. For an instant, she wondered why the girl wasn't in school, but quickly decided the reason. Mrs. Granger needed her help at home.

Della introduced herself and asked, "May I speak to your mother?"

"I know who you are," the girl said. "Your father was killed in the explosion like my friend, Heidi's father." She stared at Della for a second and shifted her burden. "I'll call Mama."

Della stepped inside the house and glanced around while the girl trudged up a stairway to the second floor. From what she could see, the first floor consisted of a living room with worn furniture and a kitchen with a stack of clothes on the kitchen table.

After a few minutes, Mrs. Granger descended the wooden stairs. Della instantly felt a pang of compassion for the woman. She had dark circles under her eyes, her hair hung in limp strands, and she wore a faded robe, cinched at her thin waist.

"I'm embarrassed to greet you this way, but I didn't want to keep you waiting until I could dress."

Della held up her hand to stop her apology. "Please. Forgive me for intruding. Mrs. Hovey told me you have a new baby and thought you might be in need of a bureau. Since my father died, I find myself short of funds and have furniture I wish to sell." She raised her eyebrows to emphasize her unspoken question.

"Please sit." Mrs. Granger made a motion toward a faded

couch with flattened cushions. Della moved to perch on the edge of it. She didn't want to keep the tired woman long.

"The baby won't need clothes for a good while, so a small drawer is enough for now." Mrs. Granger eased herself down onto a matching chair. "However, my brother, Harry, and his family arrived this week from Denver. They're staying in a boarding house at the moment, but he's found a place to rent, and I imagine they'll be needing furniture."

Della couldn't suppress a smile.

"I'll talk to my husband when he gets home from work," she continued. "He'll let Harry know."

Della thanked Mrs. Granger in the most gracious terms and took her leave with her hopes soaring.

When she returned to the house it was time to consider what to sell. Her parents' bedroom furniture could go. Perhaps Will Hovey would know of someone who could use her father's clothing. She'd save her father's pocket watch. It would be something her oldest brother would treasure.

She considered her mother's dressing table but decided she still needed it. In the living room, it would be the couch, chairs, lamp table, also the sideboard. Those things would bring enough money to pay the back rent. She spent the remainder of the day polishing each item she planned to sell.

Late the next day, a stocky man in work clothes arrived to knock on the door. When Della answered, he removed his hat and introduced himself as Mrs. Granger's brother. "I'm here to look at the furnishings you're selling."

Della motioned him to enter and he followed her, hat in his hand, as she pointed out the pieces she hoped he'd buy. His brow furrowed as he considered each one. When he lifted the cloth on the living room table, she held her breath. She knew it had a few scratches.

"The house I've rented is too small for all this," he said. "I'll take the bed, the dresser, the couch, the table and lamp. The rug too." After a pause, he gave her a side glance and made a modest offer.

Della suppressed a gasp. It wasn't near as much as she'd hoped, but what choice did she have? Mr. Wilcox would return any day and want his rent money.

She nodded. "Agreed."

"Good," the man said. "I'll rent a wagon and come to collect the furniture after work tomorrow." He nodded, replaced his hat, and went out the door into the fading light.

The man was as good as his word. He arrived with another man and a teenage boy. All three appeared to have come directly from work. He handed her the cash, and they set to work carrying out the furniture. As she watched, she fought off a sense of loss. She told herself that it was a step in the right direction.

In less than an hour they had the wagon loaded, everything tied snug, and were gone. She closed the door and wrapped her arms around herself. Without the familiar furnishings, the things that connected her to her family, the sense of loneliness was more acute than ever. But she couldn't let herself dwell on it. She had to focus on her goal, going home.

She walked toward the kitchen, her footsteps resonating in the vacant room, and sat at the table to count the bills again. She didn't know why she did it. It didn't make them multiply. What she had would pay the back rent, but it wouldn't leave much. Certainly not enough to finance her trip home. Her only hope was for her brother to send more than enough to pay for the train ticket. Her shoulders sagged. Surely, she'd hear by Friday.

The noise of knocking at the back door interrupted her thoughts. She rose and went to open it. The dark-haired delivery boy stood on the porch with a box of foodstuffs in his arms. He held the box out to her and she took it.

"Mr. Jones says you need to come to the store and pay your bill." He took a step back, shuffled his feet and looked down. "Or no more groceries." His message delivered, he hurried down the steps to where he'd tied the horse.

Della stood as if frozen to the spot, bile rising in her throat as she watched him jockey the wagon back onto the road. She would never have believed her father would let such a debt go unpaid. It had to be large for them to cut off his credit. How could he have done this to her? She whirled around and plunked the box down on the kitchen table. It wasn't fair. It just wasn't fair!

Chapter 26

Another restless night followed, but by morning she'd come to the conclusion that with the grocery bill due as well as the rent, she'd have to sell her mother's jewelry. It wasn't a large collection, mostly pieces passed on from Della's grandmother. She recalled seeing a jewelry store in the same building as the bank. Perhaps she could sell it there.

Without bothering to dress, she sat at her mother's dressing table and pulled open the top drawer. The modest wooden box, a treasure her mother had kept since girlhood, had her initials embossed in gold on the interior of the lid. It also had a tiny hasp on the front, but it was never locked. She opened it expecting to see the pieces so familiar to her.

Her back stiffened in amazement as she stared at the contents. Where were her mother's rings? Where were Grandma Dorothea's mother-of-pearl brooch and the gold pendant watch her mother had received on her eighteenth birthday? Had her father sold these valuables in order to buy the stock certificate, even the gold beads her mother had wanted her to wear on her wedding day?

A mixture of anger and grief swept over her. Tears threatened as she gazed at the only item left, a small hinged case she knew should contain an ivory cameo surrounded by tiny gems. Long ago, it had been a Christmas gift from her father to her mother. She lifted the latch to open the box. To her relief, the cameo was there. Her brow creased. Why had he left it behind? She'd always imagined it was quite valuable. "Well, this is hardly the time to figure it out," she said to the mirror. "There are bills to pay."

Della took a deep breath before entering the jewelry store. The man she saw behind the counter reminded her of one of her brother's school teachers, a gangly fellow with a stern look. He wore a black vest over his white shirt and sported a black tie. His drooping mustache matched his dark hair, both neatly trimmed, most likely something he had done at the barbershop next door.

In addition to the glass counter that held a variety of jewelry, a shelf on the wall in back displayed hand mirrors and handsome jewelry boxes. An upper shelf held fine china plates. Considering the fact that the ground shook on a daily basis, for an instant, Della wondered how they remained anchored in place.

"May I help you?" The clerk grinned and nodded as she stepped forward. "We have a lovely selection of items a young lady like yourself would like to wear." He turned slightly and motioned to the shelf in back of him. "Or perhaps you'd be interested in a mirror for your dresser."

Della ran the tip of her tongue along her top lip, then smiled at him. She opened her drawstring purse and pulled out the small case. "I have something I wish to sell," she said as she opened the lid and placed it on the countertop.

His smile faded. With a mere glance at the cameo, he straightened his back and looked down his nose. "My dear girl, we *sell* jewelry, we don't buy it from the public. There's a second-hand store just down the street. Perhaps they would accommodate you."

Della felt her cheeks flush. She snapped the lid closed, stuffed the box back in her bag, and fled from the store.

Outside on the boardwalk, she leaned against the brick building to recover her composure. "What an insufferable ratbag," she said, then glanced around to see if anyone had heard her. She squared her shoulders. Her mother's cameo would never end up in a second-hand store. Resolving to never let that happen, she moved in the direction of the post office.

Stepping inside, she recognized the same old postman she'd seen on her previous visits. When she caught his eye, she smiled, though she didn't feel like it. "Is there any mail for McCrea?"

"A minute," he mumbled. He went to a cubbyhole and took

out a stack of mail.

Della found herself holding her breath while he sorted through the pile, momentarily stopping a couple of times to peer at an envelope. Finally, he set one of them aside and returned the others to their place. "Arrived just today," he said as he returned to the counter and handed her the letter.

The postmark instantly told her its origin. She thanked him and clutched it to her chest, her heart pounding with excitement. The answer to her prayers had finally arrived.

She left the building and hesitated just outside the door, ready to open it. However, the figure of an unseemly man lingering at the corner of the building drew her attention. Remembering the assault she'd experienced, and certain there would be money inside the letter, she decided to wait until she reached the house.

Della dropped her shawl on the bed and sat next to it. She slid her finger under the envelope flap, pulled out a sheet of paper and began to read ...

April 18, 1905
Dear Sister,
Your sad news brought this family grief untold. Our father was a hard-working man and

now he can rest with Mother. Your situation added much distress. I wish we could help you but our circumstances are not good. Hail severely damaged crops this year and Gus will have to borrow to plant again before summer. Lizzie has been sick with pneumonia for nearly a month and had to leave teaching and go home to recover. I had a note from Aunt Gert yesterday and she said she would wait to tell her about Father as she was afraid that the grief would endanger her health.

Lon was here last Sunday and told me that Richard is out of work again. The bad crops closed the mill. The weather has also affected Lon's business but he looks to a better year. The children have all had bad colds but seem to be recovering. I am enclosing what money Lon could spare and some of my egg money. I will pray for you.

Lovingly,

Your sister, Etta

Della sat with the letter in her lap, turning over the currency. "Two dollars? Only two dollars? That's all?" Her stomach threatened to erupt. "What am I supposed to do?

Della held back her tears as she entered her neighbor's front door. "Cora," she called out.

"In here," Cora replied from the next room.

Della waved the letter as she entered the kitchen.

Cora was seated at the table with Georgie on her lap, helping him spoon food into his mouth. She wiped his face with a cloth and looked up at Della.

"I finally got a letter from home. But it wasn't from my brother. Etta wrote and sent two dollars. She said it was all they could spare. I had such hopes." She plopped down onto a chair opposite Cora. "And that's not all."

Della went on, the words tumbling out of her mouth about unpaid grocery bill, and her failed attempt to sell her mother's cameo.

Cora took a deep breath. "Well, it looks like you'll just have to find employment."

"Employment? What sort of employment could I get, the Fashion Saloon and Gambling House? I'd rather starve."

"No, no. I have a second cousin and her husband who run a boarding house on the other side of town. I can write a note to Pearl. She might hire you. You know how to cook and clean, and she likely needs help. I saw her at the post office several months back. She didn't say anything, but I suspect she is in a family way again. They have five rooms to rent out, plus her own family to care for, and she's no spring chicken. Lord knows, Jasper Cooper isn't much help. He parades around trying to look like a big shot. He hasn't seen the inside of a church in years, not since they married."

Chapter 27

With Cora's directions in mind, Della hiked along the slag-covered road Monday morning. As she approached her destination, she realized she was going to be living much closer to United Verde's smelter, thus the noxious fumes would be more potent. It was one of the things she wouldn't miss when she finally left Arizona.

Nearing the top of the grade, she spotted what she thought was Cooper House, a sturdy frame structure, two stories, situated on the sloping hillside. The main floor sat below road level by several feet. Wooden steps led from the ground to a portico on the front of the second story. A wooden walkway, more narrow than a balcony, ran from the bottom of the steps along the side of the main level. It had a railing and appeared to wrap around the entire building. Substantial wooden posts had been driven into the ground to support it at intervals. A set of wooden stairs attached to the walkway at the rear provided a way for a boarder to access the privy farther down the hillside. Below the main floor, at the rear, a lower level supported the upper stories as well as providing additional room for storage or other use.

Della approached the wooden walk, intent on reaching a door she deemed was the kitchen entrance since she'd noticed a vent above it on the roof. A rumble and sudden jolt of the ground below stopped her. She grabbed the railing to steady herself. Since her father's death, the daily episodes of blasting seemed more sinister than ever. It was another thing she wasn't going to miss.

She proceeded and rapped on the kitchen door. A large woman with a round, flushed face answered her knock. The woman wiped her face with her apron and looked at Della with an expression of distrust. "I don't have any empty rooms," she said. "Don't expect any either."

A bit startled by the reception, Della blinked. "Mrs. Cooper, I'm Della McCrea." She pulled Cora's note from her handbag. "My father, Joshua McCrea, was one of those killed in the explosion at the mine. I have fallen on hard times since then and need work. I bring a letter from your cousin Cora Hovey to recommend me." She handed the envelope to Mrs. Cooper, noting the woman's girth under her light-blue dress, and thinking Cora had been right.

Without any change in her expression, Pearl Cooper unfolded the single sheet of paper and stared at it for a few seconds. She handed it back to Della. "I haven't got my glasses. I can't make out all the words. Read it to me."

Della took the letter and did as she was asked.

> To Mrs. Jasper Cooper
>
> Dear Cousin Pearl,
>
> This letter is to introduce Della McCrea, a young woman in need of employment. She has been orphaned during the last month. Her character is pure and her knowledge of housekeeping and cooking is well known to me since her family became neighbors to us. I can safely recommend her for your employ.
>
> Your cousin, Cora Hovey

Pearl looked Della up and down. "Turn around."

Della complied, turning in a circle.

"I guess you'll do. I been thinking about gettin' a new hired girl. Better'n the last one, I hope. You have some other clothes to wear? Can't work in such a dark dress like that, make my boarders dejected."

Della opened her mouth to protest, but Mrs. Cooper interrupted before she could begin. "I know, I know, you're in mourning. You can wear a black ribbon on your sleeve." She stepped out the door onto the walkway. "Follow me."

Della followed her down the stairs at the back of the building to where there was a door to a room at a lower level. "This is where you can stay. Two dollars a week and room and board is all I can manage," Mrs. Cooper said as she pulled the door open. "But sometimes a boarder will ask to have a shirt ironed special or mended. You might be able to pick up a little extra that way. I don't have the time, what with the boys and all."

What Della saw through the opening was a small dim room with a single window facing the rear yard. A cot stood at the back of the room along with a narrow table, one chair, and a low, three-drawer chest. A squatty cast iron stove occupied the far corner and was vented with a pipe through the wall. In her opinion, it was a hovel. How low could a person sink? At the moment, she thought she'd hit rock bottom.

She squared her shoulders and turned to Mrs. Cooper. "This will be just fine."

"Good. I'll expect you in the morning. Be here by five and not a minute later."

It was midday when Della located Mr. Wilcox at the side of his house. He wore overalls and boots, had a shovel in his hand, and was standing over a ditch. She suspected he'd dug it to divert water around the foundation in preparation for the upcoming summer rains.

"Mr. Wilcox," she called from the road.

He leaned the shovel against the building and approached her, stomping the dirt off his boots. "I apologize for my appearance," he said.

"No need, sir. I've come to tell you that I've secured employment, including a room, so I won't be needing the house any longer."

"What about the unpaid rent?"

Della took several pieces of currency from her purse and handed it to him. "I confess I don't have the full amount."

Counting the money, he snorted.

"I'd hoped that after I remove my personals, you could sell what's left of the furnishings for the amount due."

He shaded his eyes and squinted at her. "Well ... I guess that's agreeable."

She nodded and thanked him, pleased that they'd reached a settlement, then started the long walk back to the house.

The overdue grocery bill occupied her thoughts along the way. She lacked the funds to meet the obligation. However, she wouldn't be needing any groceries delivered, so maybe it didn't matter. She supposed she could leave Jerome without paying, though it'd be something that would be a blight on the family name. But having left, that wouldn't matter either, would it? On the other hand, she supposed her conscience would probably nag her and give her no peace.

As she approached the path to the front porch, she decided she'd think about it another day and made a detour to talk to Cora.

She found her friend at the kitchen sink peeling potatoes. "Ah, here you are. Did my cousin give you a job?"

"She did. This will be my last night in the house. I've made arrangements with Mr. Wilcox to sell the furnishings I leave behind for the balance on the rent. I was wondering, when I have the trunks packed, will you store them until I can make other arrangements?"

"Of course. Just pull them out in front. Will can move them after supper. We'll put it under the back porch."

"The small trunk holds my father's clothing. Do you think Will might know someone who could use them?

"I imagine so."

"Bless you, Cora. I'm going to miss you so much. You've become like a sister to me."

"My goodness. I'm happy I was able to help you, but this is not goodbye. You can come to dinner every Sunday. Will and I will want to hear all about your new adventures. In fact, you must stay for supper tonight."

After depositing her hat and gloves on the dresser, she opened her mother's steamer trunk. The picture on the inside of the lid had always fascinated her. It was of a young lady dressed in a delicate, flowered dress and broad-brimmed straw hat. She was standing in the middle of a stream, holding her skirt out of the water. Behind her was a buggy with a broken wheel. She was looking over her shoulder, expectantly, as if she'd heard someone approaching.

Della had always conjured romantic vignettes when she looked at the picture. As a child, she'd thought it was the girl's father who was coming to the rescue, but later, while packing her mother's clothing for the move to Jerome, she'd imagined it to be some handsome young man.

"Well, there's no one coming to rescue me, so I better get busy."

She placed the quilt her mother had made for her before her illness at the bottom of the trunk, followed by her own winter clothing. It wouldn't be needed for months. The family photo from her bureau went in, plus her mother's empty jewelry box and items from the kitchen, all wrapped in spare bedding. She folded her best dresses and laid them on top. It pained her to leave them behind, but except for one to wear to church, they would go unused.

Closing the trunk lid, she turned her attention to her sewing basket, reorganizing the pockets in the lining. If one of the boarders needed mending done, she wanted to be prepared. She took the packet of sheet music from her dresser drawer, thought of putting it in the trunk, but couldn't quite bear leaving it behind either. It would be a small comfort to look at it now and then and imagine the day when she'd play it on the parlor piano at home.

Filling her valise was next, she packed her undergarments along with a spare work dress and aprons. She added two towels and a facecloth she'd need, plus her hairbrush, extra combs, and the container of hairpins. Last of all, she put in a cup, knife, and spoon she thought would be essential in the basement room. Snapping the latch, she set it near the door.

The evening was falsely lighthearted. Cora suggested Will play his banjo. They sang and clapped their hands as the two Hovey boys and Nellie danced in a circle. In a bittersweet way, it reminded Della of when she and her sisters danced while her father played the fiddle.

Later, alone in the house, Della woke several times during the night, afraid she would oversleep and be late for her new job. At three o'clock, she rose and lit the lamp. Without familiar furnishings around, the house felt cold and strange. She slipped on her undergarments and brushed her hair while her thoughts rambled. Hard to imagine Cora and Mrs. Cooper as cousins.

Cora, so thoughtful and kind; Mrs. Cooper, so stern. She'd be no more than a workhorse to her. And that basement room would be like an oven come summer. The little stove—would she have to buy her own fuel? No matter. She'd save every penny, pay her debt, and be gone home by the time cold weather set in.

From her sewing basket, she selected a black ribbon and stitched it into place around the sleeve of her light brown dress. She secured the basket lid, then shimmied her way into the dress and covered it with an apron.

A glance around. Had she forgotten anything? No. Gathering her bedding into a bundle on the bed, she tied the corners together, hoisted it over her shoulder, and picked up her sewing basket. I'll look like a beggar, she thought. I hope no one is awake to see me.

At the front door, she added the valise to her impedimenta, took one last look around, closed the door with the toe of her shoe, and set forth to start a new life.

Chapter 28

The sun had barely begun to lighten the sky when Della dumped her bundle and valise on the cot in her dismal room at the Cooper's Boarding House. She set her sewing basket on the little table and hurried up the slope to the kitchen door. When she opened it, she saw Pearl Cooper's large frame leaning over the cook stove, shoving a length of firewood into the firebox. The woman straightened and glanced from Della to the white-faced clock on the wall.

"On time, I see." She pointed to a cabinet next to the sink. "There's a big mixing bowl in that cupboard. Get it, and fetch the bowl of eggs from the pantry. Today is flapjack day. You know how to make 'em?"

Della nodded. "Yes, Ma'am."

"Well, good." Pearl turned back to the stove. "As soon as this pan is hot, I'll start cooking the sausage. After breakfast, I'll show you around the house."

The kitchen was not as large as Della expected, perhaps fifteen square feet. Her gaze swept around the room. A sink with a hand pump was to the left of the back door. She surmised there must be a cistern underneath the building. At least she wouldn't have to carry water from outside. Between the sink and the cast iron stove stood a Hoosier cabinet with a built-in flour bin and marble breadboard. Cupboards lined the adjacent wall with an ice box in the middle, and through a doorway, Della could see shelves in the pantry. Directly across from the back entrance, another door led to the dining room, she thought, or maybe a hall. Adjacent to that was an alcove with a table and chairs.

Della hustled to fetch the bowl and the eggs. She had just placed them on a work table in the center of the room when the outside door swung open. Two boys appeared, by their size, an eight and ten-year-old. Each clutched a handle on either side of a milk can and struggled to haul it to the ice box.

Pearl twisted from the stove to watch them. "Ah, good. The milk truck finally got here."

The boys set the milk can down and stared at Della.

Pearl frowned. "Get washed and changed for school now," she said, making a shooing motion. "Get going. And don't slam the door behind you."

As soon as her sons left, she said, "The tall one is Jacob, the other'n is Luther." She returned her attention to the sizzling sausages, leaving Della to prepare the pancake batter.

Barely a half-hour later, the smell of fried sausage filled the air, and the big table in the dining room was surrounded by hungry miners. Della carried in a large platter of the pancakes she'd made and another of sausages. She put them on the table next to the butter dish, syrup pitcher, and bowl of hard-boiled eggs.

Forks flew, and in less than a minute, the platters were empty. The syrup pitcher was passed and the golden liquid poured onto the pancakes. All of it was washed down with steaming cups of black coffee. The only sound in the room was the clinking of knives and forks and the slurping of coffee as they ate with an amazing speed.

As soon as they'd cleaned their plates, the men stood, one after another, and filed out of the front door, each picking up a dinner pail from the adjacent cabinet.

They're like locusts, Della thought, looking at the empty plates. And when did Mrs. Cooper prepare those dinner pails? She was beginning to feel a tinge of admiration for the efficiency of her grim employer.

After the miners left, another man entered from the stairway next to the front door. He was clean-shaven and wearing a black suit and white shirt with a tie. Della was surprised when she recognized him. He was the man she'd been introduced to at the church picnic. He took a seat at the table and pushed aside one of the miner's cups.

Pearl stepped into the room from the kitchen with a plate of steaming pancakes in her hand. "Good morning, Mr. Bennett," she said in a voice so pleasant Della was amazed. She set the plate in front of him and passed the coffee urn.

"Good morning," he replied, nodding. He gave Della a glance. "I see you have a new girl."

"Indeed, she comes highly recommended."

"Does she do shirts?"

"Oh yes, sir," Pearl and Della said in unison.

The morning passed in a whirl of activity. Della had little time to think about Mr. Bennett or his shirts. She washed a mountain of dishes and greasy skillets while Pearl tended to two of her other children.

"This is Joey," Pearl said as she put her chubby-cheeked toddler into a high chair. In between shoveling spoons of breakfast cereal into the mouth of her youngest child, Pearl grabbed her squirmy four-year-old son and pointed him to a chair at the round table in the alcove.

"That one's Wesley." She rose to go to the counter next to the stove and scooped ladles of cooked oatmeal into three waiting bowls, topped them with milk and a spoonful of sugar, and put them on the table.

The two older boys came into the kitchen dressed in brown

overalls, slipped into their places, and set to work on their breakfast. As soon as they'd finished, hats were snatched from hooks, dinner pails from the counter, and the outside door shut behind them.

The raucous breakfast hour was over, and the only sound in the house was the gurgling of the baby in the highchair and little Wesley stirring what was left in his cereal bowl.

After the kitchen cleanup and mopping, Pearl led Della through the four bedrooms upstairs, showed her where the carpet sweeper and dust mop were kept, and instructed her on the correct way the furniture polish was to be used. The upstairs would be cleaned one day, Pearl said, the downstairs on another.

The house was large, but no larger than the one Della had grown up in. The only difference was that at home, the work was shared by her sisters. In this case, the biggest part of the upkeep would be on her shoulders. However, there was one room Della wasn't to touch—the big bedroom downstairs. Pearl made it clear she was not to enter that room.

Afterward, back in the kitchen, while the baby napped in a cradle, Pearl started making pie dough. Della was assigned the peeling fresh apples for the pies. She stood at the kitchen sink, a paring knife in one hand and an apple in the other.

"Found a new hired girl, I see," a man's voice said.

Della swung around at the sound. The man smiled at her,

showing a space between two yellowed teeth in his broad grin. His handlebar mustache drooped over the corners of his mouth but was not sufficient to cover a scar on his upper lip. A white shirt stretched over his ample midsection while his dark trousers were supported by a set of red suspenders.

He moved to the stove, lifted the coffee pot, and poured himself a cup.

"This is Della McCrea," Pearl replied. "I hired her yesterday. Cousin Cora recommended her." She motioned a large spoon in his direction. "My husband, Mr. Cooper," she said to Della.

"Pleased to meet you," Della said as she watched move the cup to his fat lips

Jasper Cooper returned her greeting with a nod, his dark eyes studying her face.

She noticed his hands were devoid of traces of grim common among minors and wondered about his occupation. She returned her attention to the apples but sensed his gaze on her back.

"I'll be taking supper in town today," Mr. Cooper said.

When Pearl didn't respond to his statement, Della thought it odd. For several minutes Della heard him drinking his coffee, followed by the sound of a cup being set on the counter and the outside door closing.

While the two women worked, Pearl went over the weekly routine. "For most people, Monday is wash day, but I prefer doing it on Tuesday morning. It doesn't take long for the sun to dry everything. Today, all the sheets get changed. You can do that when we finish here."

She measured water from the sink into a cup and continued. "Mr. Bennett's shirts are done separately. Tuesday afternoon the ironing and mending are done. The men get fried chicken with fried giblets and onions for supper.

Wednesday, you clean the downstairs while I do the marketing." She patted out the dough and picked up a rolling pin. "Thursday, after the groceries are delivered, we preserve whatever fruit or vegetables I was able to find.

And so it went. Della listened without a word, trying to fix the details in her mind.

"Friday, you clean upstairs. Saturday, we bake bread and fix a double batch of stew, so there's leftovers for Sunday's soup. Most of the men go out drinking Saturday night and hardly know what they're eating on Sunday, anyway. You can take Sunday off for church. See that you go."

The rest of the day Della was kept busy with the kitchen chores and cutting up chickens for the frying pan. She hardly noticed the passing hours until noise in the building signaled that the boarders had arrived after their shift in the mine.

Pearl instructed her to set the table in the dining room and place a heaping plate of biscuits at each end, along with a dish of butter and three coffee urns.

"This bunch of foreigners are from Spain, not Mexico," Pearl said as she forked hot chicken onto a platter. "A higher grade than some of those honyocks, I think, but don't understand much English. I have rules here," she continued, narrowing her eyes. "No alcohol on the premises. One drop and I boot them out. I don't tolerate quarreling, either. Gotta keep a tight rein on young bucks like them." She put one fist on her hip. "Same goes for you. Don't encourage any advances from the miners. I don't abide such goings-on. And don't think I won't know if it happens."

Della gulped. She had a mental image of Pearl with a horsewhip, and a miner tied to a tree.

Minutes later, Della entered the dining room with the platter of fried chicken and saw that all nine of the miners were seated around the table. She set the platter in the center and expected they would begin passing it. After a day down in the mine, she figured the men would be hungry as wild lions.

She backed up to the kitchen door, ready to return with the rest of the meal. It jerked open behind her. Della spun around to face her employer, who was scowling and holding the dish of giblets and onions. "What's the hold-up? Don't be dilly-dallying, girl. Get the food on the table." She pushed the dish into Della's hands.

One of the miners grabbed the platter of chicken and forks stabbed at it as it was passed from hand to hand.

When all of the meal had been served, Della joined the Cooper family for supper in the kitchen.

Later Della stood in the dining room, looked at the table full of dishes she would have to wash, and realized how much her feet hurt. Easing down into one of the chairs, she sighed. All this for two dollars a week. It'll take over six months to earn enough for a train ticket.

She was on the verge of tears when the kitchen door opened and the three Cooper boys came clambering in, followed by their mother with her youngest child propped on her hip. She shook her head when she saw Della. "Don't think you're the only one who's tired, girlie. I still got these young'uns to put to bed. Get busy. Tomorrow's another day."

Chapter 29

Despite herself, Della found that she learned something new every day from her exacting and humorless employer. The woman ran the boardinghouse with amazing efficiency. From the punctual mealtimes to the children's schoolwork, everything ran precisely as Pearl dictated.

A good example was washday, an exercise that began at dawn. It was about the only time Mr. Cooper was any help. He built the fire under the cauldron that heated water for the galvanized tubs, helped fill them and left. The sheets were first into the washtub, next came table clothes, and then the family laundry. Mr. Bennett's white shirts were washed separately in a large bucket, run through the wringer attached to the rinse tub and hung to dry. And finally, at the end of the morning, Della was allowed to do her own laundry in the murky water.

The hot Arizona sun dried everything in record time, followed by dampening the garments to be ironed later, a delicate process in a kitchen that never cooled off. The two-pound iron was heated on the stove, then cooled to just the right temperature to avoid scorching the fabric of each garment.

Della had just finished pressing Mr. Bennett's shirts when he poked his head around the door from the dining room. "Ah, you have them ready, I see." He stepped into the kitchen and took his shirts from the drying rack.

"I'm afraid they are still a little damp," Della said.

"They'll be dry by morning when I need them." He reached into his pocket and approached Della still standing at the ironing board. As he held out a few coins, he asked, "Aren't you the girl my sister introduced me to at the church picnic last summer?"

"Yes, sir."

He dropped the coins into her hand. "I thought you looked familiar the other day. I remember you were obliging to my son."

"He's a nice boy. How is he?" Though it was none of her business, she wondered where the child was living. Not with his father, apparently.

"I have to travel so often, my sister is caring for him. But I'm having a house built up on the hill south of town, and as soon as it's completed and I find a nanny for him, we will be together again." He paused, a sudden sadness in his eyes. "I miss him. It's been very hard since his mother died. I knew my sister was the only person who could begin to fill the gap." Suddenly, his brow creased. "Oh, I'm so sorry. I believe your father was one of those killed in that explosion."

Della nodded, her feelings suddenly rising to the surface. She picked up the iron and stepped over to place it on the stove, not wanting him to see her bite her lip.

"You've done a very nice job on the shirts. Thank you." He nodded and quietly left the room.

One day ran on to the next and at the end of each week, Mrs. Cooper handed Della two dollars, her week's pay, though it was evident by her expression that she begrudged parting with it.

On Sunday, her one day off, she had the luxury of not getting up at dawn. It wasn't raining, so the chance to walk to church was also a treat. While there, she had a chance to speak to Cora and learn the news from the mine and her old neighborhood.

In between the daily chores, Della became better acquainted with the Cooper boys and found their antics amusing. The oldest, Jacob, was a serious ten-year-old with sandy brown hair and keen blue eyes. He had a ready smile and a love of music. She knew that because she recalled seeing him months earlier when she'd passed through town on her way to the post office. He'd been hanging around the door of Marshall's saloon, his foot tapping to the rhythm of a banjo.

At home, he was often charged with caring for his baby

brother, hauling in wood for the cook stove, or polishing his father's shoes.

Eight-year-old Luther helped his brother with chores if told, but his preference was teasing his younger brother, Wesley. He struggled with his arithmetic and often had to bring his papers home to finish the work.

The four-year-old was a study in perpetual motion. If he wasn't tormenting the cat, he was crawling between the legs of the miners under the breakfast table, which resulted in a spanking. His blonde hair never stayed combed for more than five minutes, and he always had a scrape or bruise on his elbow or knee.

Since their home was built on a steep slope, there was little outdoor space to play where there wasn't the hazard of snakes or scorpions and the unrelenting Arizona sun. The result was that the children had to entertain themselves indoors much of the time. Della didn't mind their noise, but the same couldn't be said for their mother. She kept telling them to quiet down.

Late one Wednesday afternoon before his mother had returned from town, Luther sat at the kitchen table, his head propped against his hand, a pencil idle in the other. "I'm no good at figuring," he said, his tone reflecting a sense of hopelessness. "Jacob says I'm stupid."

Della, standing at the kitchen work table, was polishing the silverware. "What is it that is so hard?"

He slid off his chair and brought the paper to show her. She glanced at the problems on the page and nodded.

"Look." She laid out nine table knives in a row. "How many knives do I have?"

Luther leaned forward and narrowed his eyes. "Nine."

"What if I laid out some more?" She added three knives to the lineup. "Now how many do I have?"

"You have twelve."

"Right. But what happens if I take some away." She pushed a handful aside. "How many now?"

"That's easy. You have six."

"Very good. It might help to think of the numbers on the page as knives or forks."

"I dunno." Luther leaned against the table. "Maybe Jacob is right."

"I don't believe that for a second. Let's try a different problem. Pretend you're a farmer."

Luther watched as Della laid three knives side-by-side. "Let's call these horses." She picked up a few forks and put them in line with the knives. "These will be cows." Then she grabbed a handful of spoons. "What shall we call these?"

"Pigs," he said, grinning.

"All right." She added the 'pigs' to the collection. "Now,

what's the total number of livestock in the farmer's field?"

Luther laughed. "Eleven."

"Correct. That's not so hard. But what if the farmer sells one of the cows and three of the pigs, then buys six chickens. Now, what's the total?"

Luther thought for a minute. "Thirteen!"

"Right. See. Jacob is wrong. You're smart. Just think of the numbers as pigs and chickens."

Luther grinned, his eyes sparkling. "I can do that," he said and hurried to the papers on the table.

"You'd make a good teacher," a man's voice said.

Della whirled around to find Mr. Bennett standing in the dining room doorway. He was wearing his usual black dress suit and white shirt.

"My father thought so. One of my sisters is a teacher."

Bennett smiled and held up one of his shirts. "Can I trouble you to sew on a button for me?" He held out a button in the palm of his hand.

"Sure. I'll just fetch my sewing basket. Wait here. It's in my room." She hurried out the back door and a minute later returned with the basket. A few snips, a threaded needle, and before long, the shirt button was firmly attached. She clipped the thread and handed the shirt to him.

"I am grateful," he said, accepting it. "I must hurry to be on the next train to Ashe Fork." He whirled around and was gone as suddenly as he'd arrived.

"I'm done," Luther declared. He slid off the chair, took his arithmetic paper and pencil, and ran off to his room.

Della smiled to herself, reached for the polishing cloth, and returned her attention to the silver service. The only pieces left were a few spoons. She'd finished the large ones. If she hurried, the chore would be done before time to start supper preparation.

Without her notice, Jasper Cooper had walked up behind her and looked over her shoulder. "Good job. I can almost see my reflection in that vase."

Startled, she flinched. "Thank you, Mr. Cooper."

He leaned across in front of her and picked up a soup ladle. As he did, he put his right hand on her shoulder. "You're a good worker and mighty pretty too." He let his hand slide to the center of her back.

At his touch, her instinct was to recoil, but she knew that one word from him and she'd be out on the street with nowhere to lay her head.

The outside door opened, letting in a gust of hot air. Pearl appeared with little Joey propped on her hip and a shopping bag in her hand. Her face was flushed and her hair damp with perspiration.

Mr. Cooper stuffed his hand into his trouser pocket. "Your

new girl is doing a bang-up job here. Looks like she'll work out just fine."

Della kept her eyes on the serving spoon, rubbing it extra hard with the polishing cloth. She didn't look at either direction but wondered if Pearl had noticed her husband's actions.

A moment later, she heard the dining room door close behind her as he left the room. A shiver ran down her spine. What a despicable old man, she thought. She looked over at her employer, and for a moment, felt compassion for her.

Pearl put the toddler down and dropped the bag on the table. "Put all that away," she commanded, "and get the leftover ham out of the ice box. Call those boys. We need them to bring up more wood for the cook stove. It looks like rain."

Chapter 30

The afternoon brought a thunderstorm, one of those so common to the area, where dark clouds blew over the mountain top, dumped a half-inch of rain in a matter of minutes, and rolled on across to the valley below.

At dusk, when the day's work was done, Della sat on the cot in her ground-level basement room and chewed on a fingernail. Mr. Cooper's conduct troubled her. He was a threat. That was clear. Her sister had told her about such men, had told her to be wary of his kind.

But what could she do? She guessed she could seek employment in a different boardinghouse. Or maybe a hotel. But what reason could she give Mrs. Cooper for leaving? Her financial situation hadn't changed. She couldn't claim family sickness; she didn't have any family in Jerome. And if she left abruptly, Mrs. Cooper might be angry and say mean things about her. The woman did not have a forgiving nature. Jerome was still a small city. Word traveled fast, and then no one would hire her.

She opened her sewing basket where she kept the money

she'd saved—the six dollars pay and the coins she received for ironing Mr. Bennett's shirts. Far from her goal. She sighed and closed the lid, then pulled the combs out of her hair and stretched out on the cot to consider her choices. They were too few, so in the end, her only course was to avoid him.

Much to her relief, she didn't see Jasper Cooper for the remainder of the week. One morning at breakfast, she overheard Jacob ask his mother where his father had gone. Pearl told the boy his father was in Bisbee on business.

Business? Cora hadn't mentioned Mr. Cooper having any kind of business. However, it was of little concern to her. She was simply glad he wasn't around.

On the following Tuesday, when she saw him building the fire under the cauldron to heat water for the washing, she wondered when he had returned without her notice. He gave her no attention, and as soon as there was a good blaze, he left the women to their work.

That afternoon, Della eyed the last garments in the ironing basket while she waited for the iron to heat on the cook stove. Mrs. Cooper had complained of a headache and retired to her bedroom. It could hardly be missed that her girth was expanding, and Della wondered when the new member of the family would arrive. When that happened, she knew her workload would increase enormously.

Luther was at the kitchen table, chewing on his pencil, and practicing his arithmetic at his mother's insistence.

"What's taking you so long?" Jacob scowled at his brother, anxious to play ball on the road in front of the house.

"Luther will be finished soon," Della said, smoothing a garment out on the ironing board. "You can go ahead. Take Wesley. Teach him how to play."

Jacob glanced at her, tucked the ball under his arm, and mumbled something not meant to be heard. "Come on, kid," he said in a grudging tone. The younger boy grinned as the two of them went out the side door.

"I hate takeaways," Luther said with the emphasis on "hate."

"The more you practice, the easier it will be," Della told him. "Knowing how to figure numbers is important if you want to grow up and have a business like your father."

Luther hunched over his paper, a furrow forming in his brow. "What is a wager?"

"It means to bet money on something."

He straightened and swiveled in his seat. "Like the men in the Copper town saloon?"

"Yes. Where did you hear that word?"

"I heard my dad tell my mother the suckers in Bisbee would wager on anything."

Della didn't comment but suspected she now knew all she needed to know about Mr. Cooper's business.

There seemed to be no pattern to Jasper Cooper's comings-and-goings. Sometimes he was away for several days, others, he was absent at suppertime, but appeared at the breakfast table in the morning. The atmosphere varied at the table each time he returned, some days cheerful, others gloomy. But in either case, he paid Della little attention beyond requesting a second cup of coffee, which caused Della to relax a bit.

The weekly cleaning schedule at the end of the week brought Della to the second floor where she wrapped a kerchief around her hair. She gathered the supplies from the closet in the center hallway and entered the first of four sleeping quarters. The rooms had simple furnishings: two double beds, two highboy chests of drawers, and a series of hooks on the wall for hanging clothes. Unlike her brothers, these boarders didn't leave clothes on the floor, or a clutter on the bureaus.

She swept down cobwebs, shook the curtains, and dusted every flat surface. After running the dust mop on the hardwood floors in the first room, she moved on to the next bed chamber and followed the same procedure.

With her attention on her work, she didn't notice when

Jasper Cooper came up the stairs. Hearing footsteps behind her, she glanced over her shoulder, saw him enter the first room she'd cleaned, and realized he was inspecting her work.

"Della," he called out after a moment.

"Yes, Mr. Cooper?"

"You've neglected this window. There's a spider in the corner. I see it clearly."

Della hesitated, not wanting to be alone with the man. But if she defied him, and he complained to his wife, she'd be in trouble.

Cooper raised his voice. "Hurry, Della. It's going to get away."

She grabbed the broom and went into the room. "Which window?"

"Right over here." He pointed to a spot at the top of the drapery.

Della walked over to where he was pointing and looked up for the elusive spider. She raised the broom and swept along the upper edge.

In a swift move, Cooper had his arm around her waist, pulled her to his chest, and pressed his lips next to her ear. "You're just too tempting to pass up."

Della sucked in air, twisted around, and brought the broom handle down between them. Pushing it against his chest with all her might, broke free, dropped the broom and fled.

Out in the hall, Della felt faint, her legs weak beneath her. The storage closet—she could hide there. She rushed to get inside and pulled the doorknob tight, hanging onto it for fear he'd try to enter. Her heartbeat hammered in her ears. She squeezed her eyes closed, but could still see his grin as she broke away. What was she going to do? At the moment, she couldn't think.

She listened for footsteps for several long minutes. Hearing none, she opened the door a crack to peek out. No one in sight. She eased open the door enough to see in the other direction. No sign of Cooper. Still apprehensive, she stepped out and gently closed the door. Moving stealthily as a cat, she returned to the room she'd been working in, collected her cleaning tools, and finished her work, all the while alert to any sound in the hall. When she'd completed cleaning the last room on that level without incident, she gathered her courage and returned to the first room to retrieve the broom. She found it leaning against the doorjamb.

Believing the man was somewhere in the building made Della uneasy for the rest of the workday, and by the time she finished washing the supper dishes, she'd made a decision. She knew she would miss the boys. She'd become very fond of helping Luther with his lessons. She'd even begun teaching Wesley the letters in his name. Nevertheless, she'd have to leave

Mrs. Cooper's employ.

She'd go to talk to Mrs. Sayers, the woman who ran Hanover House, where she and her parents had stayed when they first arrived the year before. With the mine so busy and new people moving to town, Della reasoned that Mrs. Sayers would need additional help.

Much to Della's relief, Jasper Cooper wasn't at the breakfast table the next morning, and likewise, missing at suppertime. It seemed he'd left on one of his "business" trips again.

At the end of the workweek, Della received her week's pay, counted her savings again, and determined to stick it out as long as possible. At church on Sunday, she managed a short visit with Cora afterward, though she never mentioned Jasper Cooper's despicable nature. Cora invited her to supper, but she declined, as it would be such a long way to walk back across town to return to the boardinghouse.

The following Wednesday afternoon, while their mother was out doing her weekly shopping, the Cooper boys were playing hide and seek, scurrying around the first floor, hiding in closets and behind furniture. Though fun at first, Jacob became bored because the younger boys were so easy to locate. The three of them came into the kitchen where Della was preparing vegetables for supper.

"You be *it*," Jacob said to Della.

She shook her head. "Your parents don't pay me to play games."

"Come on," he begged. "They won't know."

Seeing Jacob's pleading blue eyes melted her resistance. "All right. But just once and no fair going upstairs." Della began counting while the children scattered. "...Forty-eight, forty-nine, fifty," she called out.

She could hear them banging into furniture. "Here I come, ready or not." She couldn't help but smile. The game brought back memories of wintery days at home with her brothers and sisters.

She entered the dining room, rattled the chairs a bit, and then into the parlor making a big display of swishing the draperies and looking behind the sofa. In the entryway, she opened the door to the compartment under the stairway.

"Where can they be?" she said, loud enough for them to hear as she sauntered down the hallway to the boy's bedroom. She walked in heavy-footed and peeked under the beds. A giggle came from across the hall in their parent's room. She went to stand in the doorway. "What did I hear?"

Another giggle. It sounded like little Wesley, and it came from under his parent's dark walnut bed. With barely a foot of space, she wondered how he managed to wiggle underneath.

"I think someone is under the bed," she said, making her voice sound gruff.

Getting down on her hands and knees, she reached under the blue bedcover and swept her hand back and forth along the floor.

Just as she touched Wesley's foot, she felt her petticoat being lifted and a hand on the calf of her leg. She reared back, twisted around, and saw Jasper Cooper, positioned on one knee, leering at her with a grin.

Suddenly, the sound of heavy footfalls came from the hall, and Pearl Cooper appeared in the doorway, her expression a mixture of horror and fury. "What is going on in here?" By her tone, it wasn't a question.

Jasper reacted and got to his feet, sidestepped around his wife, and hustled into the hall out of sight.

Della stood and faced her employer. Pearl glared at her. "I told you never to enter this room." She advanced on Della, her eyes ablaze. "You harlot!" Pearl swung her handbag at Della's head.

Della ducked aside, held up her hand to ward off another blow, and pointed to the bottom of the bed. "The boy ..."

"Get out!" Pearl's shout fairly rattled the windows. "Pack your trash, get out of my sight and off my property! I never want to lay eyes on you again."

Chapter 31

In Della's world, the woman was always considered at fault in such situations, and she knew it. She would be labeled a loathsome temptress by his offended wife. There was no remedy. Tears blurred Della's vision as she retreated to the basement room to gather her possessions. She removed her apron, flung it onto the cot, and sat, her head in her hands with Pearl Cooper's words ringing in her ears. It wasn't fair. It just wasn't fair.

She could still feel his hand on her leg. She knew it was a sin to wish someone would burn in hell, but she couldn't help it. At that moment, that's exactly what she wished for Jasper Cooper.

She'd wanted to get away from that repulsive man, had planned to leave the Coopers, but she wanted it to be her choice, not the way it turned out. She wiped her eyes. The worst part was that the Cooper boys couldn't help but hear their mother's shouting. What would they be thinking?

Rising from the cot, she made her bedding into a roll and tied it, just as she'd done the day she'd left the rental. She folded her apron and placed it in the valise, then gathered her other clothing.

Where could she go? It would be dark before long and lingering in the streets of Jerome was out of the question. She thought of Cora Hovey, but there was no room in their home for another person, not with four children. Other than Cora, she had few friends.

She thought of Vesta and nearly laughed at the idea of knocking on the door of her parent's home. She pictured the look on Mrs. Blocker's face if she saw Della with her bedroll slung over her shoulder. It would be the same with Millie Swanson's mother.

Who would take her in? Pondering all the people she'd met at church; she couldn't think of a one. Except, maybe ...

The light from the sunset was fading fast when Della stood on the concrete step at the rear of the Methodist church rectory and knocked on the door. She waited and listened for movement inside. Her courage was starting to wane before she heard footsteps approaching. Mrs. Smith opened the door, a look of surprise spreading over her lined face.

"Why, good evening, Della. Come in, won't you? Why didn't you come to the front door?"

Della stepped inside and Mrs. Smith closed the door. In the bright light of the kitchen, Mrs. Smith's gaze swept over her, taking in the things she was carrying. Her brow creased as Della set her valise and sewing basket down on the floor.

"Mrs. Smith, I need your help. I didn't know where else to turn."

"Oh, my dear child, come sit at the table. Tell me, what has happened?"

"You wouldn't believe it. I hardly believe it myself." Della sat on the nearest chair and blinked back tears as she poured out her story. She explained how, since her father's death, her family had been unable to help her, how she'd sold the furniture to pay the back rent, about the overdue grocery bill, and then how she'd taken the job at the Cooper House and about Jasper Cooper's revolting advances. By the time she'd finished, she was sobbing. "I don't know what to do. I have nowhere to stay and with so little money, no way to get back to my family in Ohio."

Ruby Smith put her hand on Della's arm and held out a handkerchief to her. "Have you had supper, dear?"

Della took the hankie and shook her head. She hadn't thought about food until just that second.

Ruby rose from the chair. "I'll fix you something to eat and then we can talk about what to do next. Let me show you where the lavatory is, so you can wash your face." She led Della down a hall.

While Della let the warm water run over her hands, she looked in the mirror. What a sight she was, red-eyed, her dark hair disheveled with the combs loosened. For the next several minutes, Della concentrated on making herself presentable and wondered what Reverend Smith would think about her showing up at his back door. He might not be as kind as old Pastor Conklin back at her church in Ohio.

When she'd finished, she returned to the kitchen and found Reverend and Mrs. Smith seated at the table.

He stood when she entered. "My wife tells me you are in need of a place to stay." He stroked his scraggly, eight-inch, gray beard and glanced at her baggage. "I agree that it would be better for you to stay here temporarily. Mrs. Smith will help you find suitable employment. This town is a harsh place for a good Christian girl like you."

He turned to his wife who had moved to the stove and was warming sausage in a frying pan. "I'll leave you to take care of Miss McCrea. I'll be in my study."

Della heaved a sigh as she watched him leave the room. "Thank you. Thank you both. I won't be a bother, I promise."

Mrs. Smith set a plate of sausage and vegetables in front of her, and when Della had finished eating, showed her to a small bedroom on the second floor.

"I'll be very happy to do any housework you desire," Della said to Mrs. Smith the next morning as she helped with the breakfast dishes. From what she'd seen, the pastor's wife was a well-ordered housekeeper. "And I'm a rather good seamstress if you have need of one."

Ruby Smith smiled as she gave the sink one last swipe. "I certainly could use the help. In fact, our Missionary Society is due to meet here this afternoon, and they will be expecting some refreshments. You can help with the preparations."

Over the next week, Della soon learned that a pastor's wife was as involved in the work of the pastor as the pastor himself. Mrs. Smith was tasked to either host or attend Bible study each week, besides being present at the church service. She called on the sick in the hospital and sometimes in their homes, also handled the mail, and kept her husband up to date on the concerns of his flock.

But it didn't take long before Della decided that though the Smiths were very kind, staying at the rectory was not getting her any closer to buying the train ticket she longed for.

"I need to find employment of some kind," she told Mrs. Smith as she placed silverware on the table for the noonday meal. "I believe I'll go talk to Mrs. Whipple at the dress shop this afternoon. Perhaps I could do some sewing for one of her customers. And if she can't use me, I'll seek work at the Hanover House. Mrs. Sayers knows me."

Mrs. Smith nodded thoughtfully. "Certainly no harm in asking. And on the way back, you could stop at Miller's Mercantile for me. They should have our order of candles for the church by now."

May was a pleasant month in Jerome, warm enough that Della didn't need a shawl. As she walked up the sloping street to the center of town, she couldn't help but reflect on the fact that a year had passed since she'd been in the dress shop. Would Mrs. Whipple even remember her?

Della stepped inside the shop, glanced around, and noted that not much had changed, except perhaps that the floor slanted a little more acutely. It didn't surprise her. The daily blasting in the mine continued to cause slippage in the foundations of many buildings.

Mrs. Whipple came walking out of the storage closet at the back of the room with two bolts of fabric in her arms.

As Della approached, the dressmaker plunked her burden onto the cutting table. "Della. It's good to see you again. I was so sorry to hear about what happened to your father. Terrible. Just terrible." She shook her head. "What can I do for you?"

"I'm hoping you might have some sewing or mending work I could do. I have no income since my father died, and my family has fallen on hard times of late, so they have been unable to help me with funds."

Mrs. Whipple's brow creased in a thoughtful manner. "Hmm. Let me think a minute. Well, as it happens, I do have a torn dress that belongs to one of our more colorful ladies in town. She brought it in yesterday, and right now, I don't have time to do anything with it."

"Colorful ladies?"

The dressmaker pressed her lips together for an instant and glanced to the back of the room where three women were busy at sewing machines. "Uh, she lives above one of the saloons, and uh ..."

Della interrupted. "I need an income. I used to mend my brother's torn shirts after one of his quarrels. May I see it?"

"Certainly." Mrs. Whipple walked over to where a green dress hung on a rack and took it off the hanger. She folded it over her arm and exposed a three-inch tear in the bodice. Della stepped forward to examine it. It looked like someone had grabbed the tie at the waist and given it a jerk. Besides causing a tear, the seam had opened at the waistline, loosening the skirt by a good eight inches.

Reattaching the skirt would be simple, Della thought, but repairing the tear would be more complicated. She turned up the hem of the skirt. It was wide enough that she thought she could steal a sufficient amount of material to make matching wedges and then insert them into either side of the bodice.

She nodded. "I believe I can repair it well enough to make it wearable again. I'll come back in the morning to work on it."

"You sure you won't be offended by the ownership?"

Della shook her head. "Not in the least."

Mrs. Whipple chuckled. "Good enough, then. I'm obliged. Like I said, I don't have the time."

Della left the shop with a smile on her face. She'd recognized the dress and knew the identity of its owner.

Chapter 32

Della felt heartened as she waited for the clerk in Miller's Mercantile Store to wrap the candles Mrs. Smith had ordered. She let her gaze drift over the various items for sale while still thinking about the green dress and how she would achieve the repairs. Lena Larson had been kind to her when she'd needed someone. Now she had the opportunity to repay the debt.

"Here you are," the bi-spectacled clerk said. He laid the package on the countertop along with an account book and a pencil. "Sign here."

Having finished the transaction, she took the package of candles and thanked him. When she turned toward the exit, she spotted Jacob Cooper entering the store and hurried to greet him. "I'm so happy to see you, Jacob. How are your brothers?"

Jacob looked at her with apprehension in his eyes, and then averted his gaze. "My mother says you are a very bad woman, and I'm not supposed to talk to you."

Anger and embarrassment sent a flush to her cheeks. Speechless, she rushed from the store, fearful the clerk or someone else might have overheard what he'd said.

She hurried up the boardwalk and didn't stop until she reached the next block. She could only imagine what had transpired in the Cooper House that evening and what Pearl Cooper had said to those boys. Would she spread lies about her? And would they be believed? The thought of it made her shudder.

Della spent the better part of the next morning at Mrs. Whipple's repairing the green dress. With a few scraps from a basket of discards, she patched the hem where she'd removed the needed wedges of fabric to match the bodice. Basting all the parts in place took the most time, but the final stitching was done on one of the treadle sewing machines.

When Della finished, she held it up for Mrs. Whipple's approval. The dressmaker studied the stitching and nodded. "I'd say you've done a fine job. If I didn't know better, I'd think the bodice was meant to look that way."

"I hope the lady agrees." Della folded the garment over her arm. "Will she be calling for it soon?"

Mrs. Whipple shook her head. "There's a Mexican woman who makes deliveries for me. She'll be here this afternoon."

"If you'll tell me where to take it, I'm willing to deliver it myself. Then she can pay me directly for the repairs."

Mrs. Whipple pushed her glasses up on her nose and looked at Della, misgivings clear in her expression. "Are you sure?"

Della shrugged. "I have nothing better to do this afternoon unless you have more work for me, that is."

"Unfortunately, I don't." Mrs. Whipple took the dress from Della, packaged it, and tied it with a piece of twine. "You'll find Miss Larson at McBride's."

As Della approached McBride's saloon, she pondered the question of which door to enter. It might not be wise to enter directly off the boardwalk, she thought. She didn't know who might take note of her going inside and get the wrong impression. But around the corner at the side door that opened onto the narrow street, she wouldn't be noticed.

She chose the side door. Walking to it reminded her of the day she'd been assaulted. Lena Larson had been so kind that day, repairing her dress was the right thing to do.

But what if Lena was busy in her room? What would she do with the dress? She couldn't just leave it in the bar. Maybe making the delivery herself was a mistake.

While Della stood dithering over what to do, the door swung open, and a dark-haired, young man wearing a white apron appeared. He had a broom in one hand and dustpan in the other. He pitched the contents of the pan at Della's feet and looked at her. "You lookin' for somebody?"

Della swallowed. "Uh...yes. I have a dress to deliver to Miss Larson."

The man pushed the door open wider. "Well, don't just stand there. Come on in."

Della stepped into the dim interior and found herself at the bottom of the stairway she remembered. She glanced across the room. Just as the year before, the bald-headed bartender was behind the highly-polished bar. A couple of men stood opposite with drinks in their hands, their images reflecting in the mirror that hung on the wall beyond.

The sound of music pulled Della's attention to the front of the building. Near the front entrance, a man wearing plaid trousers, white shirt and a derby hat sat at a piano drumming out a lively tune. He occasionally hit a wrong note but didn't seem to notice.

Drawn by curiosity, Della walked past the men at the bar and stood next to the man on the piano stool. He stood, tipped his hat, and stepped aside.

Sensing the young bartender had followed her, she turned to him. "Is this...?"

He grinned and nodded. "Brand new, straight from New York City. A Steinway. My father, uh, Mr. McBride thinks it will bring more business. Except, George here, only knows one song. Do you play?"

Della nodded, reached out with her free hand, and ran her fingers over the ornate rosewood of the cabinet. "Beautiful," She said.

She was about to test the keys when, out of the corner of her eye, she saw Lena approaching. She straightened and turned to greet her. Without makeup, Lena was a rather plain-looking woman with small brown eyes and thin lips. Her hair, several shades lighter than the year earlier, hung loose, touching the shoulders of a pumpkin-colored dress. "Hello, again. What brings you to our fine establishment?"

"Your dress. Mrs. Whipple let me mend it for you." Della held out the package.

"Well, I'll be." Lena accepted the bundle. "Let's go up to my room. I want to try it on."

Della thanked the young man and followed Lena up the stairs. As soon as Lena closed the door, she pulled the string on the bundle and shook out the dress. She draped it over the privacy screen and began unbuttoning the dress she was wearing.

Della couldn't help but stare. Her friend slithered out of the garment, letting it fall around her ankles, and stepped out of it.

She reached for the repaired dress and wiggled as she drew it over her head and into place. Pulling the front of it together, she worked the buttons and moved to a mirror.

"I'm amazed. I had little hope Mrs. Whipple could fix that rip. But you did it, and by golly, it looks real good." She whirled around to face Della. "How much do I owe you?"

"Not a penny. You saved me from the clutches of that wicked man. It's the least I can do."

"Well, let me buy you a drink, then."

Della blinked. "Uh ..."

"Oh." Lena made a face. "I guess you're not yet old enough for that sort of treat. Well, I do thank you."

"If any of your friends have sewing needs, I'd be happy to oblige."

"Sure, honey. I'll let 'em know." Lena moved to open the door.

"I'm without employment," Della hurried to continue, "and saving to buy a train ticket to Ohio."

Lena reached out, put her hand on Della's shoulder, and shook her head. "You poor kid. The mine has made you an orphan, and now you're stuck here on this rocky hillside. I'll walk you down to the door."

When they reached the bottom of the stairs, the older, bald-headed bartender approached. "Young Douglas says you play the piano. That right?"

Della was a little taken aback by his boldness. "Yes, sir. I've had ten years of lessons."

"I'd guess the only kind of music you learned was that high-brow stuff."

"I had plenty of practice of that sort, but I learned other types of music as well."

"Is that so? Like what?"

"Well ..."

"How about, 'After the Ball is Over' or 'Dixie.'"

Della nodded. "Sure."

He pointed to the piano. "Play something."

Della felt uncomfortable and a bit annoyed, but she went to the piano. "Would 'My Old Kentucky Home' be all right?" She sat and commenced to play it. When she finished, she worked her fingers and played "Sweet Rosie O' Grady" as well.

"You play them songs on that piano, an' I'll pay you a half-dollar a night."

Della gulped and looked up at his face. "A half-dollar?"

He nodded.

Her thoughts swam with calculations. A half-dollar a night would mean she'd have nearly enough money for the train ticket in a little over two months. She'd been intent on talking to Mrs. Sayers about employment, but Mrs. Sayers would likely pay no more than two dollars a week. With luck, she could be home in time for the summer band concerts in the park. Temptation simmered.

Chapter 33

What was the risk? Her reputation? When she was back home in Ohio, it wouldn't matter.

A sudden rumble rattled the windows. The floor shuddered and the piano stool slid sideways beneath her. She sprung to her feet and watched it roll.

"I'll do it," she said and stuck out her hand to Mr. McBride.

From the foot of the stairs, Lena ambled toward Della and McBride. "I don't know, Gus. She's awful young."

"That's the best part," he said, grasping Della's hand. "Look at that face. She'll draw new, uh, patrons. It'll be good for business. The Fashion Saloon keeps getting bigger, I need some kind of edge."

Lena put a hand on her hip. "They're a rough bunch, Gus. Drunk and quarreling. She could be in danger. You gonna protect her from the likes of Ben, the bonebreaker?"

Gus scowled and looked sideways at Lena. "Don't worry. I'll take care of it." He turned to Della. "Can you be here by nine o'clock? And wear something a bit more classy. That getup makes you look like a school marm."

Della returned to the parsonage, removed her dress, and sat on the bed. Since Mr. McBride had already disapproved of the brown dress with the high collar and long sleeves she'd been wearing, she didn't have much choice. Her best clothes were in the trunk under the Hovey's back porch. Her only other choice was her blue skirt and white shirtwaist. She was trying to think of a way to make it look "classy" when Mrs. Smith rapped on the door and opened it.

"I hate to interrupt, but I was wondering if your visit to Mrs. Sayers went well. Can she employ you?"

Startled, Della stood abruptly, uncomfortably aware she was attired only in her undergarments. "Uh, no. But I found work in another place."

Ruby Smith clasped her hands together and smiled. "Very good. Where?"

"Mmm. I'll be able to use my musical talent."

"Yes, yes." The woman raised her eyebrows in anticipation. "At the school? That's wonderful. I am so happy for you."

When Della explained exactly where she would be using her talent, Mrs. Smith blanched. She put her hand over her heart. "Oh, Della. You can't, you just *can't*."

"Mr. McBride promised me a half-dollar a night to play for his customers. I'll only have to work there three more months to have enough money for my trip home."

"But you don't understand. Reverend Smith will never allow you to stay here if you work in a place like that. It would bring scandal on the church and censure from the bishop. If you persist in this plan, you'll have to find another place to live."

Della's legs turned to jelly. She plunked down on the bed. "But it's just for three months. No one has to know."

The pastor's wife shook her head. "A girl like you, working in a saloon? Jerome is a small town, my dear. I guarantee, Reverend Smith would hear about it." She shook her head, turned, and walked into the hall. "I'll leave you to think about it."

Della did think about it. She thought about the blasting that shook the earth each day. She thought about the noxious smoke from the smelter. She thought about her parents buried out in the hogback. And she thought about how she ached to see her brothers and sisters and the green trees along Chestnut Street.

She took the box that contained her mother's ivory cameo out of her sewing basket where she kept her valuables and lifted the lid. For a moment, she stared at it, then took a deep breath, pressed her lips together, and pinned it to the collar of her white shirtwaist.

When it came time to help with dinner, Della put on her apron and descended the stairs to the kitchen. She smiled at Mrs. Smith and set about gathering the table service for the dining room.

"I see you've reconsidered," her hostess said. "I'm glad. Set an extra plate tonight. The schoolmaster's son will be joining us. He's such a nice boy. I'm sure you'll find him pleasant company."

The dinner was tasty, but Della had to force herself to concentrate on the food. Musical notes kept bubbling out of her subconscious. She made an effort to join in the conversation at the table, but the young man to her left was as dull as dishwater in her opinion. He talked about his intention to enter the University of Arizona in Tucson, his talent for memorizing Bible verses, and speculated with Pastor Smith as to when Arizona would gain statehood.

The clock setting on the sideboard was in Della's direct line of vision, and as she watched the minutes tick past eight o'clock, she found herself twisting the napkin in her lap and had to restrain a fidgeting foot. It felt like the dinner would never end. A trigger was needed. She decided she'd have to rely on a lie.

Folding her napkin and placing it beside her plate, she sent Mrs. Smith a most gracious smile. After an effusive compliment about the peach pie, she turned to her dinner partner. "I'm so pleased to have had this opportunity to meet you, Mr. Milton."

She looked across the table at her hostess. "Mrs. Sayers will be expecting me very early in the morning."

Mr. Milton responded to the more than obvious hint as any well-bred young man would, offering praise for the dinner, and after a bit of awkwardness, shook hands with Pastor Smith and took his leave.

Della's hands were shaking as she helped clear the table, carrying the balance of the roast chicken to the kitchen. She took her apron from the wall hook to start washing the dishes, but Mrs. Smith stopped her. "You get your rest, dear. Tomorrow will be an important day for you."

She folded the apron over her arm. "I guess it would be best if I confessed right now. I know you disapprove, but Jerome is not where I belong, and performing in that saloon will be the quickest way for me to earn my way home."

The pastor's wife gasped. "But I thought..."

"I'm sorry to disappoint you. You've been so good to me." The hurt look on Ruby Smith's face was almost too much.

Della thanked her hostess for giving her shelter and dashed up the stairs before she lost courage. She rushed to gather her belongings just as before and turned out the light. Her heart thumped in her chest as she descended the stairs, prepared to head out into the dark.

Ruby met her at the back door with tears in her eyes. "I will pray for you."

Chapter 34

Della stepped through the rear door of McBride's saloon and peered through a haze of smoke at the men crowded at the bar. It was Saturday night and most were dressed for the evening, wearing a white shirt, coat and tie. A few women in gaily colored skirts and shirtwaists styled to be revealing, mingled, smiling and laughing.

The scene was illuminated by electric bulbs hung at intervals over the bar. An additional bartender had been added to accommodate the crowd. Each had his white apron snuggly tied at the waist and was busy pouring drinks for customers. The atmosphere was one of good cheer.

A burst of raucous laughter from the back room behind the stairway indicated a night of gambling was well underway. And near the open front entrance, the man Douglas McBride had referred to as George was pounding out "Daisy, Daisy" on the piano.

She set her satchel, bed roll, and sewing basket on the floor. Her presence caught the attention of the proprietor's son. He moved quickly around the end of the bar and hurried over to her. "What's all this stuff?" he asked, pointing to the items at her feet.

"My belongings. Is there someplace here I can put them? I can't stay at the parsonage any longer."

His brow creased. "Well, uh, I don't know. I'll have to ask." He scratched his head and retraced his path to consult with his father.

A creak from the stairs above drew Della's attention. Lena Larson, wearing the green dress Della had mended for her, was descending the staircase. "Looks like you got the boot," she said when she reached the bottom step.

Della nodded. "I'm hoping Mr. McBride will allow me to store my things here."

"And where do you figure to sleep?"

"At the moment, I don't know."

Lena pressed her scarlet lips together. "Hmm. Juanita's away just now. Her mother died. Come on. I'll sneak you into her room. But don't let McBride know. He'll want you to pay rent."

Della quickly gathered her possessions and followed her benefactor up the stairway and along the gallery to the last room. Lena opened the door and motioned for Della to hurry. The interior was dark, but Della didn't hesitate. Lena lit a lamp, giving the room minimal lighting.

A quick glance around revealed a bed with a chamber pot underneath, one chest of drawers with a mirror, a privacy screen, and clothing hanging on wall hooks. A dark green drape covered what Della guessed was a window.

"Get changed," Lena said and turned to leave.

"I *have* changed."

Lena glanced back at her and chuckled. "I doubt that's the sort of dress McBride had in mind." She closed the door as she left.

Della went to the mirror, checked her appearance, and moments later with her sheet music cradled in her arm, descended the stairs. She felt a bit breathless. She'd never stayed up all night in her whole life. The prospect of it was invigorating.

She hurried past the crowd to where George, in his plaid pants, was seated at the piano. "Excuse me," she said.

He swung his head around to look at her. "Hi, sweetie."

Della bristled at his brazen familiarity. "Mr. McBride has engaged me to play this evening," she said with a tinge of irritation. She wondered if he worked in a circus somewhere. Even his derby hat had a plaid band.

"Right you are." He heaved himself off the stool, gave a little bow, and walked over to the bar a few feet away.

Della settled on the piano stool, smoothed her skirt, and arranged her music. As she did so, she couldn't help but notice the numerous photos of almost naked prize fighters that lined the wall in front of her. She found the view a bit disturbing, but began her performance with "Sweet Rosie O'Grady," followed by "The Good Old Summertime." As she positioned the next sheet of music, the proprietor's son walked up, placed a glass bowl on the piano top, and returned to his duties.

While in the middle of playing "My Wild Irish Rose," a muscular man with a drooping mustache appeared on her left. He leaned toward her, studied her face, and straightened. "Excuse me for being so bold," he said in a gravelly voice, "but you look just like my baby sister, same color hair, same brown eyes too."

"That's nice." Della gave him a quick smile but kept her attention on her music. He lingered, leaning his arm on the piano top, staring at her for another moment, then walked away. Behind her, she heard him speak to someone at the bar. "She's such a pretty little thing. Looks just like my sister, Bonnie."

With her back to her audience, Della couldn't judge if anyone was listening to what she played, but with the front entrance barely ten feet from the piano, she was aware of movement when men left the building and others arrived. However, as she busily swapped one piece of sheet music for another, she didn't notice when Reverend Smith entered.

He was suddenly at her side. "Della McCrea, you must come back to the parsonage with me. This is no place for a Christian girl like you." He pulled a handkerchief out of his coat pocket and wiped his brow.

She glanced at him, commenced playing another piece, and shook her head. "Kind of you to ask, but I'm being paid for my talent."

"Now listen here. I insist. If your parents knew about this, they couldn't bear the shame." He'd raised his voice, perhaps thinking volume would get the desired results.

Again, she shook her head.

A man from the bar stepped over and stood next to the reverend. "I hope you're not bothering this young lady."

Della gave a quick glance and saw it was the same man who'd spoken to her earlier.

"Humph. Sir, it is my duty as head of our flock of good Christian men and women to rescue this young woman from this den of sin."

"Den of sin, huh?" the man growled and took hold of Reverend Smith's arm.

"Now see here." Smith jerked his arm in an effort to loosen the man's grip.

Della gasped, and stopped playing, fearful Pastor Smith was about to be injured. The drama caught the attention of two other men nearby and they stepped forward.

"Time you left," the first man said. He pulled the reverend to the door, opened it, and gave him a push. "Don't come back."

The parson stumbled, righted himself, and dusted his coat sleeve. The bulky man returned to Della's side. "Don't you worry, little sister. He won't bother you no more. Ol' Ben will be on the lookout." With that, he and his friends went back to their drinks.

Relieved the incident was over, Della glanced back at Mr. McBride and changed the tempo of her music with "Yankee Doodle."

As the night progressed, she played one song after another. Occasionally, one of the miners came, leaned his arm on the top of the piano, and sang along with his favorite tune. Another requested "My Old Kentucky Home" and left a coin in the dish.

Though she enjoyed entertaining, the time came when her hands needed a rest. She rose from the piano stool and turned to look for Douglas McBride. Both of the McBrides looked up from their work when the music stopped. Young McBride hurried in her direction. "What's wrong?"

She massaged one hand with the other. "Time for intermission."

"Oh." He went over to the man in the plaid trousers at the bar, tapped him on the shoulder and motioned him to the piano.

Della headed for the stairway and a moment later, "Daisy, Daisy" emanated from the far end of the building.

As she reached the top of the stairs, she glanced back at George and saw young McBride put a foam-topped glass on the piano top.

Abruptly, the pop-pop sound of gunshots came from the street out front of the saloon. Della flinched, rushed to Juanita's room, and locked the door behind her. She took a deep breath, lit the lamp, and then struggled with her clothing to use the chamber pot. Thus refreshed, she flopped on the bed, and in less than a minute, her eyelids grew heavy.

Chapter 35

Della bolted upright, eyes wide, and shook her head. Fearful of falling asleep, she rose from the bed. A basin and big pitcher of water sat on a table by the privacy screen. She went to it, poured a portion into the basin, then splashed her face and dried it with a soft cloth she found on a hook.

Had she ever played for such a long stretch of time, she wondered as she massaged her hands. She didn't think so, not even when practicing for a recital. Thinking back on her recitals, by comparison, they had been easy. But so much had changed since then that it all seemed like a dream.

She turned out the light and went out onto the gallery. The scene below was like the ones she'd read about in her brother's dime novels. She could hardly believe she was actually watching it all, the men with their drinks at the bar, the laughing women flirting. A wry smile formed on her lips. Richard and Lon would be so envious when she told them. But this was real, not a book, and she had to play her part if she had any hope of earning her way home.

Directly below, one of the painted ladies whispered into the ear of the man standing next to her. He threw back his head and laughed, then took her arm and led her to the staircase. The woman's sartorial was a tight-fitting, blue cotton fabric with a ruffled neckline. Rather pretty, Della thought.

Coming up the stairway, the woman noticed Della watching them. "Don't try to horn in, girlie. Or you'll be sorry," the woman said when they reached the top step. She glared at Della as she opened the door to one of the rooms and the two went inside.

Della quickly turned away. Why would she even think such a thing? I'm not that kind. Is that what everyone is going to think of me? Well, I don't care. I won't be here much longer, anyway.

She went to the staircase, hurriedly descended, and kept her eyes straight ahead while passing the men at the bar. She heard one make a comment but didn't look back, even when she reached George at the piano. "I've returned," she said.

"Sure thing," he said, stood, and grinned. "I kept the seat warm for you." He chuckled, took what was left of his drink, and sauntered to his place at the bar.

Settling on the piano stool, she was acutely aware of its warmth. She squirmed a bit, rearranged her music, and began the next phase of her performance with "Carry Me Back to Old Virginny."

She'd just concluded that piece and was about to start the next when two men burst out of the back room where gambling had been going on. "You're a cheatin' bastard," one man shouted.

Startled, Della turned in time to see a man in overalls grab the other fellow around the neck and swing his fist into the man's ribs.

Mr. McBride hurried around the end of the bar to the back door and opened it. "Not in here," he commanded. "Take it outside."

The second man sent a punch into the first man's belly, then slung his arm around the neck of his attacker. The two scuffled, pushing and shoving as they tumbled out into the darkness.

A buzz of comments from the crowd continued even after the door closed. Della looked around at the faces at the bar. No one seemed disturbed by the altercation. She shook her head and returned her attention to the music, choosing a toe-tapping tune.

The night wore on without incident, and when the crowd began to thin out, Della played "After the Ball," then concluded with "Three O'clock in the Morning."

The sun was high in its course when Della came down the stairs the following day with her purse in one hand and blue parasol in the other. She was hungry and had dressed in a hurry, intent on finding something to eat.

Mr. McBride blocked her passage when she reached the bottom step. "Did you sleep well? he asked with a smirk.

A bit surprised by his greeting, she replied, "I did, indeed. Thank you."

He nodded upward toward the gallery. "I charge for the use of those rooms up there, no matter how they're used. I'll be deducting rent from your pay."

Della's appetite evaporated, replaced by a sick feeling.

"I heard that, McBride. You're a scoundrel." The voice came from the gallery above.

Della swiveled and looked up at Lena standing on the top step. She was wearing a brown skirt and cream-colored shirtwaist, plus a matching hat with a feather in the band. "I happen to know Juanita paid you in advance to hold the room for her. And besides that, Miss McCrea is attracting more than just the regular crowd."

Lena continued coming down the stairs tapping each step with the ferrule of her parasol. "How many extra glasses of your watered-down whiskey did you sell last night? I'd venture a guess it was enough to cover the rent three times over."

"Keep your nose out of my business," McBride said, his face darkening.

"Oh, you old reprobate. Give the kid a break. Her father was killed in that mine explosion."

McBride grumbled something Della didn't quite catch and strode toward the gaming room, grabbing a broom along the way.

Della didn't know what to make of what had just happened. She looked at Lena. "Is he going to withhold part of my pay?"

"I doubt it," Lena said, stepping off the last step. "Let's go find something to eat. I'm hungry." She led the way to the front exit, swinging her parasol as she walked.

"Can I ask you something?" Della said as they stepped out onto the boardwalk and into the hot afternoon sun.

"Fire away," Lena replied, pausing a moment to raise her parasol and watch the townspeople rushing about their business.

"Do you know the men who come into the bar all the time?"

Lena gave her a side glance. "I know many of them. Why?"

"There was a man last night who said I look like his baby sister. He made Reverend Smith quit bothering me. He referred to himself as Old Ben. You know him?"

Lena gave a little chuckle. "Big guy with drooping a mustache and a scar on his cheek?"

Della nodded.

"That would be Ben Murray. We sometimes refer to him as Ben, the bone breaker. He handles one of the big drills down in the mine. I've heard he doesn't take any sass from anyone. Busted a guy's arm once for cussing at him."

"Oh. He sounds dangerous. I'm sure glad he's fond of his sister."

Continuing along the boardwalk, they soon reached Thornbeck's bakery. Della sucked in the aroma of fresh-baked bread. "I hope they have some fresh scones."

"I'm partial to the muffins," Lena said, stopping in front of the window.

The sun shining on the glass made it hard to see the interior though it reflected the traffic behind them and people on the walkway across the street very well.

"Um. I need to see Doc Jones," Lena said. "Been feeling some poorly this last week. You go on in. Try one of their apricot scones, if they have them." She tilted her parasol as she moved down the sloping street and went out of sight at the next corner.

Della wasn't fooled. She'd noticed the reflection of two matronly women across the street pointing at Lena and her and making quiet remarks to one another.

Della scowled, her hunger momentarily forgotten. She thought to run after her friend and tell her she didn't care about the old biddies' opinion. She didn't though, knowing Lena was protecting her from gossip. Lena had a good heart. It wasn't fair. How could people hate someone they didn't even know? It just wasn't fair.

Chapter 36

Della's consternation regarding the social morays of Jerome was interrupted when she saw a buggy approaching from down the street. She realized she recognized it and its occupants. The man at the helm was Hiram Bennett and at his side was his sister, Mrs. Samples. Between them sat Mr. Bennett's young son, Davie. As the buggy passed her, Mr. Bennett tipped his hat in greeting, and his sister, resplendent in a lavender dress and matching hat, nodded. The boy politely waved. Della responded in kind with a nod and a smile. They were coming from church, the service she'd missed because she'd been asleep in a prostitute's bed.

She felt her cheeks flush at the thought. Would she dare show her face in church ever again? Likely not, she supposed. Word of her new employment would be spread all over town by the end of the week. The women at church would think she was on her way to Hell. Could that be true? Della scowled at her reflection in the bakery window and squared her shoulders. No! That was not where she was going. She was going home, home to her family, home to the tall maple trees and the green grass along

Carson Avenue. It didn't matter what they thought. With a swish of her blue skirt, she stepped to the bakery door.

A few minutes later she was out on the boardwalk again with two apricot scones in a paper bag. In the next block, she stopped at the meat market. The butcher always kept a large glass jar of pickled eggs on the counter. When she'd purchased one of those, she walked on down the sloping walkway to the next block, her thoughts on her meal.

At the sight of the grocer's, she halted, abruptly reminded of her debt. She looked in the window. Mr. Jenkins, the grocer, was standing behind the counter dressed in his usual white shirt and black vest. Beside him was a shallow box heaped with fresh red strawberries, a favorite of hers. If she went inside to buy berries, she'd have to pay the debt her father had left. Standing there, she thought about the eight dollars in her purse. The idea of parting with any of it pained her, but if she were going to frequent this store, she had no option.

She opened the door, walked in and glanced around. A man was standing on a ladder retrieving a can from an upper shelf for a woman waiting below. Two other women were adding items to baskets they carried.

Della approached the counter and stood next to the cash register. "My name is Della McCrea," she said in a tone just above a whisper. "I've come to pay what I owe for the groceries."

Mr. Jenkins stroked his dark mustache. "It's about time." He reached under the counter and brought up a thick tablet. Laying it on the counter, he thumbed through until he found the page marked McCrea and put his finger on the bottom number circled in red. Even upside down, Della could easily read the figure.

"Eight dollars," he said. "I hope you plan to pay all of it."

Della suppressed a groan. It meant there'd be nothing left from her month's work at Cooper House. She raised her chin. "Yes sir. That is my intent." Pulling the money out of her purse, she laid it on the countertop. He wrote paid on the page and put the bills in his cash box.

"I'd like a few of those strawberries too," she said and produced the coinage, pennies that had been left in the dish on the piano top. With a handful of strawberries in a second bag, she left the store heartsick over the fact that she was now virtually penniless again.

Eager to silence her complaining stomach, she hurried further down the street to a bench near the bandstand and turned her attention to her small repast.

By the time she finished eating, the sun had crept to the top of Cleopatra Hill. She dipped her hand in a nearby horse trough, shook them and dried them against her skirt. Knowing it would be her only meal that day, she kept one of the scones wrapped in her handkerchief to eat later before she began another night's performance.

The next few nights passed without incident. Business at the bar was brisk with miners coming and going. If one of them became overly inebriated and approached her, Ol' Ben stepped in to intervene, cautioning them to mind their manners. His presence made her feel more at ease. If one of the men dropped a penny or two in her dish, she rewarded him with a smile.

She wasn't certain if Lena's chastising Mr. McBride was the reason or not, but on Friday before she approached the piano, he called her over to the bar and held out his fist. He motioned with a nod that she was to accept what he held there. She reached out and he dropped seven half-dollars coins into her open hand. She stifled a gasp. At the sight of the shiny coins, she grinned. "Thank you." He hadn't subtracted anything for the room.

Elated, she dashed up the stairs to hide her treasure in her sewing basket. Ten more weeks, she thought. One week gone and ten to go. She simply needed to keep focused.

The Saturday night crowd was louder and more boisterous than during the week. Della had an uneasy feeling as she settled herself at the piano, though she didn't know why. She glanced one way and another, watching for the now familiar faces, the man with the Santa Claus beard, the short fellow with a limp, and of course, George in his plaid trousers.

It was almost midnight when Della heard a familiar voice behind her. "Well, what do you know? Here she is, little Miss Prissy. I heard you'd found a new job."

A shiver shot down Della's spine as Jasper Cooper sauntered up and stood directly behind her. She gave a quick look over her shoulder for Ben but didn't see him.

Cooper's hand clamped down on her shoulder. She made to shake it off. "Get away from me. I'll have nothing to do with you."

"That's what you think. Your situation has changed."

"My opinion of you hasn't changed."

"That doesn't matter. I'll pay whatever McBride asks and bed you tonight." He guffawed and walked off.

Stunned, Della spun around and scanned the room for a place to hide. Her stomach whirled. The men at the bar were staring at her. McBride couldn't do that, could he? What sort of agreement did Lena and the others have with him? She'd never thought to ask.

It wasn't long before Cooper returned. "Come on. Time's a wastin'. Let's go up to your room."

Della glared at him, her heart pounding in her chest. "You're lying!" She turned her back on him, the color draining from her face.

"Listen, you little hussy. You're mine for the night. I paid for you." He grabbed her by her upper arm, lifting her off the stool.

"Let go of me!" She made an effort to hit him with her free hand. Where was Ben?

Just then the saloon door swung open and Ben Murray walked in. When he spied what Cooper was doing, a snarl formed on his face. With three swift steps, he had Cooper's arm in his grip. "Let go of her," he growled.

"Get lost, buddy," Cooper responded. "Wait your turn."

In the background, McBride was watching and motioned to one of the miners at the bar. The man slipped out the back door.

Ben Murray towered over Jasper Cooper. He bent Cooper's free arm around his back with a jerk. Cooper bellowed in response. Ben's big fist came up and connected with Jasper Cooper's chin. He fell to the floor, releasing Della's arm.

The big man hauled him up like a rag doll, dragged him to the front exit, and threw him out on the boardwalk. Cooper didn't move. Ben brushed his hands together, stepped inside, and pushed the door closed.

Della looked up at him with big eyes. "Did you kill him?"

Ben turned his reddened face to her. "Would it be so bad, if I did? He's scum, known in these parts as a lying weasel."

A minute later, Deputy Marshall Durain came through the same door with Cooper right behind.

"Arrest that man!" Cooper said, pointing to Ben. "He nearly broke my arm. He's got no business interfering with my dealings with that little whore."

Ben stepped forward, his fist ready to punish Cooper again.

The deputy raised his hand. "Now hold on here," he said, looking at Ben. He turned to Della. "Tell me what happened."

"Well, sir. Mr. Cooper came in and thought to force his way on me. But ..."

"Not so!" Jasper moved up close behind the deputy and glared at Della. "She's lying. They all do."

The deputy gave Cooper a shove with his elbow, causing him to step back. He looked at Ben. "Speak your piece."

"I came in and saw this bunghole dragging Miss McCrea off her seat. She ain't no chippy. It was agin her will. I couldn't abide it."

"That's right, sir," Della chimed in.

"McBride!" the deputy called out.

As McBride approached, the deputy asked him, "Is what he's saying true?"

McBride nodded. "From what I could see. Yes."

The deputy turned to Cooper. "Get lost."

Jasper Cooper cursed under his breath but moved toward the door. Just before stepping out, he turned and shook his fist in Ben's direction. "You watch your back, hotshot. I'll be getting even, you hear?"

Color rose in Ben's face again and his eyes narrowed. "Anytime, toadface. Anytime."

Chapter 37

Della rubbed her arm where Jasper Cooper had pressed his fingers into her flesh. There'd be bruises there in the morning, for sure. She turned to Ben Murray, her heart barely slowing its gallop. "A room full of men, and you were the only one to come to my aid. I can never thank you enough."

He reached over with his big paw and gently patted her shoulder. "It's all right now, Missy. He won't bother you again."

"I would a helped ya," George in the plaid trousers chimed in. "But Ben here got to 'im first."

Deputy Marshall Durain glanced down the line of men at the bar, nodded to McBride, then to Della, and walked out the door into the dark.

McBride watched him leave, then fixed his gaze on Della. "I don't pay you for standing around. Play something lively, like a polka."

His tone propelled Della's Irish blood to a simmer. If I were a man, she thought, I'd put a lump on that bald head of his. She drew a deep breath and returned to the piano, settled, and reached to sort her sheet music. As she did, she noticed the stitching of her shirtwaist sleeve had pulled loose in the scuffle. She scowled. Repairs would have to wait till morning. She fished through the pages and played "Ta-ra-ra Boom de ay." George started singing along, and soon others joined in. When she reached the conclusion, someone clapped and shouted, "Play it again." And she did, three times, before moving on to another piece, and then another and another.

Despite coins gathering in the dish on the piano top, time dragged until finally, the crowd thinned out, and young Douglas McBride gave the signal. After playing her usual final number, "Three O'clock in the Morning," she stood, scooped up the coins. and hurried to the narrow stairway that led to the gallery. Lifting her skirt, she climbed the steps and met one of the miners on his way down. As he passed by, he stepped on the hem of her skirt, briefly halting her progress. Another one I'd like to thump, she thought with sarcasm.

When she reached the top step, she looked up and saw the woman Lena had called Rita. She was leaning in the doorway to the room next to hers. Lifting her burgundy skirt, she exposed one of her high-topped shoes. "Hey, kid. You need one of these." She pointed to a small knife in a leather sheath tucked in next to her ankle. "If you figure to hang around here much longer, you better get yourself some protection."

Della drew a quick breath. She looked from the knife to the cynical smile on the woman's face. "Where would I find such an item?"

"Down near the livery. There's a leather goods store. Tell Mr. Jones Rita sent you."

Della bit her lower lip. It was clear Rita had witnessed her run-in with Jasper Cooper. "Thanks. Maybe I will."

Della didn't sleep much that night. The scene from earlier repeated in her head like a flickery movie. She kept seeing the hate in the eyes of the two men, and somehow, couldn't shake the notion that it would be her fault if they chanced to meet again and one of them killed the other. But what could she have done? If she'd had a knife, could she have brought herself to actually use it? The thought was appalling, yet had a certain appeal.

And what if Jasper Cooper turned up again to torment her? The prospect sent shivers across her shoulders. Her plan for earning money to go home was not as simple as she'd figured. It would be weeks before she'd have enough. She turned over and over on the bed, recalculating the days. It wasn't until a glimmer of morning light began to penetrate the window curtains that she managed a restless slumber.

The lack of sleep left her feeling out-of-sorts that evening as she approached the piano to begin another performance. A number of the men she passed at the bar spoke a greeting, but she didn't respond. She settled on the piano stool and started with a slow waltz, then moved on to more lively songs. Each time the outside door opened, she half expected to see Jasper Cooper. But an hour later, he wasn't the one who entered McBride's saloon.

As she sorted through her sheet music between numbers, the sudden presence of Hiram Bennett at her side startled her. She gasped, then recognized him and his expression of dismay.

He removed his hat and cleared his throat. "Miss McCrea, I've looked all over town for you. I learned from Mrs. Cooper that she'd dismissed you and that you were working in a saloon. This is no place for a girl like you."

Annoyance shot up her spine. "Well, I don't intend to do this forever. As soon as I earn enough money for a train ticket, I'll be on my way home."

"And how long is *that* going to take?" he asked in a fatherly tone.

She gave him a curdling glance. "I don't see that's any concern of yours."

With the sharpness of her tone, Mr. Bennett's face blanched. He withdraw a step and made a sound, a cross between a croak and a cough. "I suppose you're right. It's just that..." With another step, he slowly replaced his hat. "Perhaps I misjudged ... Excuse me for intruding."

Della scowled as he backed away and left the building. Seems like too many people are keen to meddle in my affairs, she muttered under her breath. First Pastor Smith and now Mr. Bennett. She jutted her jaw, put her fingers on the keys, and pounded out "Camp Town Races" louder than ever.

During the following days, whenever Della left McBride's in the afternoon, she kept a watchful eye out for Jasper Cooper. Even though Lena had assured her that he would never dare accost her in public, she couldn't shake an uneasy feeling. It was enough to make her consider locating the leather goods shop Rita had mentioned.

When Gus McBride handed her the fifty-cent pieces she'd earned that week, she dashed up the stairs to add them to her cache. With her treasure safely hidden, she dropped the coins the miners had left in the dish into her purse. Pinning on her straw hat, she grabbed her parasol and gloves and headed for the outside door.

Out on the boardwalk, she glanced at the sky before raising the small umbrella. The day was going to be warmer. It was already June, she realized. The acknowledgment brought a scowl. Pressing her lips together, she determined she'd write to her brother. After all, he was her guardian. Perhaps he'd found another job by now.

She made her way down the sloping walk and entered the bakery. The smell of fresh bread made her mouth water and her stomach grumble. As much as she wanted a buttery scone, she decided to forego it. Instead, she settled on three simple biscuits. Saving her pennies for a sheathed knife was more important.

Exiting the bakery, she advanced along Main Street toward the butcher shop. Before long she sensed someone approaching close behind her. Thinking it was Jasper Cooper, she collapsed her parasol and whirled around ready to fight him off, but saw Hiram Bennett instead.

He halted and removed his hat, his expression flustered. "I mean you no harm," he insisted. "I'm sorry I alarmed you."

Della expelled a breath. "It's not you, Mr. Bennett. I'm just a little jumpy." She gave him a weak smile.

Holding the brim of his bowler hat with both hands, he said, "I just wanted to apologize for upsetting you the other night. I talked to the pastor's wife. She told me ..."

Della bristled, interrupting. "How dare that woman betray my confidence?"

He held up his hand and shook his head. "Now, now. No harm done. It's just that now I understand your situation better."

"That hardly matters. I'm determined to make my own way, however trying it might be." Della turned her back, raised her parasol again, and started to walk away.

"Wait," he called after her. "To make up for my interference, I'd like to take you to supper at the Connor Hotel this evening."

Della paused and slowly pivoted around. She thought of the two lonely biscuits that would constitute her evening meal. With the merest hesitation, she stepped forward, tilted her parasol, and smiled up at him. "Why, Mr. Bennett. That would be most appreciated."

Chapter 38

Hiram Bennett's face lit up with an expression of relief. He suggested he'd call for her at seven that evening and she agreed. He gave a brief bow, replaced his hat and they parted.

The prospect of a full meal at a real table had Della almost dancing down the street as she headed toward the butcher shop. Supper with the Smiths at the rectory seemed like a dim memory now, though in reality, it had been only three weeks. Since then, a napkin on the nightstand in her room had served as a table, and she'd sat on the side of the bed to eat her supper, a far cry from family dinners at home. Her determination to spend only the coins the miners left in the bowl on the piano was beginning to take its toll. The waistband on her skirt would soon need to be altered.

She hurried to purchase her usual hard-boiled egg from the butcher and a piece of fruit at the grocery store. At the park, she dusted off a spot on a low brick wall and sat. While eating her meal, she debated about what she would wear that evening. Since her nice dresses were packed away in the trunk under the

Hovey's porch, she had few options but decided that the thinnest of her shirtwaists and the blue skirt would be the best choice for the evening.

It was nearly sunset when Hiram Bennett pulled his buggy up in front of McBride's Saloon to call for Della. He'd chosen to wear his best Sunday suit for the occasion.

Della was watching for him at the front window, so she stepped out quickly. When he saw her, he fairly jumped from the carriage and hurried to assist her. He smiled and offered her his arm. She accepted, lifted her skirt, and climbed into the buggy. As soon as he had gained his place, he swung the vehicle into the street.

"I think you'll like dining at The Connor Hotel," Mr. Bennett said. "It's quite nice and the staff are pleasant."

Della smoothed her skirt. "I'm sure I will." She'd heard the hotel was quite modern and that fact piqued her curiosity. So many of the buildings in the town were rather unremarkable.

Their destination was not far and soon they entered the two-story red brick hotel. A slender man in a black frock coat greeted them, and after a brief exchange of pleasantries, they were escorted to the dining room and seated at a corner table.

The room was larger than Della had expected with dark wood pillars at intervals to support the high ceiling. Lighting came from elegant chandeliers that hung in the space between the pillars. She noted a dozen or more tables evenly distributed around the room. A few of them were already occupied. Each table was draped with a white tablecloth and displayed a small vase of flowers that Della thought must have been imported from Verde Valley. No plant of that sort would survive the sulfurous fumes that plagued Jerome.

A waiter brought menus to them and drifted away.

"May I order for us?" Hiram asked.

Della nodded. "Of course."

"I've been told they serve an excellent roast chicken." He glanced over the menu, made a motion with his hand, and the waiter hurried back to record the selection.

With that settled, Mr. Bennett turned to Della. "This is a bit of a celebration. My house is finally complete. My sister helped me choose the furnishings. I've settled in and now can have my son with me. I grew tired of living in a boarding house." He continued, describing the difficulties of getting the house built since every bit of the materials had to be brought up by train.

"It isn't as large as the home we had in Chicago, but I believe I will enjoy the absence and inconvenience of so much snow."

Della listened intently, murmuring approval at intervals and asking polite questions. As he spoke, she studied his round face and decided that he wasn't as old as she'd originally thought when she first met him the summer before, though he surely had to be at least forty.

The meal soon arrived, and Della was delighted at the sight of a sumptuous chicken dinner. She'd saved a biscuit from her noon meal to eat while dressing, fearing she'd be so hungry she'd devour the food in an unladylike manner.

A bottle of red wine was offered and glasses filled. Della left hers untouched. Having never been allowed spirits of any sort due to her mother's Methodist background and her father's weakness, she was not inclined to imbibe.

She cut into the chicken and with the first bite, she was certain it was the best meal she'd had in years. The potatoes were fried and seasoned just right. They both ate in silence for a several minutes, then Hiram spoke up.

"As I told you a few weeks ago, I travel a good deal for business. I hired a woman to do the cooking and cleaning and she is quite adequate in that respect, but her attitude toward my son is rather ah ... formal, and not at all what the boy needs. His mother's death seems to have affected him even though he was very young at the time. He has become overly shy and is inclined to have nightmares. I don't know what to do for him."

Della didn't know what to say. She could tell by his tone that his concern for his son was genuine, an admirable feature in a man. "I recall he is a sweet boy. Having other children to play with would probably help." She forked a bite of summer squash into her mouth.

Bennett nodded, broke a dinner roll in two pieces and reached for the butter dish. "Unfortunately, I am unable to make such an arrangement. I wish to offer you a proposition. I could tell by the way you talked to the Cooper boys that you have a way with children. If you would be willing to live at my house and care for my son, I would pay you a fair wage."

She stared at him in surprise and laid down her fork. So *this* was the real reason for his supper invitation.

"Surely, you can't be satisfied with your accommodations at the present time," he said.

Della bit her lip, glanced at the plate in front of her, and tilted her head to one side. "It's not quite as bad as you think. I have always wanted to play for a bigger audience than my family. Of course, it's not the audience I had in mind, but they do seem to enjoy my music." She paused and looked directly at him.

"Such an arrangement would not be fair to your son. You see, as soon as I have acquired sufficient funds, I intend to buy a train ticket and be on my way home to Ohio." She clutched the napkin on her lap. "The time I've spent in this place has been dreadful." Her voice cracked. "Losing both my parents … I wish to put it all behind me."

His shoulders sagged. "I understand." He laid his napkin on the table and took a deep breath. "I had such hopes. Please consider it. That's all I can ask."

Della nodded, though she had no desire to continue the discussion. She turned and glanced at the window that overlooked the street. Beyond the thin curtain, it was dark outside. "I wonder what time it is. I mustn't be late to work."

Hiram pulled a watch from his pocket. "A quarter to eight. I suppose we should be on our way." He motioned to the waiter.

The delicious chicken and Mr. Bennett's surprise offer of employment still occupied Della's thoughts as she played for the miners who lined the bar. The mood in the room reflected the fact that it had been payday. A few of the miners requested songs that had special meaning for them and dropped a coin in her little dish.

By midnight the crowd was getting rather boisterous. She heard a deep voice yell out the name of a song. She ignored him. I'll not be hollered at, she muttered and continued what she was playing.

A minute later she felt a heavy hand on her shoulder and the same voice said, "Hey, honey. Are ya deaf? I said play "Hello Ma Baby.""

Della pushed his hand away, swung around on the piano stool and glared up at him. His hooded eyes indicated his degree of drunkenness. "Don't touch me," she said through gritted teeth.

"Pretty uppity," he said, "for your kind." He walked away making a hissing noise.

She wished she had a knife like Rita's. She'd like to trim his ... mustache. What did he mean, her kind? Did he think she was one of the soiled ladies who occupied those upper rooms? Would all those men begin to think that? Would the whole town? The thought made her clinch her teeth. She spun around and began another piece of music. Maybe she *should* consider Mr. Bennett's offer. She shook her head. He would never pay her like McBride.

Later, as it neared three o'clock, an inebriated miner waddled over to the piano, leaned over the keyboard, and breathed the stench of liquor in her face. "Play something snappy, honey," he slurred. Della recoiled and her stomach churned. Seven weeks, she thought. Just seven more weeks.

The following Monday morning Della was in the middle of bathing when she heard a knock at the door. "Who's there?"

"It's me, Lena."

Della grabbed Juanita's robe, slipped into it, and stepped over to let her in.

"I have some news," Lena said as soon as she entered. With a huge smile on her face, she continued, "You'll never guess who got shot dead Saturday night."

Della pulled the robe tight around her. "Who?"

"Jasper Cooper. He was killed in a gambling house in Bisbee." Lena raised her hands. "The devil takes his own. He'll not be bothering you or anyone else."

A sense of relief flooded over Della. But then she thought of his children. Their mother could support them, but still, it would be a devastating shock.

Lena gave Della an up-and-down look. "Hey, hurry up. Get dressed. Let's go find some sweets to celebrate."

With the threat of Jasper Cooper gone, Della moved about town on her errands with confidence that week. So that Friday when she descended the stair to collect her week's pay from McBride, she was feeling lighthearted. By her mental calculation, she would now have accumulated fourteen dollars. Almost half of what she needed. She could almost imagine the train ticket in her hand.

She smiled at Mr. McBride as he handed her the coins. By his grimace, it was clear he begrudged her the money despite his increased business.

"I thank you, sir," Della said. She kept smiling as she headed back to her room to add to the cache in her sewing basket. Kneeling, she reached under the cloth covering the bedside table and lifted the lid. She felt for the little cotton, draw-string bag she'd fashioned. Failing to immediately put her hand on it, she groped the corners but didn't find it. Panic gripped her. She dragged the basket from under the table, opened it wide, and pawed through the contents to no avail. The bag was gone!

Chapter 39

Della felt bile rise in her throat as she searched the basket again as if the bag of coins might magically appear. A sob escaped her throat. She crumpled onto the floor. "It's not fair," she moaned into the rug. "Who would do this to me?"

After sobbing for several minutes, she sat up straight, her thoughts in a whirl. "Who *would* do this?" she demanded with a scowl. "Lena?" She shook her head. Her eyes narrowed. Could it have been Rita in the next room? Or that other woman, who'd accused her of thinking to horn in on her business? She pressed her fingers to her temples. Mr. McBride? Unlikely. It could have been anyone who came up those stairs last night.

Her stomach sickened as she unclenched her fist and looked at the few coins she had left. What could she do? Going to the Deputy Marshall would be useless. Thievery was common in this town. She wiped her eyes with the back of her hand and rose to her feet. No use crying, she muttered to herself. It won't bring the money back. And I'd better get something to eat. I'll need my strength last out the night.

With some effort, she washed her face and prepared to leave the building. She pinned her straw hat forward so it would shade her eyes, hoping her misery would be less evident to anyone she met.

When she'd made her usual purchases of biscuits and hard-boiled egg, she found a sliver of shade beside one of the brick buildings near the park and mulled over her situation. At her current wage, it would be the end of October before she'd have enough money for a ticket to Ohio. Another four months of playing for people who, despite what she'd said to Mr. Bennett, had little appreciation for fine music. It seemed like an eternity.

The men in the saloon had become accustomed to her presence. A few, in their drunkenness, had become more bold. It was plain she couldn't depend on Mr. Ben, "Bone-breaker" Murray for protection. He hadn't been around for several nights. And what if the thief returned to steal her money again? The only bolt on the door was on the inside—to keep an intruder out while a lady "entertained."

She supposed she could take Mr. Bennett's offer of employment, but then it would take even longer, maybe three times longer to accumulate sufficient funds. It seemed an impossible dilemma. How she wished she could talk to her sister, Etta, though she had to confess Etta hadn't been much help recently. What would Cora advise? Perhaps talking to her would help her figure it out.

Sunday morning Della forced herself out of bed after a restless sleep. She'd decided to attend church. If ever she needed heavenly intervention, it was now. Though she wondered what her reception at church would be, she dressed in her blue skirt and white shirtwaist, pinned on her straw hat, and gathered her parasol, bag and gloves. The saloon building was quiet with no one in view as she left by the side door.

It wasn't a great distance to walk, but the air was rather sulfurous, and the warmth of mid-June was enough to cause perspiration. As she entered the Methodist Church, the usual buzz of conversation could be heard. Some of the pews were already filled. She scanned the room and felt the critical eyes of a number of the women. No one approached or greeted her, so it wasn't a surprise when she found herself sitting alone in the last pew. She folded her hands in her lap and gazed up to where the sun filtered through the stained-glass windows.

"Miss McCrea," a voice said. She turned and found Hiram Bennett standing at the end of the pew. He held his hat in one hand and gave a quick bow. "I'm glad to see you here."

Della smiled up at him. "Good morning, Mr. Bennett."

When he paused and didn't move on, she wondered if he was waiting for an invitation to sit next to her. It would not be proper and he knew it.

He cleared his throat. "I do not mean to speak impertinently, but have you given my offer any consideration at all?"

"I have, sir. It has been on my mind, and I wish to consult with a dear friend before making such an important decision."

"Ah, yes. A wise choice." He nodded again and moved off to his usual place in the congregation.

Della shifted in her seat to watch the people file into the modest building. In time, she saw the Hovey boys push between others to gain passage and knew Cora and Will would be close behind. When the couple appeared, Will was carrying little Georgie. Della waved her gloved hand to catch Cora's attention and noticed her friend appeared to be wearing a new dress, or at least one Della hadn't seen before. It was light blue cotton with loose-fitting sleeves and a tie at the waist.

As soon as Cora noticed, she squeezed past two women and sat down next to Della. "It's a relief to see you here," Cora said. "I was surprised when I heard you were working in a saloon." She reached to squeeze Della's hand. "No matter. I want to hear all about it. You must come to Sunday dinner today."

Della's spirits instantly lifted. "I have so missed your friendship. I'd be grateful to dine with you and your family."

"Will has the horse and buggy tied at the side of the building," Cora said with a gesture indicating the direction. "Meet us after the service." She glanced toward the front of the church. "I must go corral those boys before they upset something or tromp all over people's feet."

Cora scooted out of the pew and hurried on to join her family. Just then a bell rang and the congregation settled and quieted. Reverend Smith stepped up to the pulpit and delivered a blistering sermon about the sinful gambling secretly going on in their midst.

After the final amen, Della quickly slipped out by a side door. She had no desire to encounter the withering glances of the local gossips. She searched the line of buggies along the side street of the church. All were black, and at first, Della couldn't pick which one belonged to Will Hovey. But when she spotted Nellie's rag doll on the back seat of one of them, she walked over and stood next to it to wait.

A few minutes later, Billy and Buster came bounding out the door of the church and rushed in her direction. Nellie soon followed. Della grinned as the children crowded around her.

"Are you gonna come eat dinner with us?" Billy asked.

"I shot a lizard with my slingshot," Buster announced.

Nellie climbed into the buggy, picked up her doll, and offered it to Della. "You can hold her."

"Why, thank you, Nellie." Della cuddled the doll, knowing the offer was a great compliment.

Will and Cora soon approached with Georgie wiggling to escape Will's arms.

"Get on in," Will said to the children, placing his youngest son on the back seat. He nodded and smiled at Della. "It's good to have you with us."

He reached out to assist Cora into the buggy and then aided Della into the seat next to his wife.

A mere ten minutes later, Will Hovey guided the horse and buggy to a stop in front of their home. The boys jumped out and ran toward the porch. Della gingerly stepped to the ground and handed the rag doll back to its owner. "She's a lovely dolly," she said to Nellie. The girl smiled shyly, dipping her chin.

"I'll be back as soon as I take care of the horse," Will said to anyone listening.

Cora helped Georgie climb out and took him by the hand. "Don't tarry. Dinner will be on the table soon."

"I can help," Della commented, her gaze drifting to the house next door. There was no evidence that anyone lived in it.

Cora caught her friend's wistful look. "People are fearful the disease lingers inside. The landlord will have difficulty finding a tenant."

"I scrubbed it until my hands were raw," Della said.

"Yes, you did." The two stood in silence a moment until Cora said, "Let's go inside."

Within minutes of entering the house, both women had donned aprons and were busy in the kitchen. Della handed plates to Nellie, who busied herself setting the table.

When Will returned from the stable, several steaming dishes were ready, and the family gathered to take their seats. Will said the blessing, and Cora scooped portions of food onto the children's plates.

Will tucked the tip of a napkin into the neck of his shirt. "I understand that the city fathers are struggling to enforce the new gambling law."

"They've been talking about it long enough, it's high time they did something about it," Cora remarked.

Will forked a slice of meat from the platter to his plate. "There's talk of hiring another deputy."

Della listened but made no comment. If that happened, Mr. McBride's back room would soon be shuttered. There'd be less income. She wondered if it would affect her status.

The meal progressed and it wasn't long before the boys asked to be excused. Cora wiped Georgie's face with a napkin and released him from his stool. Will drained his coffee cup and retired to the next room, leaving the women to their chores.

Della helped Nellie clear the table, stacking the plates next to the sink. "There's something I'd like to talk over with you," Della said to Cora as she poured hot water from a large tea kettle to fill the dishpan in the sink. She looked at Della and raised her eyebrows. "All right." Cora put the milk-clouded glasses into the dishwater. "Nellie, you can go play. Della is going to help me with the dishes."

As soon as the girl had left the room, Cora said, "If it's about working in that saloon, I'd say find better employment. What happened to the job at my cousin's?"

Della quietly explained her experience at the Cooper House while she wiped the clean dishes and placed them on the shelf.

Cora shook her head as she listened. "I'm so sorry to hear it. My cousin picked the wrong man. Word is he was shot by a man for cheating at cards."

"I feel much concern for those boys. They are bright and lively and need a father."

"Indeed. Now tell me what brought you to be working in that saloon."

Della continued her story, explaining how mending a dress led her to playing McBride's piano, and concluded by telling Cora about Hiram Bennett's invitation to supper at the Connor Hotel and his offer of employment.

Cora turned her head to look at Della. "What makes you hesitate? Seems like a golden opportunity to me."

"I'm afraid he might turn out to be like Jasper Cooper."

"Well, if he's anything like his sister, he's an upstanding citizen." She handed Della a large bowl to dry. "You're in far greater danger where you are now. From what I've heard, Hiram Bennett was a devoted husband and wants only the best for his son. And who knows. He might turn out to be a suitable husband for you."

Della's face blanched. "Oh, no! He's much too old."

Cora chuckled and handed her another dish.

Chapter 40

After a pleasant afternoon with the Hovey family, Della made her way up one of the many sloping roads on her way back to McBride's Saloon. She tilted her parasol to block the rays of hot sun and recalled Will and Cora's many kindnesses during the years she'd lived next door. What would she have done without them? She could not conceive of any way she might have coped. Cora had always given solid advice, but as Della thought about it, right that day, Cora's thoughts on the subject of Mr. Bennett were certainly wrong. Della absently shook her head. How could Cora even consider Hiram Bennett a suitable match for her? Not now, not ever. Ohio was her destiny, not drying up like an old prune in Jerome.

The following day Della was sitting on the side of the bed when a rap on the door startled her. Still in her nightdress, she hardly had the energy to get up to answer it. It had been a difficult time the night before. There'd been another mine accident. One miner was dead and three others were in the hospital with serious injuries. She'd observed that some of the men had hardened themselves to such events, while others brooded, leaning on the bar over their drinks. Both groups drank far more than usual and occasional pushing and shouting matches occurred. No amount of lively music had had any effect on the mood.

Della reached for her shawl and wrapped it around herself as she rose to open the door. When she saw it was Lena Larson who stood there, she stepped aside. "Please come in."

Lena was fully dressed, including a hat and gloves. She handed Della an envelope. "A messenger left this for you. I hope it's not bad news."

Della frowned. "Thanks." She tore open the envelope and unfolded the enclosed paper. It read:

> *Miss McCrea,*
>
> *I must leave town in a few days. If you are still considering my offer of employment, please respond by coming to my home to meet my son at two o'clock today. Our house is the white one at the southeast end of High street.*
>
> *Sincerely, Hiram Bennett*

Lena hesitated near the door, watching as Della read the note. "By the way, Juanita will be returning on Thursday."

Della's head jerked up. "What?"

"Juanita will need her room again."

Della blinked and stared at Lena as the realization crystallized.

Lena stared back. "You knew the room was only a loan."

"Of course." Della folded the paper. "I must talk to Mr. McBride. I've been offered employment elsewhere."

"Ooh. He's not going to like that."

"I suppose not. What time is it?" She tossed the shawl on the bed. "I must get dressed."

An hour later, she'd packed her valise, tucked her other belongings into her sewing basket, and sat in front of Juanita's mirror to adjust the combs in her hair. She stared at her reflection and bit her lip. Was there no other way? It seemed not. She had to vacate the room before Thursday, and renting a room in a boarding house was out of the question. She couldn't spare the money.

If she wormed her way back into the parsonage, she wouldn't be allowed to work for Mr. McBride, plus she'd have to face Reverend Smith's reproach and show an appropriate degree of repentance. She sighed and reached for her hat and gloves. No. Mr. Bennett's offer was her best option. He had a housekeeper, so it's wouldn't be like working in a boarding house. At least she'd have a place to lay her head and a means of deriving some income, but the train ticket to Ohio seemed very far from her grasp.

As she stepped out of the building and raised her parasol, Della fixed a smile on her face as if she were certain of the future. She started down the sloping boardwalk at a brisk pace, her valise in one hand, her sewing basket hanging from the crook of her arm, and her parasol in the other hand. She's left her bed role behind. Perhaps she'd pick it up later. She supposed people would stare at her, but she couldn't be bothered to give it any notice. Time was short.

She'd spent precious minutes talking to Mr. McBride. He had been more than huffy when she told him she was leaving. But in the end, when she assured him that she was not going to work for his competitor, he wished her well and allowed that she had brought him new customers.

On the other hand, parting with Lena was bittersweet. Della had been almost tearful when she thanked her for her friendship. They hugged as good friends do and each promised to keep in touch, though both knew it was unlikely.

High Street was indeed high and at the southeast end of town. It would be a good long walk. While she hurried along, her thoughts ranged between apprehension and relief. The relief was that she'd have a place to hang her hat, so to speak, and the apprehension, about the amount Mr. Bennett would pay her, since he hadn't been specific in that regard.

She had the same amount of anxiety about Mr. Bennett himself, since she really knew little about him, except that he was a widower with an almost five-year-old son. Was he well off? Cora seemed to think so. His sister seemed to be. He dressed nicely, but not in expensive suits like some of the businessmen in Dayton. She knew nothing about his business, though she suspected it had something to do with mining. Why did he have to travel so much? Did he have an investment in one of the local mines as well as in other places? She had no idea and could only speculate.

Another concern was her inexperience with the care of children. She guessed she'd have to rely on her natural inclinations. Besides, how much trouble could one little boy be?

After taking a steep shortcut between two houses, she stopped in the shade of one of the houses, set down her burden, and pulled a handkerchief out of her purse to dab her brow. It wouldn't do to arrive in a sweat.

After a few minutes rest, she readjusted her hat and made the final ascent to High Street. There, she found herself on another slag-packed road that curved along the hillside. Soon she stood at the foot of a set of wooden steps that led to a two-story white house with a light tan roof. The wood construction was much like the other better homes in town with windows facing the valley in the distance. And like so many, it sat on a carved-out section of the hillside. The area around it was without foliage and lacked a place where a child could play outside.

She glanced back toward the main part of Jerome, noticing that smoke from the smelter could barely be seen. That alone would be a benefit of this new position. Those repulsive fumes would be a some distance away.

She climbed the steps to a broad, covered porch. After collapsing her parasol, she used a door knocker to announce her arrival. Jitters gripped her as the minutes passed before the door opened. Was she late? Without a timepiece, she couldn't tell.

Presently, a chunky, brown-eyed woman no taller than herself stood in the open doorway. She wore a white apron over a brown dress. Her dark brown hair had been pulled to the back of her head, fixed in a tight bun. She stared at Della with a blank expression.

"I'm Della McCrea. I've come to see Mr. Bennett."

The woman grunted, turned her back on Della, and walked into the dim interior and down a hallway. Although unsure of what to do, Della stepped inside what seemed to be the parlor and pushed the door closed with her foot. To her relief, the interior was several degrees cooler than out on the porch. She also noticed a faint scent of pine left over from the new construction.

A moment later, Della heard a brief exchange of words from a room down the main hall and soon Hiram Bennett appeared, slipping into his suit jacket as he walked toward her.

He paused in the doorway and smiled as his gaze swept over her and her baggage. "Miss McCrea. I am so very glad to see you. It is my good fortune that you have decided to accept my offer." He made a gesture with an open palm. "Please deposit your belongings. Mrs. Molina will take them up to your room. May I offer you a cool drink?"

"You certainly may," Della replied, putting her burden down and removing her gloves. "The afternoon is quite warm."

"Please, have a seat while I call Davie. I'm eager for you to see him and become better acquainted." He turned back to the hall and gave instructions to the woman who had been waiting in the doorway.

As soon as they were out of sight, Della glanced around. The room was nicely furnished with a brown cushioned sofa and three upholstered chairs, plus floor lamps arranged to provide suitable lighting.

She settled on the sofa and noticed a library table nearby. On it sat a stereoscope and a box of cards. It reminded her of a similar one she'd used many times at home. A narrow bookcase stood against that wall. Curious about the books it held, she was tempted to get up to look at the titles. But from somewhere in the back of the house, she heard Mr. Bennett's voice. "Come down, Davie. A nice lady is here. I think you'll remember her."

Light footsteps could be heard on a stairway, and Della saw Mr. Bennett in the hall as he took the hand of the little boy. As they reached the doorway to the parlor, the boy pulled away from his father and stopped.

Della thought he hadn't grown much since she'd seen him at the church picnic. He tilted his head slightly as he stared at her with soft brown eyes.

She stood. "Hello, Davie. Remember me?"

He took a few steps forward and hesitated. Then slowly approaching, he looked up at her, squinting. "Are you my mother?"

Chapter 41

Hiram Bennett took a quick step toward the boy, but Della held up her hand to stop him. She knelt on one knee. "Oh, Davie. No. I'm not your mother. I'm a friend of your father's, and I'd like to be your friend, too." She smiled. "Would that be all right?"

The boy's shoulders sagged. He looked down at his shoes for a second, then spun around and ran down the hall and out of sight, his footsteps clattering up the stairs.

Mr. Bennett sputtered, his expression a combination of confusion and embarrassment. "Why I ... I never said ... why would he think that?"

Della stood and gave her skirt a brush. "He misses having a mother."

Mr. Bennett shook his head. "But he was so young. He can't possibly remember her."

She lifted one shoulder. "Other boys his age have one. He must have noticed. Perhaps it's something like that."

His brow creased. "I ... I should go talk to him."

Mrs. Molina entered carrying a tray with a glass of water and a plate with a slice of buttered bread on it. Hiram directed her to place it on the library table. The sudden sound of a telephone down the hall intruded.

Mr. Bennett grimaced and turned to Della. "I'm sorry. I've been expecting this call. I must answer it. Please, have a seat and refresh yourself." He started toward the ringing phone. "Mrs. Molina, please show Miss McCrea her accommodations upstairs whenever she's ready."

He didn't hesitate, but hurried off, and within seconds a door down the hallway could be heard closing.

Mrs. Molina muttered something in a guttural tone Della couldn't make out, then picked up her satchel and basket. "Foller me."

Della grabbed the glass, took a gulp, quickly set it aside, and hurried after the housekeeper. The older woman paused at the end of the hall, glanced back at Della, turned left, and started up a steep, narrow stairway. Trailing behind, Della hurried to catch up, lifting her skirt to climb the stairs.

At the top, Mrs. Molina stepped into a small bedroom, and with a huff, placed Della's belongings on the bed.

From the doorway, Della's gaze swept the room. It had a single bed, a chest of drawers, a dressing table and an armoire, clearly better than the basement room she'd stayed in at the

Cooper's Boardinghouse or the noisy borrowed room at the saloon. A lone window let in ample light through the thin curtain. The sun was now in the west on the opposite side of the building.

She thanked Mrs. Molina, laid her parasol on the bed next to her satchel, and removed her hat. She placed it and her gloves on the bureau. When she turned around, Mrs. Molina was gone. She went to the doorway and caught sight of the top of the woman's head near the bottom of the staircase.

Since she had the opportunity, she decided to explore the rest of the top floor before unpacking. Stepping out into the hall, she noted that the door to the room next to hers was open. Looking in, she saw Davie curled up on his bed facing the wall. She felt a surge of pity. What a dreadful thing to be motherless at so young an age. At least she had her memories of her own mother.

She felt inclined to speak to him, but then considered he might react unfavorably to the intrusion. They'd already gotten off to an awkward start, better to wait until his father was present. How would she engage the boy? At the picnic, he'd trusted her with his shoes. Perhaps she'd remind him of that, maybe talk about that day. For the moment, it would be best to leave him be.

Across the hall, a closed door drew her notice. Even though this was going to be her home for a while, she felt like an intruder as she reached for the knob and opened it. Inside, a window blind shut out most of the sunlight, but with the light from the hall, she could see that it was being used as a store room. It contained two steamer trunks, two large, sturdy-looking, wooden boxes, even bigger than the trunks, plus a dozen smaller boxes of varying sizes. Those were likely filled with household goods still to be unpacked, she thought. She closed the door and continued her exploration.

She opened the door to the room next to the storage. It was of similar size, but empty. At the end of the hall, a large bedroom encompassed the breadth of the building with a four-poster bed, two four-drawer chests and matching armoires. A traveling bag lay across the bed with several pieces of men's clothing laid out next to it. Mr. Bennett, it appeared, had been preparing for his trip.

She turned around and wondered if there were bathing accommodations somewhere on the premises. Not outside, she hoped. And where was Mrs. Molina's quarters?

Other questions crowded in, but she decided that unpacking would be the best thing to occupy her time until supper.

The task didn't take long. She put her extra change of underwear in one of the dresser drawers and arranged her hair brush and extra combs on the top of the chest, then ambled over to the window. Pulling aside the thin curtain, she gazed out. The expanse of dry desert was broken only by a ribbon of green in the valley below and the open blue of the sky above. It seemed like she could see halfway across Arizona. She drew a deep breath, returned to sit on the bed and wondered what to do next. Go downstairs or wait to be summoned? She opted for going down stairs to locate the privy. Since Mr. Bennett was from Chicago, she reasoned, he would not wish to be without indoor plumbing.

Her search was interrupted at the bottom of the stairs when Mr. Bennett approached. "Oh, Miss McCrea. I must speak with you. That phone call has placed a strain on my plans. I am sorry to report that I must leave on the morning train. I had thought to be here to help you and Davie become acquainted. Let us retire to the parlor."

He extended a hand to escort her. Preceding him, she took a seat on the sofa, while he settled in a chair nearby.

"Mrs. Molina will be preparing supper for us soon. She always places dishes of food in the oven before she leaves at six o'clock." He edged forward as he spoke. "Since Davie and I moved into this house, I've been dining with my son. But now that you are here, I'll serve Davie first, and we'll serve ourselves at seven. If that meets your approval." His gaze searched her face for assent.

Della smiled. "My family had the same custom when I was a child. But perhaps this may not be the time to make a change—for Davie's sake. I suggest I join you and Davie for supper. But you said Mrs. Molina leaves? Where does she go? Does she have a family?"

"She does indeed. A husband and three grown sons who work in the mine. I was lucky to be able to hire her, if only for part-time. She agreed with the condition that she would be able to return home in time to prepare supper for her men."

For Della, the implication took less than a second to sink in, that she'd be alone in the house at night with a four-year-old for protection. "How long will you be gone?"

"I should be back by next Monday."

"I see." The matter of her remuneration was still unsettled. Della opened her mouth to ask about it, but the sound of a buggy pulling up in front of the house interrupted her.

Mr. Bennett craned his neck as he looked out the window. He held up a hand. "I believe that's my sister. Excuse me." He rose from the chair and went out on the front porch, failing to close the door.

Annoyance prickled Della. She rose and stepped over to the door, expecting he would be escorting Mrs. Samples into the house. Instead, what she saw puzzled her. He didn't extend his hand to his sister, and she made no effort to exit the buggy. He spoke, but with his back to her, Della couldn't make out what he was saying.

Mrs. Samples shook her head and leaned toward him with a glower of disapproval. "I just heard that you've hired that saloon girl to take care of my nephew. How could you do such a thing? You must dismiss her immediately."

As though a hand clutched her heart, Della felt her knees weaken. She grabbed the edge of the door. Harriet Samples was a moving force among the women of the church, and not just that. She was head of the opera company, the library committee, and heaven knows what else. One word from her and Della would find no other work in town.

Though his back was to her, Della detected the tenor of Mr. Bennett's response, but not the words.

His sister's face registered surprise, then horror. "What?! You can't mean that. Why such a thing would disgrace our family?"

Chapter 42

Harriet Samples shot her brother a look that would curdle milk, gave the horse's reins a snap, and guided the animal around until the buggy was headed back the way she came.

Hiram Bennett stood for a moment watching her go, shrugged, and turned back to the house.

Della returned to the sofa, arranged her skirt, and did her best to appear calm as he came through the door, though her nerves were on edge wondering what would happen next.

"My sister declined my invitation to come inside," he said with an uneasy smile. "She has some other engagement."

"How unfortunate," Della responded, but only for politeness sake. "It's so uncomfortably warm outside this afternoon."

Mr. Bennett rubbed his chin. "Indeed." He paused as if to collect his thoughts. "I must talk to my son, and then finish packing for my trip." He made a move to leave the room.

"Sir, excuse me, but I must inquire. You have not been specific about the amount and at what intervals I am to be paid."

Mr. Bennett drew an audible breath. "I thought I had. How thoughtless of me. I meant to offer you three dollars a week, to be paid at the end of each month. Including room and board, of course." His eyes widened, seeking her assent.

She nodded. "Quite satisfactory. There *is* one other thing." Looking up at him, she smiled. "There's a trunk of mine being stored at the home of my friends, the Hoveys. I would very much like to have it here and have the benefit of the extra clothing."

"Certainly, certainly. You may use the telephone to call for a wagon anytime you're ready to transport it. I want you to be comfortable living here."

"And could I have a scrap of paper to write to my family and advise them of my improved situation?"

"Well, of course. You'll find some on top of the bookcase, there." Excuse me now." He left the room, his shoes making a soft sound along the hallway.

Della leaned against the sofa back. Three dollars a week. It meant another four months in Jerome. With a sigh, she rose from the sofa before heading toward the kitchen, the location of the privy still on her mind.

She approached the kitchen doorway and saw Mrs. Molina, her hands padded with kitchen towels, pulling a loaf of bread out of the oven.

"Excuse me. Where might I find a place to wash up?"

The older woman placed the pan of bread on the stovetop, straightened to look at Della and laid the towels aside. "Door there. I show you."

The only door Della saw was one on her left with a curtainless window that revealed a path that led from the back door to a small building. She felt a rush of disappointment.

Mrs. Molina wiped her forehead with the corner of her apron and motioned toward the hallway. She led Della to a door opposite the foot of the stairs. "You like," she declared as she opened it.

Inside Della saw a water closet and a wash sink on a pedestal. She peeked behind the door. "Is there no tub for bathing?"

Mrs. Molina scratched her midriff. "For the boy, a metal wash tub. The mister, he go to the barber's, like other men."

With a little shrug, Della said. "I guess I'll have to ask you to show me where that tub is stored."

"Not now. I cook." Mrs. Molina turned her back and returned to the kitchen.

"Thank you," Della called after her, stepped into the room and closed the door.

Fifteen minutes later, feeling somewhat refreshed, Della returned to the parlor. She had in mind using the time until supper to look at the books she'd seen on the shelf. Pulling one of the chairs into position, she settled down hoping to find something suitable to read to Davie. Most prominent was the Bible with a gold cross on the spine. She pulled it out and paged through parts, noticing a number of illustrations. She nodded and pressed her lips together. This will do, she thought, as she put it back on the shelf. Running her finger along the spines of other books, she spotted *Grimm's Fairy Tales*. "Perfect," she said and pulled it off the shelf.

Hearing footsteps in the hall, she swiveled around just as Davie appeared at the doorway.

"Father says I have to say I'm sorry," he said, looking at his shoes.

"You're a good boy to obey your father."

"Father says you're going to take care of me like Aunt Harriet." He raised his eyes to her and put a hand on his cheek. "She scrubbed my face so much it hurt."

"Oh. I won't do that, I promise."

A hint of a smile flickered and was gone. "Can I go now?"

"Sure, but I'd like to show you something. Come. Look here. I found a book of stories I think you'd like." She held up the book of fairy tales.

The boy tilted his head and squinted at the cover, then edged closer.

She opened it to one of the illustrations. "There are so many, it's hard to choose the best one. There's one about a wolf who follows a girl to her grandmother's and another where seven dwarfs save a princess. And there's a wicked witch too. Maybe you'd like to pick one for me to read to you tomorrow."

He half-turned, giving Della a sideways look.

"You can ask your father if that would be all right."

The boy gave her a quick nod and scurried back into the hall.

Hearing his footsteps on the stairs, Della glanced upward and grinned.

It was still daylight outside when Mr. Bennett indicated it was time to put supper on the table. Della followed him into the kitchen to assist. She looked around the room. The stove was a more recent model than the one in the rented house, she noticed. Lucky Mrs. Molina, she thought.

The plates, cups and glasses were on an open shelf next to where canned goods and glass jars of vegetables were kept. She gathered the needed tableware and carried it to the dining room while Mr. Bennett followed with the hot dishes from the oven.

With everything in place, Mr. Bennett called his son, and they seated themselves. Mr. Bennett said the blessing, shook out a napkin and handed it to his son before positioning one of his own.

"Please, help yourself," he said to Della, passing her a bowl of white beans in a red sauce. The aroma hinted of a spicy mixture. Della decided on a small amount as she wasn't sure if it would be to her liking, but with the first mouthful, she decided they were delicious.

Mr. Bennett reached for a dish of cooked greens and leaned over to put a scoop on Davie's plate, followed by a ladle of beans. He helped himself to a serving of each, as well as a thick slice of bread, and passed the plate to Della. "Davie tells me you found the book of stories you think he'd like to hear." He glanced at his son.

The boy, spoon in hand, was staring at the greens on his plate.

"Mmm, yes," Della said, helping herself to a serving of greens. "Grimm's folk tales, and with lovely pictures, too.

"I've had that book since I was a child," Mr. Bennett said. "Before I learned to read, my grandmother read those stories to me. As I remember some are rather scary."

Davie's head jerked up. "I want to hear about the wooff." He scooped some beans into his mouth.

Mr. Bennett smiled and winked at Della. "I think you have won yourself a friend."

Chapter 43

That evening before retiring for the night, Della availed herself of one of the sheets of paper on the bookcase. She took it to her room and sat at the dressing table.

Jerome, Arizona Territory
June 26, 1905
Dear Lizzy,

    I hope this finds you well. I suppose you are spending the summer at home. I envy you. You have no idea how much I wish I could be with you. However, I do have good news. I have been engaged to care for a little boy. His widowed father travels a good deal and needed someone to look after him. He will be 5 years old in October and is well-mannered and charming. He has brown eyes and the cutest turned-up nose. I plan to start teaching him his letters and numbers. So you see I have come into teaching as Mother wanted.

I have been promised $3 a week and am saving every penny in hopes of being able to be home by Thanksgiving.

My accommodations are quite satisfactory. I have a room upstairs next to the boy's, and though the nights are only slightly cooler than the days, I often get a breeze through the window.

Give my love to all.

Your sister, Della

She folded the paper and laid it on the bureau next to her hat. She would post it when she went to fetch her trunk.

With some effort, Della rose the next morning, dressed and arranged her hair. She'd spent a restless night. Having been accustomed to retiring at three in the morning, she'd lain awake until that hour listening to the noises of the night, those that drifted up from the center of town, and an occasional coyote howl.

Though still feeling a bit groggy, she wanted to make a good impression on her new employer by being present when he left for the train, so when she descended the stairway, she went to the kitchen in search of coffee.

She found Mrs. Molina at the work table cutting a piece of beef into smaller chunks.

"Good morning. Is that coffee?" Della asked, nodding at the blue-and-white speckled pot on the stove. It was an unnecessary question since the smell of simmering coffee filled the room.

Mrs. Molina pointed to the shelf of dinnerware with her elbow. "You take," she said.

Della obtained a cup, filled it from the pot, and holding it with both hands, drew in a deep breath of the aroma. She'd taken only a few sips when she heard Mr. Bennett's voice coming from the parlor.

"Now Davie, be a big boy. I'll be back on Monday."

Della set the cup next to the sink and hurried to the hall in time to see the front door close behind them. Anxious to make her presence known, she rushed to catch up and found a buggy and driver waiting outside on the road.

Mr. Bennett was standing on the porch looking down at his son. He had a perplexed expression on his face. Davie's lower lip protruded in a pout, clearly unhappy about his father leaving.

Mr. Bennett looked up when Della stepped out. "Ah, here's Miss McCrea. She'll take good care of you. She'll read to you and tuck you in at night."

Della moved next to the boy, leaned over to face him and smiled. "We'll have a wonderful time. We can read a new story every day."

The boy's demeanor remained the same, though he didn't turn away from her.

Mr. Bennett picked up his suitcase with one hand and lifted his hat with the other. "I'll say goodbye now." He stepped off the porch and placed the bag behind the seat of the buggy. As he was about to get in, he turned back to Della.

"Oh, yes. I hope you approve. I've made arrangements for Bosko here to bring a horse cart to take you to fetch your trunk. He can come at ten if that is convenient." He turned to the driver, who nodded his agreement.

With a flash of gratitude, Della thanked him. His kindness meant she wouldn't have to part with any of her precious savings to hire someone. But then she was taken aback when she realized she recognized that the man he called Bosko was the same man who had been so rude to her the week before at McBride's, the one who said she was uppity and put his hand on her.

She didn't have time to comment. Mr. Bennett was in the buggy and gone before she could have voiced her misgivings.

As ten o'clock rolled around, Della pinned on her straw hat and waited on the porch for the cart and driver. She'd determined she'd take Davie with her. Having a child along would likely deter any comments from a man, even one like him.

The conveyance arrived several minutes late. As it slowed to a halt, Della felt certain that Mr. Bennett had never laid eyes on it. It looked like someone had dismantled a buggy, assembled boards on the rear and added a bench seat. She supposed it would be adequate for the task, despite the appearance of the contraption.

Bosko had brought along another man, a younger fellow he introduced as his brother. Both men were dressed in blue denim work clothes and wore common broad-brimmed hats. The younger man hopped off the wooden seat, went to the back of the cart, and hoisted himself onto the flatbed to sit with his feet dangling.

Della assisted Davie onto the seat, placing him between herself and the driver. When she settled next to the boy, she gave directions to the destination and noticed that Mr. Bosko didn't act as if he recognized her. Perhaps his drunken state that night had erased his memory.

The cart jostled along the slag road so much that Della was fearful of being thrown off the seat at every turn. It was a great relief when they arrived at the Hovey house.

Cora stepped out to meet them when the wagon rolled up in front of the house. Della quickly left the vehicle. She didn't want to give either of the men a chance to offer her a hand.

"We've come to relieve you of that trunk," Della told Cora. "I'm sure you'll be glad to have it out from under your porch,"

Cora hurried forward to give Della a hug. "Goodness me. There was no hurry. It's not in our way."

While Davie and the Hovey boys played chase, Core directed the men to where the trunk was located. Loading the trunk took only a few minutes, which left no time to visit.

"Come for coffee some afternoon, soon. And bring the boy. I miss you," Cora said.

"I shall. I promise." She waved at Cora as she hurried back to the horse cart. "Come along, Davie. We mustn't delay these men from their work." She motioned to the sky in the west to add weight to her reasoning. "Look, rain clouds are forming."

Back at the house with the trunk parked in the parlor corner, Della handed the older of the two men a few small coins. He glanced at them, nodded and hurried to leave.

When they were out of sight, she opened the trunk and quickly realized the contents held a musty smell. Every garment would need to be aired out or washed. But it would have to wait until the next day. She'd promised the boy she'd read him a story, and so after the noon meal and the table had been cleared, Della brought the fairytale book from the parlor and began reading out loud.

As the story progressed Davie listened intently when Red Riding Hood entered the woods and was approached by the wolf. Even Mrs. Molina seemed interested. Della noticed her peeking around the corner from the kitchen with a quizzical look on her face.

The boy squirmed in his chair as the wolf entered the grandmother's house. At the climax, Della heard Mrs. Molina gasp. Davie's expression was one of horror.

"That's not the end," Della said and continued reading to the end of the story.

"See. It has a good ending," she said, smiling.

The boy scowled. "I hate that wooff." He slid off his chair and headed up the stairs.

At suppertime, Davie watched while Della ladled the soup Mrs. Molina had left for them.

"Why didn't that woodman shoot the wooff before he ate Grandma?" he asked. "I woulda kilt him dead."

"Maybe he didn't have his gun with him." She sat and took her napkin on her lap.

"I'd get him Papa's gun."

"Your father has a gun?"

He looked up at her, his eyes shining, and nodded.

"Where is it?"

"Up in the storeroom," he whispered, pointing over his head. "I can show you."

"I don't need to know," she said. "You must never touch it."

But later that night, after she'd tucked the sheet under Davie's chin and closed his door, she went to check out the storeroom across the hall. She turned on the hall light and soon acknowledged that the boy had been right. Propped in the corner in back of the boxes was a shotgun. Della nodded to herself. Well, if a wooff ever gets into the house, I'll know where to find it.

Chapter 44

Later that night, a coyote's howl woke Della, sending a shiver across her shoulder blades. She'd heard them before, of course, many times, out somewhere on a hilltop. But this time it seemed so close, like it was poised right outside her window, which was impossible since the bedrooms were on the second floor. She left her bed and went to look out the window anyway.

Light from the full moon flooded the dry hillside, giving her a clear view of the area. No sign of a coyote. It didn't surprise her. They never lingered after waking people.

A faint breeze moved the thin curtain, cool enough to make her step back. June days were hot, but at night a blanket was sometimes needed.

She wondered what time it was as she closed the window. Some people could tell the time from the position of the moon. She wasn't one of them.

She was about to go back to bed when it occurred to her that Davie might have heard the eerie sound and been frightened. She thought to check on him and opened the door to the hall. In the dim light coming from her window, she saw him standing there in his nightshirt like a small ghost.

She reached to take his hand. "It's all right, Davie. It was just an old coyote out on the hill." When he didn't move or look at her, she stooped down to his level and realized that he wasn't awake at all.

Cousin Freddie had been a sleepwalker, she recalled. Her mother had commented that Aunt Betty always tried to wake the boy when she found him wandering around the house, a practice her mother thought was a mistake. With that in mind, Della led the boy to his bed and arranged the cover over him.

Back in her own room, she wondered if Cousin Freddie had ever gotten hurt walking around in his sleep. She had no way of knowing since she'd only seen him a few times. His family lived in Muncie.

Della pushed those thoughts aside to consider Davie and the possible danger of such behavior. Perhaps she should block the stairway in some manner to prevent an accidental tumble. Why hadn't Mr. Bennett warned her? And why would a sweet little boy develop night-time wandering? She wished she knew more about such things. She'd seek Cora's advice, but at that moment, the only person she could consult was Mrs. Molina.

In the morning, after seeing that Davie was settled at the table eating his cooked cereal, she approached Mrs. Molina in the kitchen. The woman was wiping off the work table and looked up when Della walked in.

"I understand from Mr. Bennett that you have sons," she said and reached for a cup on the shelf.

The older woman nodded and held up three fingers.

Della smiled as she went over to the stove. "Did any of them ever walk in their sleep?"

"*Si*," Mrs. Molina replied. "Juan." She tossed the cleaning cloth into the sink.

"What did you do about it?"

The woman shrugged. "Mister, he tie rope to boy," she pointed to her ankle, "and to bed."

"What happened?"

"Boy get up, fall, wake up." She walked over, reached for the coffee pot on the stove and filled Della's cup.

Della had to admit the mental picture was somewhat amusing, but she didn't think Mr. Bennett would approve of such treatment. Thoughtful, she sipped the coffee.

Reading Della's expression, Mrs. Molina said, "The boy, he grow up, no more walk in sleep."

Della nodded and took another sip. "I guess all your sons are miners now."

"*Si*. Carlos, Javier, *y* Juan." She straightened her shoulders in an expression of pride. "Work hard. Juan, *mi hijo menor*."

Though she didn't understand those last words, by Mrs. Molina's demeanor, it was something good. Della responded with a smile and a nod.

Walking to the parlor, Della finished her coffee, set the empty cup on the table, and turned her attention to unpacking her trunk. She carried her dresses upstairs to her room, hung them in the armoire, and left the door open, hoping any mustiness would disappear, and returned downstairs.

The sight of the framed photo of her family brought a sense of loneliness. She took it and her mother's jewelry box upstairs and put them on top of the chest of drawers. The quilt, she hung over the railing of the porch to air. The rest of the items could remain in the trunk.

Though awkward, she managed to drag the half-empty trunk up the stairs. Once at the top, she positioned it next to the railing, planning to use it at night to block the stairway in case Davie should take to sleepwalking again. She'd leave the door to her bedroom open. That way she would hear if Davie left his room again.

When time for the noon meal arrived, Mrs. Molina brought something different to the table. The plate she placed before each of them contained a single pancake. Both Della and her young charge stared at their plates. Della supposed that such an offering would suffice, but thought it an unusual choice, and an odd specimen, clearly made without leavening. Mrs. Molina went back to the kitchen, returned with a bowl of fragrant beans, and placed it on the table.

She made a motion indicating that they should spoon some beans onto the pancakes. Della scooped a heaping portion onto Davie's pancake first and then her own. Then Mrs. Molina made additional motions, a folding gesture. Della did what she thought she understood, creating a package of beans.

The cook made eating gestures, and they each carefully lifted the bundle to take a bite.

The hot, juicy concoction tasted wonderful. Della smiled at Mrs. Molina and nodded. "This is good," she said with enthusiasm. "I can't think of a better way to eat your delicious beans."

Mrs. Molina displayed a wide grin, proud of her accomplishment.

As Davie bit into his, juice from the beans ran down his chin. Della quickly dabbed his face with a napkin to prevent the red sauce from soiling his shirt.

It didn't take the boy long to finish his part. He gulped down the last of the milk in his glass, then squirmed on his chair while he watched Della eat her part. Della smiled at him. It didn't take a mind reader to know he was anxious for the afternoon's story time.

Mrs. Molina was standing in the doorway to the hall watching them. "You have *hermanos aquí?*" she asked Della, making a sweeping motion with her hand.

After a second, Della thought she understood. "Family? No, not here. My family is in Ohio."

Mrs. Molina shook her head, the corners of her mouth drooping. "Mmm. No good, *solo en la noche.*"

Della was surprised at the woman's concern. Though she didn't understand all of what she'd said, she imagined the cook meant that being far from her family was bad. And she couldn't agree more.

That Friday night, Della was sitting in a parlor chair reading after putting Davie to bed. The boy had balked, but when Della said she would tell him a story, he soon relented.

She sat at the foot of his bed and tried to remember the one she'd heard her grandfather tell when she stayed at his farm. He'd been a skilled storyteller.

Her version involved a young rabbit and before long Davie's eyelids became heavy. When she finished, she quietly left the room, pulled the trunk over as a barricade, and descended the stairway.

Mr. Bennett's library was small, only two shelves, but she found a history book to page through. There was bound to be something interesting in it to read. She would have preferred a novel, but it would do.

She was still having trouble getting to sleep at night, so the summer evenings dragged like those of midwinter. She'd already finished what mending she had the night before. Daylight lingered until nearly eight o'clock, and the air was slow to cool, adding to her sleeping difficulty.

After spending a good deal of time reading about the queen of England, she was beginning to feel the fatigue from her morning's work and glanced at the clock on the bookcase. Midnight was not far off. She closed the book and decided a glass of milk might help her get to sleep. It was something her grandmother always recommended.

Standing to replace the book, she thought she heard the sound of voices outside somewhere. Noise from the town below was often carried on the breeze from the valley. However, she turned out the table lamp she'd been using and went to the front door.

Opening it part way, she was surprised when what she heard was much closer. She peered out and spotted the figures of two men moving along the road in the moonlight. Strange, she thought, uneasiness sweeping over her. It might not have given her pause, except that Mr. Bennett's house was situated at the end of the road. There was no good reason for anyone to be out there at that late hour.

Chapter 45

Della strained to hear what was being said. As they drew closer, her stomach knotted. That gravelly voice was one she'd heard before. It belonged to that man, Bosko. An instant recall of his hand on her shoulder at McBride's made her shudder. The other fellow was likely his brother. Her hands shook as she eased the door closed and fumbled to turn the lock. With her heart thumping in her chest, she thought of the shotgun.

Whirling around, she lifted her skirt and made a dash for the stairs. When she reached the storeroom door, she turned on the hall light. Inside the store room, she had to move several boxes in order to get at the weapon, pushing them right and left. As soon as she had the gun in hand, she headed back down the stairs. It gun was heavier than she would have thought, and she almost tripped. Managing it and her skirt as she descended was treacherous.

At the bottom step, her thoughts turned to operating the weapon, realizing she didn't know if it was loaded. Stopping in the dim hallway, she tried to force open the breach. It wouldn't budge. Did it have a release? She sucked in a deep breath and wished she had a pistol instead. She'd fired her grandfather's pistols many times during visits to his farm, but she'd never fired a shotgun, though she'd watched her brothers do it.

As she struggled with the weapon, the silence in the front of the house seemed more ominous than the voices earlier. Those men might be sneaking up onto the porch that very minute. Another deep breath. She'd have to fool them into thinking she knew how to use it. Perhaps just the sight of it would be enough.

Hurrying to the front window, she peeked around the drapery. The moon was bright and the sky was clear. The two were standing out on the road, their heads together. Plotting, she figured. She didn't dare let them get up onto the porch. They might break in and rush her.

Easing open the door, she stepped out and stood in the shadow of the roof. Her nerves were on high alert, her focus sharp.

The fellow she knew as Bosko nudged his companion. Even though she'd made an effort to be quiet, they'd heard the door. He stepped forward. "Hey there. I figured you'd like some company tonight, what with ole man Bennett away." His voice was husky with liquor and his head swayed as he made an effort to peer into the darkness to the porch. The other man moved up behind him. "Let's do it. You know she's there."

Both men took another step forward. Della gripped the gun and put her finger on the trigger. "I warn you. I'm armed."

"Bosko chuckled. "Is that so?"

She lifted the gun to her shoulder, pointed it over their heads, and squeezed the trigger. A resounding click was heard.

Bosko guffawed and put his foot on the bottom porch step.

A sudden pistol shot pierced the night. Bosko yowled, cursed, and grabbed his left ear. Both men stepped back and crouched against the roadbed.

"The neex one will be betwin you eyes," a man's voice said. "Git going. And don come back."

Della gasped. Confused, she pressed against the outside wall.

"Git!" the man bellowed.

Bosko uttered a stream of foul words, but the two of them, still hunched, scurried backward, then turned and ran down the road.

Watching them go, Della let out the breath she'd been holding. But then she stiffened, not sure if it was safe to relax or not. She waited, listening.

After a moment, she said, "Please show yourself."

A hand holding a hat waved over the top of the porch railing. A second later, a short, dark-skinned young man in miner's clothing stepped into view in front of the porch.

"Who *are* you?" Della demanded.

"Juan. Juan Molina. *Mi madre,* she sent me to watch."

Della put her hand over her heart and poured out words of gratitude.

"They not bother no more. I go now." He backed away, bowed and replaced his hat, then slipped into the darkness down the hillside.

Still shaken by the confrontation, Della clutched the shotgun and hurried upstairs to check on Davie. She wondered if he'd heard the pistol shot, but when she pressed the light switch and peeked in on him, he was sound asleep.

Her lack of knowledge about how to operate a shotgun was disturbing. Under the light, she studied the action part of the gun, found a lever and pushed it aside. The barrel fell forward, exposing the empty chamber. At least she'd be able to do that if the occasion arose. The weight of the gun was another issue. If it hadn't been for her excitement, she didn't think she could have held the long barrel up much longer. It wasn't fair that women should be so helpless, but perhaps Mr. Bennett had a pistol that would be more suitable for protection if needed.

She closed the breech and shifted her attention to the store room. After returning the gun to its place, she looked around for a box of ammunition. It would be needed in case of another threat. Not immediately seeing a packet like the one she envisioned, she wondered where it would be kept. Likely in one of the boxes stored in that very room. Though tempting, it didn't seem appropriate for her to search her employer's belongings. Her questions would have to wait for his return on Monday.

When Mrs. Molina arrived in the kitchen the next morning, Della was waiting for her, anxious to relate the events of the previous night. Her emotions were close to the surface as she spoke, and tears threatened as she thanked her for sending her son to guard the house. "But how did you know there would be trouble?"

The older woman held up her hand, rubbing her thumb and fingers together. "Payday. Too much drink."

Della touched her forehead. Of course. It was the end of the month.

"No more trouble now," Mrs. Molina said as she reached for a pan to begin preparing the morning meal.

Della marveled at the woman's calmness. "But won't your son be in trouble with the law? The bullet nicked the ear of that awful man."

Mrs. Molina made a face and shook her head. "He not know who shot."

Della blinked. "I guess you're right. Your son didn't show himself until after they ran away." She drew a deep breath. "I was so scared when the shotgun didn't work. If he hadn't been there …"

"Time to cook now," Mrs. Molina said, turning to the ice box. She took out a package wrapped in butcher paper, placed it on the work table and pulled the string.

Seeing her unwrap the side of bacon, Della recalled an idea she'd had. "Let me have the clean part of the paper," she said. "I've been thinking the boy could learn his letters if I show him."

After Della helped clear away the dishes from breakfast, she spread a long sheet of the brown paper on the table. "Look here, Davie." Picking up one of his crayons, she began to print the alphabet across the top. He got onto his knees on one of the chairs and watched.

"These," she said, pointing to what she'd written, "make up all the stories I've read to you and articles your father reads in the newspaper. When you go to school, you'll learn to read too. But for now, I'll show you how to print your name. You'll need to know how to put your name on your school work."

The morning was spent with Della helping her pupil put the letters together. The boy caught on quickly, and even though his name was somewhat lopsided, it was readable. He wanted to do it again and again, but after he'd broken the third crayon, she decided it was time for a rest. She read one of the fairy tales to him and then sent him upstairs to amuse himself with his toys while she washed two of his shirts in the washroom sink.

It wasn't until late in the day, almost sunset, that Della focused on the fact that it was her birthday, her eighteenth birthday. She guessed that officially, it made her an adult, something to celebrate. She snorted. In her situation, it hardly mattered. There was no one to celebrate with. If she were at home, her family would celebrate with her. She sighed. Well, maybe next year.

During the evening hours, after the boy had been put to bed, she chose one of the few books on Mr. Bennett's shelf. The one on mining made for dull reading, so it wasn't long before she was drowsy enough to sleep.

Late Monday afternoon Hiram Bennett arrived home like Caesar returning from the wars. When the buggy pulled up in front of the house, Davie, who had been watching for it all day, ran out the front door and was jumping up and down on the porch.

"Papa! Papa!" He scrambled down the porch steps and into the arms of his grinning father.

"How's my big boy?" Hiram said, picking him up.

The boy flung his arms and legs around his dad and buried his face in his shoulder. "You were gone so long."

Della stood on the porch watching them. She couldn't help but smile at the tender scene. It almost brought tears as she thought of her own father and how she wished she could hug him just one more time.

Hiram set the boy down and nodded to Della before turning back to the buggy. "I've brought some packages." He reached to pick up a parcel from a wooden box attached to the back of the buggy. "You can carry this one," he said to Davie, who'd started fidgeting. "Take it into the parlor, but don't open it just yet."

The child grabbed the package and raced up the steps, almost bumping into Della.

The buggy driver, a stranger to Della, looped the horse's reins around the pole that held the canopy in place and stepped out. He took Mr. Bennett's luggage, a suitcase and a satchel, and carried them to the porch. Bennett retrieved two more packages, then reached into his vest pocket and handed the driver some coins as he passed by to return to his seat. "Thanks, Joe. I'll be needing the buggy again tomorrow at nine."

The man nodded, climbed into the driver's seat, and guided the horse around to return to the livery.

Mr. Bennett gained the steps to the porch, and with his free hand, held the door for Della to enter the house. He placed the parcels he was carrying on the sofa and returned to bring his other belongings inside.

Davie was sitting on the sofa holding the package tight, one foot bobbing up and down, so anxious to know what was inside.

His father grinned. "Okay, son. You can open it."

Paper and string flew. The box inside was red and white with a picture on the side. Davie pulled open the lid and revealed a miniature locomotive and two train cars. The child gave out a yelp and slid off the sofa to the rug on the floor. In no time, he had the cars hooked together and began making a chugging noise.

His father chuckled as he watched.

Della smiled. "A good choice. A perfect toy for a boy his age."

"Indeed." Mr. Bennett nodded, then stepped over to the sofa. He picked up the round box he'd placed there. "By the way," he turned and handed it to Della, "I brought something for you, too."

Chapter 46

Della was startled by having the box thrust into her hands and
several thoughts converged in rapid succession. By the shape of
it, the box was designed to hold a hat, an improper gift
considering the difference in their social standing. She was a
mere *servant*. And then it occurred to her that perhaps he
planned to deduct the price of it from her pay. She should refuse
it. But, how would she? It was already in her hands. It would be
rude to shove it back at him. She needed this job. She didn't
know how to react. Lifting her gaze, she saw that he was
grinning.

"Go on, open it," he said, a sparkle in his eyes.

Still feeling uneasy, she pulled the string and lifted the lid.

Inside, nestled on blue satin, was a straw hat, white with a
blue band and a handsome red feather. She couldn't keep her
mouth from falling open, certain it must have cost over a dollar.

"Here. Let me help." Still grinning, Mr. Bennett took the
open box and held it out for her. "I thought anyone with hair as

beautiful as yours should have a hat like this for the Independence Day celebration tomorrow."

He watched as she gently eased it from its bed. "When I saw it in the window of a millinery shop in Chicago, I couldn't leave it behind."

He turned aside, put the empty hat box on the sofa, and snatched up the other package. "I bought red-white-and-blue ties for Davie and me to wear. We'll all look very patriotic."

Della thought the hat must be the latest style. Her friends back home would be so envious. But she wasn't in Dayton, and she had only one friend in Jerome. What would people think, especially Cora, when she showed up on Main Street wearing that hat, and in the company of Mr. Bennett and his son? She knew good and well what they'd think.

"Well, put it on," he said.

Della turned toward the mirror hanging next to the front door, placed the hat on her head, and looked back at his reflection in the mirror. "I ... I don't know what to say. It's a most generous gift." She braced herself, thinking the next thing he'd say was that it wasn't a gift as such, but something she'd have to pay him for.

But he didn't say anything like that. He just stood there, smiling and nodding. "We're going to have a wonderful day tomorrow, but we must be ready for the buggy by nine in the morning."

Della couldn't help herself. As she removed the hat, her thoughts ran to how best to arrange her hair. She turned the hat in her hands, admiring the red feather. It rose above the star-spangled blue band by nearly ten inches. Which dress? she mused.

Mrs. Molina came to the doorway. "I go," she said. "Food on stove."

Mr. Bennett nodded. "Tomorrow is a holiday, Mrs. Molina. We celebrate Independence Day. You can have the day off."

She scowled, hesitated, then turned and started toward the kitchen.

"Wait," he said. He followed her as far as his office. "Wait here." He stepped through the door, and a moment later, returned to where the woman stood in the hall. "Payday," he said, handing her an envelope. "No work tomorrow. Holiday."

She slipped the envelope into her apron pocket and nodded. "Holy day. *Bueno.*" She hurried toward the kitchen and a moment later the back door was heard closing.

An hour later, after Hiram Bennett had unpacked his belongings, Della made a pot of coffee and readied the dining room table for supper. She brought in the tureen of savory-scented stew and returned to the kitchen for the platter of biscuits Mrs. Molina had left for them. She had been thinking about Mr. Bennett's surprise gift. Her father had never been interested in her mother's hats, so Mr. Bennett's interest in such things was curious. Of course, the hats her mother chose had been rather old-fashioned and unattractive in Della's opinion.

Mr. Bennett came into the room with Davie at his side. "That smells so good," he said. "I'm tired of hotel food. And that woman makes the best stew on earth." He pulled out a chair for Della, another for Davie, and then one for himself. He sat and took a napkin onto his lap. "Will you serve, please?" he said, looking at Della.

She obliged, putting a ladle of beef stew on each plate. After passing the biscuits, she filled Mr. Bennett's coffee cup.

They ate quietly for several minutes. Della waited for her employer to begin a conversation if he so wished. But it was his son who began talking.

"I can write my name now," he said in a proud tone of voice.

"Is that so? Who taught you to do that?" his father asked.

Davie pointed his fork across the table at Della.

Mr. Bennett looked at her. He raised his eyebrows. "You taught him to write?"

She dabbed her mouth with her napkin and nodded. "He learns quickly. I predict he will be a good student when he starts school."

"It shouldn't surprise me. I remember how you taught that boy at the boarding house about his arithmetic."

Della's smile started to fade at the mention of the boarding house. It brought immediate thoughts of the Cooper boys, and she wondered how they were getting along. She'd enjoyed coaching young Luther. Maybe she should reconsider her mother's advice and become a teacher.

Mr. Bennett took a swallow of coffee, then said, "I saw several handbills in the Junction terminal announcing that the circus school in Phoenix will be performing for the public in the middle of the month. That would be a swell outing for us." He turned to Davie. "You'd like to see clowns and acrobats wouldn't you?"

The boy nodded vigorously while chewing his food.

Mr. Bennett turned his gaze to Della. "What do you think, Miss McCrea?"

"It sounds like a fine idea." She cut her biscuit and reached for the butter dish.

"Yesiree, that's what we'll do. The three of us will take the train to Phoenix and go to the circus."

Della blinked. "You mean I am to go, too?"

"Well, of course. It wouldn't do to leave you behind." Hiram tilted his head toward his son. "Don't you agree, Davie?

Davie gaped, looking from one adult to the other.

Mr. Bennett turned his gaze to Della. "Have you ever been to the circus, Miss McCrea?"

Della put down her fork. "No, I haven't, but when I was a little girl, I had a chance to ride a camel."

Hiram chuckled. "I was not aware that camels were native to Ohio."

"They're not," she said with a grin. "The Shriners came to Dayton and after the parade, they gave us children a chance to ride a camel. I was pretty scared, but my brother dared me, so I had to do it."

Hiram blinked. "What was it like?"

"Kind of herky-jerky, a back-and-forth movement."

"Sounds interesting. I'd like to try that sometime." Hiram laid his napkin on the table. "The folks in Phoenix don't have camels, but I understand they have some pigs that put on quite a performance, and the people who perform the high-wire act are something to behold."

He pushed back his chair. "You must excuse me. I have some office work to attend to." Mr. Bennett rose and left the room to Della and the boy.

Davie slipped off his chair and stood looking at her. He'd left most of the vegetables from the stew behind on his plate, but Della knew he was anxious to play with his new train, so she waved her consent for him to leave.

She cleared the table and washed the dishes. As she did so, her thoughts ranged from which dress to wear the next day to the prospect of seeing circus performers, finally settling on the problem of finding the right moment to talk to her employer about the incident the previous Friday night.

Chapter 47

After Davie had been tucked into bed and his new train safely sheltered underneath it, Della settled into one of the parlor chairs. The evening was still hot, only a few degrees cooler than midday. She pulled the hem of her skirt up to her knees. All the windows in the house were open to allow in whatever breeze might come up from the valley, 1500 feet below.

She'd taken a book from the shelf to serve as a solid surface for letter paper and was contemplating how to explain the last few weeks to her sister when Mr. Bennett entered. At the sound of his steps, she quickly returned her skirt to a more modest level.

"Oh, Miss McCrea. I'm sorry," he said when he noticed the letter paper and pencil. "I see you are busy. I won't disturb you." He started to retrace his steps.

"Not at all, Mr. Bennett. It's been some time since I've written to my sister, and I'm not sure how to tell her about my change in circumstances. Please stay. There's something I must report to you."

"Is that so?" He returned to sit on the sofa and leaned back, relaxed.

Della set the book and paper aside. "Last Friday night ...." She described in detail the intended assault perpetrated by the scoundrel named Bosko and how Mrs. Molina's son had intervened.

As she spoke Hiram Bennett's expression morphed from surprise to anger to obvious distress, his eyebrows drawn together in a scowl, his hands fisted.

When she finished, he leaned forward. "I am deeply sorry for your appalling experience. I blame myself. If I could, I would take you and Davie with me when I travel, but some of the places I must visit would be unsuitable, if not dangerous." His eyes narrowed. "I'll speak to the sheriff about Leon Bosko, and I'll see to it that the Molina lad is rewarded." He ran his index finger back and forth across his chin. "That old bird gun is no kind of weapon for a woman. I'll find a suitable pistol for you. But you'll need to practice with it."

"Thank you, sir. My grandfather let my sisters and me practice with his pistols several times when we visited his farm. He had an old revolver he claimed was just like the one Jesse James carried."

Mr. Bennett's brow relaxed, deep in thought. "Good. Very good."

Della rose early the next morning in order to help Davie dress and still have time to attire herself for the day. She'd chosen the white batiste dress she'd worn the year before and was glad she'd taken the trouble to steam out the wrinkles when she'd had the time. After a quick sponge bath and donning the garment, she arranged her hair. She placed the new hat on her head and secured it in place with a hatpin, then with the aid of her hand mirror, turned this way and that to admire it from different angles. Mr. Bennett is right, she thought. It's perfect for the holiday.

"The buggy is ready," Hiram called from the bottom of the stairs. "I made arrangements for us to eat at the hotel. Come along, Miss McCrea."

Della quickly slipped on her gloves, grabbed her purse and parasol, and hurried to join them. After a week of confinement, excitement made her stomach feel fluttery as she descended the stairway. When she reached the bottom, Mr. Bennett and Davie were waiting in the hallway, both wearing their new patriotic ties. Davie pulled on his father's hand. "Let's *go*."

"Hold on son," Hiram said as he stared at Della. He took a deep breath. "Doesn't Miss McCrea look splendid? I knew that hat would be just the thing. Yesiree. Splendid."

Turning his focus to Davie, he said, "All right. Let us depart. We're off to have a first-rate holiday."

The morning meal at the hotel was delicious, though Della could barely consume half of what was on her plate. Davie was too excited to eat. Hiram, however, made up for both of them, and even enjoyed an extra sweet roll.

Back out on the street, people lined the boardwalk on either side. The fire department's band had begun to parade down the center of town with the nation's flag carried in the lead. Men doffed their hats at the passing and a great deal of applause was heard as the band played "The Washington Post March."

Coming along behind the band, the mayor waved from an automobile driven by the town clerk. The city council followed, each of them riding in a very handsome buggy drawn by a fine-looking horse.

Soon after the parade, the young boys in the sack race formed at the starting point. Della spotted Will and Cora Hovey across the street, and the three of them joined the Hovey family to watch Buster Hovey compete. Always a source of much laughter each year, the people called out encouragement as the boys hopped and tumbled along the cobbled surface. But unlike the year before, Buster Hovey finished first. His parents beamed and everyone cheered as the town mayor pinned a blue ribbon to his shirt.

The donkey race was the next competition. As the crowd waited for it to begin, Cora leaned close to Della. "Billy thought he was too big for the sack race. I admit, he's grown a foot this year, but I'm not sure he has muscle enough to handle a donkey."

Down the block, the donkeys were being hauled in place at the starting line, the first challenge. But soon the older boys got them more or less in a row, and the pulling and pushing began. Billy made a good showing, however, in the end, he came in next to last. His disappointment was clearly written on his face.

Will Hovey tried to cheer the boy. "Next year, Billy. You'll be bigger and stronger then." He went off with Billy to take care of the donkey and Buster tagged along with them. Georgie began to squirm and fuss in Cora's arms. "Time to take this one home," she said. "Come along, Nellie." She bid Mr. Bennett, Della and Davie goodbye and headed off to where their horse and buggy were tied.

The highlight of the day was the fire hose cart race between the firemen from Bisbee and the crew in Jerome. Della looked for Vesta's brother in the assembled group but didn't see him. She looked up and down the street hoping to see Vesta or Millie. It'd be fun to have them see her new hat. Then Millie and her family appeared in the crowd across the street and a half-block away.

Della waved but didn't manage to catch Millie's attention. It had been almost a year since she'd spoken to her. She heaved a sigh and turned her attention to the racers.

The contest was a crowd-pleaser with both teams straining to move the heavy carts. Men on the sidelines shouted encouragement. Fifteen minutes later it was over, but unfortunately, the local squad didn't win.

As the people began to disperse, Hiram said, "Let's walk down to the bandstand. I think the mayor is going to make his speech there."

As they walked along, it seemed like half the town had the same thing in mind. By the time they arrived, the band had assembled on the stand ready to entertain. New benches had been installed around the venue, but it was obvious the number would not be adequate. Hiram hurried ahead and found space for Della at the end of one of the benches. She stepped up, collapsed her parasol, and was about to take a seat when the woman already seated turned, and Della found Harriet Samples looking up at her.

Both women instantly recognized that they were wearing identical hats. Della didn't know how to react but felt her cheeks flush.

The look of horror on Mrs. Samples' face was like she'd seen the devil himself. She huffed and rose from the bench. Pushing past Della, she jammed her elbow into Della's ribs in the process and blended into the crowd.

Della gasped, swung around to say something, but her breath caught in her throat. She clutched the injury with one hand, her eyes filling with tears.

Hiram gaped after his sister. "Harriet!"

Chapter 48

"I don't know what has gotten into my sister," Hiram remarked. "Are you injured? Do take a seat."

Della rubbed the sore rib as she sat and composed herself. "I...I just need a moment." She raised her parasol to shade herself and forced a weak smile. Glancing at Davie, who looked a little puzzled, she said, "Let's not let her spoil the day."

Mr. Bennett bent forward, his brow still furrowed. "Well...if you're sure..."

"I am, indeed." She wasn't about to let that woman rob her and the boy of the opportunity to be away from the confines of the house and enjoy the festivities.

"Very well then." He straightened and stood beside her with Davie at his side.

Presently, a smattering of applause was heard as the mayor, a portly man in a black suit and white shirt, climbed the steps to the bandstand. He removed his hat and raised a hand to quiet the audience, then pulled a piece of paper from his coat pocket.

"Ladies and gentlemen," he began and launched into a prepared speech about the freedoms the people of Jerome enjoyed, a speech long enough to make people squirm in the hot July sun. When some began to wander off to seek relief, the mayor soon noticed and concluded his rhetoric, after which the band took over the entertainment.

Della was not a bit drowsy when she slipped under the sheet on her bed that night. She had too much to think about. She pondered Mr. Bennett's unusual behavior that evening. Soon after arriving back at the house, Mr. Bennett had muttered something about talking to his sister and left again. When he returned two hours later, it was clear that his visit had not ended well, for his demeanor indicated he was exasperated. He'd shut himself in his office and didn't come out until after she and Davie had retired. She'd heard his footsteps on the stairs after the lights were out.

Was that his usual manner when displeased, she wondered. Her father had been one to storm and curse when someone upset him. Most often, when her mother pleaded for quiet, he'd leave the house and return smelling of alcohol.

She touched the tender rib where Mrs. Samples had assaulted her. That crazy woman didn't have to be so mean simply because we were wearing the same hat. Sure, it might be embarrassing, but hardly enough to make one violent.

But then Mr. Bennett had been so kind and concerned for her welfare, she couldn't imagine any other employer like him. The early supper at the hotel had been superb, a delicious roast beef with all the trimmings. Huge fans had not only made the room almost comfortable despite the later afternoon heat but also had kept the flies away. And Davie, bless him, had behaved well.

She turned over to face the doorway. She'd left it open to encourage the night air from the window to pass through, and also to be able to hear Davie if he went sleepwalking.

So far, her new employment seemed quite satisfactory. Since the house had been recently constructed, it had none of the problems of an older home. The boy wasn't difficult to manage. Reading stories and teaching him his letters was something she enjoyed. And Mrs. Molina was pleasant enough. As her eyes closed and she drifted off, her last thought was of the hat with the red feather.

Two days later, Mr. Bennett left the house before eight o'clock. He returned late that afternoon and called out to Della from the dining room. When she approached, she saw a wooden box in his hand. He opened it and unfolded a brown cloth to reveal a .38 Smith and Wesson revolver, the newness barely worn.

"I purchased this from one of the merchants in town. I hope it will make you feel more secure in my absence."

She was surprised. Since he hadn't mentioned the frightful incident again, she'd begun to think he'd forgotten about it. "My goodness, thank you. I'm sure it will be satisfactory."

"I wanted you to have it today because I must leave on the early train tomorrow. Rest assured, I'll return before our trip to Phoenix to see the circus performance." He placed the box on the table and removed the gun.

"Let me show you." He flipped open the cylinder and closed it again, then handed it to her. She did the same as it seemed that he was expecting a demonstration of her skill.

He reached back into the box, took out a small cardboard carton, and opened it to show her the required ammunition. "Let's go outside."

He slid the container into his trouser pocket, took the pistol from her, and led the way toward the back door. As they passed through the kitchen, he grabbed a can of beans from the open shelf.

She followed him out and around to the other side of the washhouse. "Stand here," he said and walked twenty paces to the side of the hill. He jabbed out a crevice in the sandy soil with the toe of his shoe and placed the can in it.

"You're not going to waste that can of beans, are you?" she said as he walked back toward her.

He smiled and gave a quick chuckle. "I'm not much worried about that can of beans."

Her eyes narrowed. Clearly, he hadn't believed her when she'd told him about practicing with her grandfather's pistols.

He pulled the packet of bullets from his pocket, loaded the cylinder, then handed her the weapon. "Now, take it in both your hands." He stepped behind her and reached around her to position it. "Hold it like this, and use your left hand to cock it." He pulled back the hammer with his thumb. "Like this. Now you can pull the trigger." He let go and stepped back.

She held the pistol out in front of her, lined up the sites and fired. The can hopped into the air. The picture of the cowboy on the front had a hole in it.

"Huh. Well, that'll do, I guess." He took the gun from her. "I think the best place to keep it is in my desk drawer in the office. It will be handy enough, should you need it."

Late Saturday afternoon Della gathered the rugs from the hallway and took them out on the front porch. She shook one and then the other. She'd already used the carpet sweeper from the closet under the stairs on the living room rug. She flopped the rugs over the railing and paused to stare out over the rooftops of the houses on the hill below. She counted and thought she could pick out the roof of the Hovey's house.

Looking off to the right, beyond the hogback, she could just make out the green trees that grew along the riverbank in the valley. In the other direction, gray clouds were bunching together above the highest peak. It meant the rainy season would soon be upon them.

Gathering the rugs, she went inside to put them back in their usual spots and pulled the drapes against the afternoon sun. The sound of the whistle at the mine reminded her that Mrs. Molina would be leaving soon. She went to call Davie for supper. Thinking he was in his room, she went to the bottom of the stairs. "Come along, Davie. Let's wash our hands. It's time to eat." He was a growing boy, always ready for mealtime.

When he didn't respond, she climbed the steps to look in his room. Surprised when she didn't find him there, she returned to the downstairs hall and went into the kitchen where Mrs. Molina was preparing to leave. The cook nodded toward the back door.

Della glanced out the window and saw the boy sitting on the side of the slope in the shade of the washhouse. He was busy digging in the sandy soil with his shovel and pouring scoops of dirt into his little wagon. She smiled for a second, thinking it was just like a boy to dig in the dirt, but then noticed a slithery movement several feet beyond where he sat.

Feeling as if she couldn't move fast enough, she dashed out the kitchen door, grabbed the boy under both arms and pulled him away—first backing—then turning to set him on his feet. "Run into the house! Quick! Go!"

She followed, sprinted into the office, jerked open the desk drawer and snatched the revolver. The snake was the biggest she'd ever seen, easily three inches across. If it got under the washhouse, she'd lose her chance to kill it. Her heart pounding, she fumbled to load a few shells, then dashed back out.

Halting at what she thought was outside its striking range, she took a breath, cocked it and raised the pistol. The rattler began to coil, its head up, its rattles making a buzzing sound. With her heart in her mouth, she aimed. She was a good shot, but was she good enough?

Chapter 49

With intense focus, she pulled back the hammer and squeezed the trigger. The revolver jerked in her hand. She aimed and fired again. Sulfurous fumes stung her eyes and nose. Stepping back, she watched the snake flail back and forth, its body pierced by the bullets.

Mrs. Molina was in the kitchen doorway saying something Della didn't understand and made the sign of the cross on her bosom.

Seeing the creature still had life in it, Della determined to finish it off. She went into the washhouse where she remembered seeing a shovel, laid the revolver on a shelf, and returned to where the snake lay, still twitching, its blood oozing out around it.

She took a wide stance and plunged the shovel, severing its head. Stepping quickly to one side, she shoved the blade into the soil to remove the blood and looked back at the house, wondering about the whereabouts of the boy.

Davie, standing in the doorway next to Mrs. Molina called out, "Can we keep it? Uncle Dan has one up on a board in his office, a really big one." He stretched his arms wide to demonstrate.

The thought of touching the vile creature made Della's stomach turn. "No. We're not going to keep it. I'm going dig a big hole and bury it."

Davie's lower lip stuck out. "If Papa weas home, *he'd* want to keep it."

After supper before the sunset, Della went out to bury the snake. She scanned the ground in all directions as she went to get the shovel and chose a spot. Though the snake was certainly dead, she edged past it just the same and walked some distance to a flat stretch of earth big enough to serve her purpose.

The digging wasn't difficult, except for a few rocks. When she judged the pit deep enough, she returned to where the snake lay, scooped up its head and carried it to the hole. She'd heard somewhere that the most venomous part should be at the bottom. Returning to the remaining body, she considered the task. It was clear that fitting a three-foot snake onto a ten-inch shovel blade wasn't practical. At that moment, she dearly wished one of her brothers would magically appear. Neither of them would have had qualms about grabbing the tail of the creature. They'd probably slice off the rattles and put them in a pocket.

What she needed was gloves, preferably thick, heavy gloves, but she didn't remember seeing any since she'd arrived at Bennett's house. What would serve as a substitute? A kitchen towel? She went into the kitchen, glad that Mrs. Molina had left and was not there to question her actions. After a glance to see that Davie wasn't around to watch, she took a dishtowel from the shelf, wrapped it around her right hand and headed outside.

Standing over the dead snake, she reflected that she'd had worse duties. She held her breath, leaned to clutch the snake's tail and straightened. The weight of it was more than she expected. Holding it at arm's length, she carried it to the pit and dropped it in. Stepping back, she flung the dishtowel to the ground and took a deep breath. She'd wash it later.

Determined to remove all signs of its presence, she retrieved the shovel and returned to scoop up the blood-stained soil, adding it to the grave before filling it in.

After giving the area a good stomping, she looked around for rocks to pile on top.

A half-hour later she'd scavenged enough to complete the chore. With a sigh, she raised her arm, wiped the sweat from her brow onto her sleeve, and saw Davie watching her from the doorway.

After putting the shovel away, she retrieved the pistol and shooed the boy into the kitchen. "It would be best if I went with you when you go to play outside," she said as he watched her put the gun back in the desk. "Snakes like that one bite, and when that happens, it's very painful."

Davie looked up at her, concern in his eyes. If her caution scared him a little, good enough.

As bad as she wished to put the whole distressful experience behind her, there was one more thing to be done. Her grandfather had gone to great lengths to teach her brothers how to clean a gun, so she knew it was important, though at the time she'd been bored watching.

Later that evening, after Davie had been put to bed, she went to the storage room upstairs to look for supplies. She turned on the light and searched among the boxes until, back in the corner, she spotted a metal box that resembled the one her grandfather had owned. She lifted the lid, found what she needed, and commenced the procedure, and returned it to the desk drawer.

Late on Monday afternoon, a fast-moving thunderstorm raced across the sky from the southeast sending huge drops to clatter on the slag road in front of the house. Della ran to snatch the clothes off the clothesline, and then hurried upstairs to close the windows.

As if someone had set a timer, in the week that followed, Della would later write to her sister, the summer storms arrived. It seemed as though Mother Nature had decided to park over Jerome and deliver all of July's rain in one week. As a result, a washout occurred in one of the canyons and the railroad trestle supports became too unstable to allow train travel in or out of the mountain community.

When Mrs. Molina brought the news that the track's underpinnings would require several days of work by a railroad crew to make it safe, Della knew the trip to Phoenix to see the circus performers was out of the question.

She did her best to keep the boy occupied while rain pounded on the roof and poured into the ditch along the road. Besides reading his favorite stories for the third time, she fashioned a puppet using one of his socks and spoke for it in a squeaky voice. When her stories lost their luster, she left him to amuse himself. Most often she found herself standing at one of the windows, watching the water dig furrows in the hillside.

At the end of the week, when Mrs. Molina didn't come to the house, Della wasn't surprised, nor did she blame her. The roads were impassable by any conveyance and treacherous on foot.

It wasn't until midmorning on Friday, a week later, that Hiram Bennett finally arrived back in Jerome. Della had just finished running the carpet sweeper on the dining room rug when she heard the crunch of wheels on the road out front. She snatched the dust cover off her hair and put it with the sweeper in the hall closet.

Davie, who'd heard the arrival, came scrambling down the staircase. He dashed past Della and out the front door. "Papa!"

Hiram Bennett stepped from the buggy and held out his arms. "How are you, my little man?"

Davie whooped and ran down the steps to jump into Hiram's embrace, nearly dislodging his father's hat.

Della stood on the porch smiling and watching the now familiar tableau. She noted that though Mr. Bennett looked especially tired, his expression was one of joy.

"Did you bring me something?" Davie asked as soon as his father set him on his feet.

"Yes. Two somethings."

"What, what?" In his eagerness, Davie couldn't keep his feet still. He made little hops as he waited for Mr. Bennett and the buggy driver to unload the baggage.

Davie grabbed the handle of one, trying to pull it toward the steps.

"Hold on, son," Hiram said as he handed the buggy driver a sum of money. "That one is too heavy for you." He reached for a parcel on the buggy seat. "Here, take this and give it to Miss

McCrea." He looked up at Della on the porch. "Good morning, Miss McCrea."

"Welcome home, Mr. Bennett." She accepted the package Davie offered and held the door while Mr. Bennett carried his luggage up the steps and into the front room.

"Wait here while I take my bags to my room," he said over his shoulder as he walked into the hallway.

Della made herself comfortable on the sofa and laid the package at her side. Davie crawled up to sit next to her and wiggled as he eyed it.

Minutes later, Mr. Bennett returned with a paper bag. He settled in one of the chairs. "Come here, son, and see what I brought you."

Davie bounced off the sofa and squeezed in next to his father. He stuck his hand in the bag and pulled out the first of two books. It had a picture of a rabbit on the cover. When he extracted the second, Della could see, it was titled, *The Jungle Book.*

Della nodded approval. "Good choice, Mr. Bennett."

Davie clutched the books to his chest, slid off the chair and settled down cross-legged onto the floor. He opened one of them and began looking at the pictures.

"Open *yours*, Miss McCrea," Mr. Bennett said, nodding at the parcel on the sofa.

Della felt a flush rise in her face. "I dare say. This is most unusual, Mr. Bennett." Curious, she pulled the string on the package, unfolded the brown paper covering, and set it aside. The inner wrapping had pink roses printed on it. Such gifts were quite improper, she knew, but peeled away the paper, uncovering two flat boxes. She quickly surmised the narrow one contained some sort of jewelry and lifted the lid. Nestled on blue satin was a pink mother-of-pearl pendant attached to a silver chain. Hardly a gift for a hired girl. "Oh, Mr. Bennett. This is too much. You shouldn't... I can't..."

"Nonsense. A girl your age should have pretty things. Open the other box."

She lifted the lid on the larger box and drew a quick breath. It held a hand mirror, the back and handle of which were made of beautifully carved cherry wood. Della gulped. It had to have cost more than two dollars.

Glancing at her employer, she could see by his smile that he was pleased with himself. It took a couple of seconds for her to form a comment. "I do declare, Mr. Bennett, you treat your hired help better than family."

"I am the fortunate one, Miss McCrea," he said with a wry smile.

Davie, who'd been paging through pictures in *The Jungle Book*, looked up. "Papa, Papa." Pushing the book aside, he sprang to his feet. "You shoulda seen the snake Miss McCrea kilt. It was *this* big." He stretched out his arms.

Hiram Bennett blinked, leaned back, and looked from his son to Della, his astonishment well apparent. "Is that so?"

"She got the gun," Davie continued, holding out his arms, hands together, two fingers pointing at the floor. "Bang! Bang! It wiggled and wiggled." He twisted his arms around to demonstrate. Then he scowled. "I wanted to keep it, but she wouldn't let me."

Della covered her mouth with her hand to hide her smile, his antics so amused her.

Mr. Bennett turned to Della and raised his eyebrows. "What *did* you do with it?"

Della assumed a serious face. "It received an appropriate burial."

Hiram ran a hand across the back of his neck. "Well, Davie, I can see you are well protected in my absence. Miss McCrea is quite capable."

Chapter 50

Hiram Bennett fixed his gaze on Della. "Tell me more. How did you happen to come across this snake? And why didn't you just avoid it?"

"It was out by the washhouse and threatening Davie. I had to act." She bit her lip recalling her fright, but continued her account of the incident.

When she finished, Mr. Bennett grinned and shook his head. "Well, Miss McCrea, you have become a true westerner."

"Not quite. I'm almost afraid to go out the washhouse for fear another snake might come crawling out from under it."

Concern flashed across his face. "Your fear is justified, I think. The slope of the hill makes it impossible to prevent such an invasion. But I've heard there's a man in town who is an expert at exterminating snakes from under buildings. I'll locate him and talk to him about what can be done."

Davie picked up his books and climbed onto the sofa next to Della. He held up the one with the rabbit picture on the cover. "Read this one to me."

Della took the book and laid it on her lap. "You mustn't interrupt your father when he is talking," she said in a firm tone.

The boy's lower lip instantly protruded.

Mr. Bennett put both hands on his knees and pushed himself to a standing position. "I must unpack, and then I have some calls to make before noon. You'll excuse me, please."

Throughout the remainder of the day, Della's thoughts kept returning to Mr. Bennett's gifts. The import had not escaped her. At face value, it seemed he meant to change their relationship. Or perhaps he thought such gifts allowed him the freedom to take advantage of her like Mr. Cooper? However, nothing in his demeanor suggested such a thing.

What course of action should she take? She supposed she could boldly ask his intentions but quickly shook her head, rejecting that idea. He might propose marriage.

Never in her wildest dreams had she entertained the notion of marriage to a man of his age. Though he wasn't homely, he wasn't handsome either. And she hadn't been around him long enough to get a true sense of his personality, though she supposed he had an ugly side too. Most men did.

On the other hand, instead of proposing, he might laugh in her face. Even the thought of such a scene felt shameful. In that case, she'd be obliged to look for employment elsewhere. No hotel or boarding house would pay like Mr. Bennett. She rubbed her temples. What to do? What would Cora advise?

August arrived and with repairs made to the railroad, the work in the mines resumed. Life in the city of Jerome returned to its normal routine. Della decided it was a good day to check the mail. She still held onto the hope that her brother would send her money. It would be a chance to visit Cora as well.

When she'd conveyed her plan to Mr. Bennett at breakfast, he reached into his pants pocket and pulled out some coins. He handed them to her. "Stop at the bakery and buy a few treats to take along. I'll be out all day. I must meet a businessman at the hotel at noon."

Davie could hardly contain his excitement at the prospect of an outing. He gobbled his meal and later squirmed as she helped him get dressed and combed his hair. She sent him to sit on the sofa with his books while she dressed.

She chose her blue dress for the day, and after she'd arranged her hair, added a matching ribbon to her straw hat. Her feelings were close to Davie's. It seemed like it had been such a long time since the July 4th festivities.

They left the house at mid-morning, and since their route was nearly all downhill, it wasn't long before they reached the center of town. By the number of people hurrying in and out of the businesses along Main Street, it was evident that folks were catching up after the storms.

They entered the post office and found a line of like-minded people intent on collecting their mail. As they waited, she still held out hope of receiving some news from home, but that wasn't to be. The only mail she was given was two envelopes for Mr. Bennett. Her spirits sagged as they left the building and headed in the direction of the bakery.

They'd hardly walked a block when Davie stopped to gawk at a man leading a donkey with bundles of firewood strapped to its sides.

"It's just a donkey," Della said. "He's probably taking the wood to the Chinese laundry."

A man on a motorcycle passed going in the opposite direction, causing the animal to balk at the noise. When it refused to move, the man began beating it with a thick leather belt.

Della cringed at the sight of it. "Let's go, Davie. I can't bear to watch."

The boy was reluctant to leave, but she took his hand, tugged him away, and hurried down the boardwalk to the bakery.

She paused a moment in front of the glass window, admired her reflection, and sucked in the aroma of fresh-baked goods, recalling how hungry she'd been while working for McBride. At least now, though the pay was less, her stomach never growled.

She closed her parasol before entering, her thoughts on what to choose. After a few minutes of waiting for a woman in a gray dress to make her purchase, Della bought a dozen apricot scones, a far cry from what she'd afforded in the past. Did the man behind the glass counter remember her and her purchase of three scones? It didn't seem so, but she couldn't help but grin as she handed over the money before leaving.

It didn't take long to reach Cora's house. Davie fidgeted while Della collapsed her parasol and knocked on the door.

It soon opened and a look of delight brightened Cora's face. "Oh, my goodness. I am so glad to see you." She enveloped Della with both arms, then swung the door wide. "Come in, come in."

Buster and Billie dashed around the women and Buster shouted a greeting at Davie. "Hey, kid. Let's play stickball." Billie snatched a ball from one of the chairs on the porch and all three ran to the road out front.

Della propped her parasol in the corner by the door and held up the bakery sack. "I brought something to have with our coffee."

"Wonderful. Let's go into the kitchen." She motioned for Della to precede her. "I'll make a fresh pot. You must tell me all about life in that big house." Cora handed Della a plate for the scones and soon had coffee brewing.

Della laid her purse on the table and carefully emptied the sack onto the plate. "Well, it's very nice, and I have a room all to myself. Davie is an easy child to manage. Mr. Bennett has a very nice Mexican lady who cooks for us." She settled onto the kitchen chair.

Cora placed cups on the table and took a seat opposite her friend. "A cook? Golly, it sounds like you're living in the lap of luxury."

"I suppose so, but there are complications."

"Really? What sort?" Cora stood and went to the stove, returning to pour steaming coffee into the cups. She retrieved a sugar bowl from the shelf and a small pitcher of milk from the icebox and placed them on the table, then sat again. "Bennett didn't turn out to be another Jasper Cooper, did he?"

"No. Not at all." Della added a dash of milk to her cup. "You saw the hat I was wearing on Independence Day." She took a sip of coffee. "It was a gift from Mr. Bennett."

Cora paused as she lifted her cup. Her eyebrows raised and she tilted her head. "Is that so? I thought you'd purchased it with the money you earned."

"Hardly. What I earned at both Cooper House and McBride's was stolen from the room I was occupying. I left there with a total of three dollars and change." She picked up one of the scones and went on to explain that the usual occupant of the room had been about to return. "I saw no choice but to accept Mr. Bennett's offer."

Cora nodded and drank from the coffee cup. "So what are the complications?"

Della described the gift of the necklace and the lovely hand mirror. "He's been very proper in every other way. I tried to discourage his generosity, but his response was that a girl like me deserved nice things. I also worry that he might deduct the value of the gifts from my wages. I've yet to receive the first month's pay. I'd really be in a pickle then. I just don't know what to think."

Nellie and little Georgie came into the kitchen. The boy spied the plate of scones and started trying to reach them. "Cookie, cookie."

Della handed each child a scone while Cora stood and went to the stove, brought the coffee pot to the table, and refilled the cups. "Take your brother out on the porch," she said. "Keep him out of mischief while Della and I visit."

Nellie made a face, but took Georgie's hand and led him away.

In less than a minute, the screen door banged. Buster and Billie rushed into the kitchen like a whirlwind. Davie wasn't far behind.

"Nellie said you got scones," Buster said, panting and sweaty from play.

Della smiled and handed them each a treat.

"Say thank you to Della. She brought them."

"Thank you," they said in unison and proceeded to stuff their mouths.

"Now scoot," Cora said, returning the pot to the stove.

She settled again. "You're probably not going to like my advice. But if I were your age and a rich & honorable man took an interest in me, I don't think I'd discourage him. The likes of Mr. Bennett might not come along again."

Chapter 51

Cora was right. Della didn't think much of the advice she'd been given. As she and Davie climbed the sloping road back to the house that day, it seemed to her that Cora never had any other ambition beyond her marriage and children. They were a nice family and all, but Della wasn't sure she'd be that easily satisfied.

Becoming a concert pianist had been her dream. She'd imagined herself poised on a stage with an audience waiting for her performance. It would be so moving that the people would rise to their feet and applaud when she finished. She glanced at her gloved hands. It had been over a year since she'd practiced her best pieces. Lessons would have to begin all over again. There'd be an expense involved. Surely her brother would support her in that. Or would he? She drew in a deep breath. One thing was certain. She wouldn't know until she reached home.

Anyway, it had been nice to spend time with Cora. She'd heard the news about the church's Ladies' Aid Society, that Mrs. Samples was no longer in charge and rather unhappy about it. Also, that there was some new ventilation system in the mine that had caused an old fire to go out, which made the work a shade less miserable for men like Will Hovey.

Davie had had a good time playing with Cora's boys, though he'd scraped his knee and now needed a bath. He'd run off a good deal of his energy and was lagging behind by the time they reached High Street.

"Let's hurry," she said, reaching for his hand. "It's almost noon, and I'm sure Mrs. Molina will have something good to eat waiting for us."

Hot summer days wore on, often broken by afternoon rain storms that rushed over the town with thunder and lightning frightful enough to make people cringe and sometimes even disrupt the power supply.

And then on the first day of August, Mr. Bennett emerged from his office and approached Della in the dining room where she was using a set of dominos to demonstrate to Davie how numbers could be counted.

He handed her one of the envelopes he had in his hand. "I believe this is the amount we agreed upon, including the last week of June."

She took the envelope, thanked him with a quick smile, and tucked it into her apron pocket. If she were honest, she'd have to admit she'd been thinking about the fact that it was payday all morning. She'd calculated the sum and mentally added it to the small amount she still had saved. The total wasn't half what she needed for the train ticket.

Later when she looked at the contents of the envelope in private, it was evident that the gifts were in reality, just that, gifts. That fact didn't do much to relieve her anxiety over her association with her employer.

At dinner that evening, as Mr. Bennett passed the dishes of food, he announced he would be leaving again on Thursday's train. "I may be away longer than usual as my business partners have a mine they want me to inspect. Perhaps when I return, we could go on a picnic trip to the lake."

"Can we go fishing like Uncle Dan?" Davie asked.

"We shall see, we shall see," Mr. Bennett responded. "Do you favor fishing, Miss McCrea?"

"Why yes. There's a fine lake just a few miles from my home. It was our favorite place for picnics. And my grandfather's farm had a small lake with plenty of fish."

"Uncle Dan goes to a big lake," Davie said. "He catches lotsa fish."

Mr. Bennett chuckled and picked up his knife and fork. "Yes, son. I agree your uncle is the best fisherman. Now let's eat our supper."

When Thursday morning arrived, Della watched the same parting scene between father and son as before, however, this time, Mr. Bennett left so early that Davie was still in his nightshirt when they both waved their goodbyes.

The day followed with what was becoming a routine. First a lesson of some kind, then a lively game before the noon meal. During the hot afternoon Davie entertained himself in his room while Della worked on the doily she was crocheting.

That night, screams coming from Davie's room woke Della. She bounded from her bed, pressed the light switch and rushed to his bedside. She found him sitting upright in bed, his unseeing eyes wild with fear. She wrapped her arms around his rigid body. "There, there now. You're alright. I won't let anything hurt you."

It took several minutes before she felt him finally relax. Oddly, he hadn't seemed to fully awaken. She laid him down, pulled the sheet over him, and returned to her room. As she settled once more, she wondered about his sleepwalking and the nightmare. Were they related to his father's frequent trips? She'd never had such experiences herself but thought it seemed like a terrible thing for a child.

In the morning, he didn't remember his bad dream when she asked him. He ate his breakfast and hurried to take his train out on the front porch to play.

After Della finished her coffee, she carried the breakfast dishes to the kitchen sink. She took the heating kettle from the stove and poured the steaming water into the dishpan. She could have left the cleanup to Mrs. Molina, but she valued the woman's company. As she washed the dishes, she related the problem.

Mrs. Molina stopped mixing flour in the bowl on the table in front of her and listened. When Della finished her account of the night, she asked. "Do you think he'll *always* have nightmares, even when he grown up?"

"*Si, si. Los ninos...* how you say ... grow up ... *muy rápido.*" With her hands covered with flour, she continued in Spanish, sentences Della didn't understand but got the impression that her opinion, like Della's mother, was that her children grew up too soon. It didn't seem that Della had communicated her concern very well. Though perplexed, she nodded and smiled, then excused herself to go tidy the bedrooms.

When she returned downstairs sometime later, the aroma of spicy beans simmering on the stove filled the air. She stepped to the kitchen doorway and found Davie watching Mrs. Molina. She stood at the work table with a ball of dough in her hands, flipping it back and forth and stretching it until it flattened out.

"Davie, come away," Della said. "Don't bother Mrs. Molina."

He twisted around. "She's making pancakes." He pointed to the short pile of circular flat dough. "See."

The cook grinned. "*Es no* pancakes. *Es tortillas.*"

Davie grinned. "I like ... *tortiyas*," he declared.

Chapter 52

Much to the delight of his son, Mr. Bennett arrived home late the following Monday just as the sun was setting. The boy had been waiting on the porch for hours, climbing the railing in one place or another.

When the buggy came into view, he scrambled down the steps to greet his father with boisterous enthusiasm. The noise brought Della out the front door. Mr. Bennett nodded to his son while he listened to his chatter, extracted his suitcase from the buggy and paid the driver. He carried the bag up the steps and inside, where he set it down. "I'm famished, but I must get washed up first. Is there anything left from supper?"

"I'll prepare a plate for you whenever you are ready," Della said.

"Good." Hiram headed for the hall and disappeared up the stairs with Davie tagging along behind.

Della went to the kitchen, stirred the coals in the stove, and added a piece of wood from the woodbox. She filled a plate with a slice of meat from the icebox, added leftover potatoes and a scoop of boiled carrots, then put the plate in the oven to warm before grabbing a fistful of utensils to set the table.

When Hiram returned downstairs and entered the dining room, he looked refreshed. His face was clean, his hair combed and he'd shaved. He seated himself at the table and Davie quickly scooted onto the chair next to him.

Mr. Bennett grinned when Della set the plate in front of him and began his meal with a forkful of potatoes.

Della poured a cup of coffee for her employer and one for herself before seating herself across the table. While Mr. Bennett ate, he described the mine he'd inspected and the town near where it was located.

Sunlight coming in the dining room window had all but faded by the time he'd finished. He heaved a sigh, thanked Della, and excused himself to go to his favorite chair in the parlor, leaving Della to clear the table and cart the remains of the meal to the kitchen.

Davie followed his father and leaned over the arm of the chair as Hiram switched on the lamp. He patted the boy on the back. "Son, it's been a very long day. How about you slide my bag over here? I have something for you."

Davie wasted no time in pushing the suitcase to his father's feet. Hiram bent forward and opened the latch. Lifting the lid, he extracted a box wrapped in brown paper and handed it to the boy, who quickly ripped off the covering.

Davie squealed when he found a toy train car inside. "Gee whiz. Thanks, Dad." He looked at his father expectantly for permission to go play. Hiram smiled, motioned his consent, and reached for a copy of the Mining News on the lamp table.

The boy rushed past Della in the hall as she approached the parlor. "Is there anything else I can get for you?" she asked Hiram when she entered the room.

He stood and motioned to the blue-cushioned sofa. "No. Please come and rest yourself."

Della stepped forward, gathered her skirt, and settled herself, happy for the chance to relax for a moment. She pulled out the sewing basket she kept at the side of the couch under the lamp table and removed one of Davie's socks that had a hole in the toe.

Mr. Bennett laid the newspaper beside the lamp and moved to sit on the sofa next to her, an action that made her a little uneasy. She allowed the mending to rest in her lap, turning her attention to her employer.

He cleared his throat. "There's something I must tell you. The Four Kings Mining Company has bought a mine in Illinois. I am to run the entire operation. To do that, I'll need to relocate to Chicago."

She stiffened. It meant she'd be out of a job and still didn't have enough money for a train ticket to Ohio.

"I want you and Davie to go with me," he said and reached for Della's hand.

She pulled it away. "It would be unseemly for an unmarried woman to travel unchaperoned with a man." She dropped the sock back into the basket and rose abruptly. "I'm sure I can find work elsewhere."

Consternation flooded his face. "I wasn't thinking in that manner. Please. Please sit down."

She lowered herself to the edge of the sofa, her brow furrowing as she did so.

He folded his hands in his lap. "My son is almost five years old. He needs a mother. You need a home and someone to provide for you. I know I'm a good deal older than you, but if you would consent to marriage, it'd be a good bargain, don't you think?"

"A bargain? I've never thought of marriage as a *bargain*. I, uh. Sir, I don't know quite how to respond. You have taken me by surprise. I need time to think."

"Understandable, I'm sure. However, I must tell you I'm expected to be settled in Chicago by the end of the month. Please, give it some consideration." He stood. "I have an urgent matter I must take care of. I'll be in my office."

As soon as he was out of sight, Della rose, still reeling from this new development, and went out to stand on the front porch. She gazed out over the town and toward the valley below without really seeing it and wrapped an arm around the porch post. "Dear God, what should I do?" she whispered.

His offer would be a chance to get out of Arizona Territory and Chicago was a lot closer to home. But marriage! What would it be like married to someone so much older than herself? It was obvious he was well off, and he traveled so often he couldn't be much bother. He'd likely provide a good home. She'd become very fond of Davie. Parting with the boy would be most distressing.

Her knees turned to jelly. She clung to the pillar for several minutes weighing the alternatives. The prospect of saloon work again with sleepless nights and unruly miners was appalling. Was this her only option? She returned inside and went to knock on the office door.

"Yes? Come in."

She eased the door open and saw that he was sitting at his desk, a folio of papers spread open before him. He looked up, expectantly.

"Sir, a lady needs time to consider such an important decision. I would like to 'sleep on it,' as the saying goes."

He nodded thoughtfully. "Perfectly understandable."

Della nearly wore the sheets out that night, tossing and turning. And it wasn't the desert heat that kept her awake. She ran all her choices through her mind a dozen times before hearing the grandfather clock downstairs strike four, but by then she'd made a decision.

When she'd excused Davie from the breakfast table, she folded her napkin and turned to Mr. Bennett. "I suppose your proposal could benefit both of us. But I have something to toss into the *bargain*."

He leaned back in the chair, his eyes widening. "What is it?"

"I want you to promise me that you'll take me home to visit my family as soon as we reach Illinois."

Crinkles formed around his eyes as he smiled. "We'll need to get settled first, but I think we can manage that."

"No. I want more assurance. I want you to promise."

He tilted his head. "All right. I promise." Then looking directly at her, he said. "Well then, if we are in agreement, we'll take the train to Phoenix and be married at the end of the week."

"I'm afraid that will be too soon. My oldest brother is my guardian. I'll have to write to him for permission."

"I don't see why. There are no such rules in Arizona Territory."

"Well, what about Davie? Who will care for him while we are away?"

"We can take him with us."

Della threw him a look of disdain. "Perhaps Cora Hovey would be willing to keep him for a few days."

"Good thought." He nodded. "Yessiree. That settles it." He rubbed his hands together and grinned. "We'll take the train to Phoenix and be married on Friday. We can spend the weekend there. And when we return, we'll pack our belongings and be off to Chicago."

Della took a deep breath and let it out, still not sure she'd made the right decision.

Chapter 53

More than once, Della came close to knocking on Mr. Bennett's office door and reneging on their agreement. The thing that stopped her was the thought that if she refused him, he'd likely dismiss her, and no one else in this wrenched town would pay near as well. Everything considered, she had no sensible alternative.

When they reached Chicago and he took her to visit her family, she would simply refuse to return with him. With the help of her brothers, she would divorce him, though the thought of how it would affect the boy nearly brought tears.

The next day she dressed Davie in play clothes and walked down the hillside to talk with Cora. When Della told her about her upcoming marriage and the reason for her visit, Cora's mouth opened in surprise.

"You won't be sorry," she said. "He will provide a fine living. You may not realize it now, but you're a very fortunate young woman. Yes, he's much older than you, but someday you'll be a rich widow."

Della took little comfort in Cora's view of her situation. She might be right, but Della had never envisioned herself married to a man so much older than her. Could she ever be like her friend, satisfied with her lot in life? Somehow, she doubted it.

Cora readily agreed to have Davie stay with her family as long as needed. After an hour of catching up on neighborhood news, Della gave Cora a hug and told Davie it was time to leave. He scowled and pouted, but when Della told him he would be returning to stay for a few days, the boy grinned instead.

When Friday morning rolled around, Della rose soon after dawn and went to the armoire. She decided the gray dress would be best for traveling. She dressed quickly. Deciding that the white batiste would be her wedding dress, she took it out, laid it on the bed and carefully folded it. Opening her valise, she filled the bottom with the necessaries, plus her hair brush and extra combs to fix her hair, then laid the dress on top.

A veil. She'd need a veil. The only thing she had was a white linen handkerchief. It would have to do. She opened her sewing basket, reshaped the handkerchief with her scissors, and trimmed it with lace stolen from her spare petticoat. After brushing and arranging her hair, she was ready as she ever was going to be.

The distance between Jerome and Phoenix was 111 miles, the first leg being the narrow-gauge railway out of Jerome. The second was on the Santa Fe line, continuing another five hours to reach Phoenix.

When they arrived at their destination, the sun was high in the sky. Hiram engaged a buggy at the station to take them to a hotel. The building had five floors with a glass door at the entrance. Inside, he rented a room for the weekend and after depositing their bags there, he led her into the dining room for the noon meal. After he'd ordered the food, he reached in his pocket and took out a small box. Popping open the hinged lid, he watched Della's reaction. Inside, a ring with several translucent stones reflected the sunlight filtering through the curtained window next to the table.

He removed the ring and reached for her hand. "A fine ring for a beautiful lady," he said, sliding it onto her ring finger.

Della drew a quick breath, knowing it had to have cost a great sum. "Oh my! It's stunning." She flashed him a smile, hardly able to concentrate on the forthcoming meal. She kept admiring how it sparkled and how her sisters would be aghast when they saw it. Between the gift of the ring and her nervousness, Della ate very little of the meal.

When Hiram finally laid his napkin aside, she said, "I wish to change into a dress more appropriate for a wedding."

"By all means," Hiram said, smiling. "I wait here for you."

She rose and made her way to the room where she removed the gray dress and slipped into the white batiste. She took the time to adjust the arrangement of combs in her hair. Before leaving, she studied her likeness in the mirror. "This should be the happiest day of your life," she said to her reflection. "Look at you. You look like you're going to a funeral."

She stepped out into the hall, fixed a smile on her face and closed the door, returning to where Hiram was waiting.

"You look lovely," he said, his eyes shining with admiration. He reached for her hand. "I have the buggy waiting outside."

Phoenix was a small city, so it didn't take long before the buggy driver came to a stop in front of a red brick building with a sign in front indicating that it was the county courthouse. Hiram climbed out onto the road's rough dirt surface and turned to assist Della. When she was safely on the ground, he signaled to the driver. "Please wait. We won't be long."

He held the door open for Della, and inside, she trailed along behind him, their footsteps echoing in an empty hallway. The doors to the various offices had frosted glass windows with gold lettering to identify the different departments. When they reached the office of the Justice of the Peace, Hiram escorted Della inside.

A baldheaded man with bushy eyebrows rose from behind a desk and walked to the counter. "How may I help you?"

Hiram grinned. "We're here to be married," he said.

The official took a paper from a nearby shelf and laid it in front of them. As he asked questions to fill out the form, Della discovered Hiram wasn't as old as she had guessed. The fact distracted her, causing her to hesitate while answering the man's questions which in turn, caused Hiram to give her a quizzical glance.

With all the information filled in, the man turned the document around on the countertop for each of them to sign. Signatures in place, he grinned. "Congratulations. I can see you're a very lucky man."

"Yessiree." Hiram beamed and leaned to tenderly kiss Della on the cheek.

Back outside, her new husband took her by the elbow and assisted her into the waiting buggy. They returned to the hotel where they would have their wedding dinner. Hiram spoke to the hotel staff about a special meal. They were gracious and bubbled congratulations.

Della wasn't a fool. She knew where babies came from and how they got there. She'd spent many summers visiting her grandfather's farm. Plus, her sister had shared some of the particulars of her own wedding night and had lectured her on the duties of a wife in hopes that it would prepare Della when her turn came.

But even with that knowledge, Della was surprised. Hiram had said he would be gentle, and she supposed he was, by his standards. But afterward, when she heard him snoring, she felt confused. She'd thought her wedding night would make her love him. Lying there she wondered if that could ever happen. He was so much older. Her parents had been closer in age, but even then, she'd never seen any open signs of affection between them. It seemed that their everyday actions defined their feelings for each other. Was that what marriages were supposed to be like?

Quietly turning over, she stared at the lights of the city through the hotel window and vowed to make him keep his promise. She knew it would be sinful, but nonetheless, when she finally reached home and her family, she would seek a divorce. But what about the boy? She shook her head and turned over again. He wasn't her child, not her responsibility. Her fondness for him was of little consequence.

As they sat at the breakfast table in the hotel dining room the next morning, she smiled sweetly as she filled his coffee cup a second time from the coffee urn. "You won't forget your promise, will you?"

He looked up at her. His expression puzzled her. Had he not understood that the only reason she married him was because of that promise?

He lifted the cup and took a sip. "Of course not," he finally said. "We'll visit your family in due time."

Chapter 54

Following the morning meal, they gathered their belongings from the room, descended the stairs, and climbed into one of the waiting buggies at the entrance of the hotel to take them to the train station. The distance wasn't long and there was the usual flurry of noise, bustling people, and smoke from the engine.

Once settled for the return train trip to Jerome, Della allowed her thoughts to wander, thinking about the upcoming move to Chicago, the next step to going home.

The last leg of the trip on United Verde's narrow gauge was just as nerve-wracking as the day she'd first arrived in Arizona Territory. She couldn't help but hold her breath when the train passed alongside the ragged drop-offs, but the knowledge that she would soon be leaving all of it behind served to lift her spirits.

When they finally arrived in the center of Jerome and had left the coach that had brought them there, she raised her parasol and walked along as Hiram led the way to the post office to collect the mail.

"I'm anxious to hear from the Four Kings Mining Company," he said as they entered the building. He made his request to the postman and watched as the man dug into one of the many cubbyholes along the post office wall. The man extracted two envelopes and handed them to Hiram, who opened one of them and scanned the page.

"The purchase of the mine in Illinois will take at least another sixty days," he said. "Looks like we'll have to remain in Jerome until I receive word to proceed."

She didn't comment. Her shoulders sagged. Two more months on that god-forsaken rock pile.

A few weeks after they returned to the house in Jerome, Della woke one morning feeling unwell. She dressed, but neglected her hair, and went to the kitchen thinking a cup of tea would settle her digestion. Her stomach revolted at the first sip. She bolted out the kitchen door and deposited the contents in the bushes beside the wash house.

Mrs. Molina, who had been kneading dough on the work table, gave her a quizzical look when she returned from outside.

After Della visited the same shrubbery on two subsequent mornings, all doubt faded. She recalled her sister's complaint before her first baby. She dragged herself up the stairs, and flopped on her back on the bed. "My life is ruined," she declared, covering her face with her hands. "My family will never condone a divorce when I'm carrying the man's child."

Rolling over, she sat up. "What am I to do?" Her father would say a man had a right to know when he was about to be a father. But how would Mr. Bennett react to the news? If she told him, he might postpone the resettlement to Chicago for the sake of her health. Leaving the desert hillside was her greatest desire.

Della could barely raise her head off the pillow the following morning. Her stomach felt sour. She reached under the bed for the chamber pot in case she couldn't make it down the stairs. She gritted her teeth and lay quietly in an effort to control the nausea. Time didn't help, so she eased out of bed, dressed, and combed her hair.

The following weekend, when she appeared at the breakfast table looking like she'd been visited by a vampire, Hiram set his coffee cup on the saucer and reached for her hand. "My dear, you seem unwell. Perhaps you need to see a doctor."

She took in a deep breath. "No, Mr. Bennett. A doctor is not required. The simple fact is that in due time Davie will have a new brother or sister."

Hiram broke into a broad smile. "I can't tell you how happy this makes me. Don't you worry about a thing, my dear. I will see to it you get the best of care." He released her hand and leaned back. "And after the child is born, we'll find a nanny to help you." He was still grinning when he laid his napkin aside. He stood, then leaned over and gave Della a kiss on her cheek. "I must meet Mr. Daily at the bank. I'll be in town most of the day. You need your rest. Tell Davie to be quiet and amuse himself."

Indeed, her enthusiasm for playing games with the boy had faded. Between the morning nausea and a listlessness she'd never experienced before, she found herself distracted. The boy spent most of the morning playing in his room which led her to think his father must have said something to him.

By afternoon that day, she was feeling better and decided she'd take Davie and visit Cora. But first, she stopped in the kitchen to talk to Mrs. Molina. She found her busy slicing a slab of bacon.

She stood in the doorway for a moment before approaching. "Has Mr. Bennett told you that we will soon be leaving to live in Chicago?"

The older woman nodded. "*Si.*"

"But it won't be for another couple of months. We're going to miss your cooking."

Mrs. Molina's expression didn't change, she simply smiled and nodded.

Della wasn't sure if the woman understood, but hand signals wouldn't work in this case, so she gave up. She went to open the back door and call Davie. "Come along now," she said to him. "I want to go visit Mrs. Hovey."

It was late September but the mid-day was quite warm, the heat radiating off the sandy surface and roadway. They took every shortcut they dared and when they reached the Hovey's front door Cora greeted her like a long-lost sister.

The Hovey boys were in school, so Davie had only little Georgie to play with, but he didn't seem to mind. Cora made fresh coffee and they sat at the kitchen table as before.

"Tell me all the news," Cora said. "How is married life treating you?" So many questions tumbled from Cora's mouth that Della had a hard time keeping up.

Finally, she interrupted. "Cora, I've come to say goodbye. We'll soon be moving to Chicago."

"Chicago?" Cora said with a slight scowl. "I've heard it's a crime-ridden city. I hope you'll find a safe place to live."

Della laughed. "It's probably no more crime-ridden than when we first arrived here in Jerome. It was a hothouse of gambling and painted ladies not too long ago."

The two of them chatted for over an hour, sharing all the news of the neighborhood, the most recent mine accident, and even the price of eggs.

"I'm anxious for the move," Della said. "It's been a long two years since I've seen my family and he's promised me a visit. But I will miss you. I'll write. I promise. And maybe I can send you a photo of the baby."

"You're going to have a baby? You scamp! You leave the most important news for last."

Della nodded and grinned, then glanced out the kitchen window and noticed the late afternoon haze from the mine works. "I must be on my way." She stood and called Davie.

Cora rose from the chair and gave Della a hug. They parted at the door, each with tears barely controlled.

Shortly before noon the next day Hiram entered the house and called out, "Della. I have something to show you." He stood at the dining room table and smoothed out a page torn from a catalog. He turned as she entered the room. "Here's a picture of the house in Chicago where we'll be living."

She walked over and stood beside him. Looking at the picture, she almost gasped. The dwelling was impressive, a mansion compared to the family home where she'd grown up. The two-story house had a turret on the front with a wrap-around porch, plus a grassed yard, a place for Davie to play. But what she felt was the best part was that it sat on flat ground with a paved street. No more struggling along slag-covered roads that twisted and curved. "It'll be a fine place to raise our children," he said. "It's a good neighborhood with a trolley system within walking distance, and I think there's even a park not far away. We'll be settled in well before Thanksgiving."

A month later, as the Southern Pacific railway train carried them northeast and away from the desert, the vast plains in the middle of the country stretched out in golden wheat fields on either side of the tracks through Kansas and Nebraska. But Della's mind was not on the rich scenery. She was anxious for the miles to slip rapidly under the wheels of the locomotive. She had packed every single bit of clothing into her trunk for she never intended to return to the stark hills of Arizona Territory.

Instead, her mind was on the home of her childhood, the maple tree branches that hung over the streets, the cool breeze from the river in the evening, and the smiles and laughter of her brothers and sisters. She wondered if motherhood had made Etta fat like so many women. She hoped not. Would Lizzie be there, still recovering from her bout of poor health?

Would her brothers be taller and more handsome and have girls mooning over them? She smiled at the thought. They, like their father before her mother's illness, had ready smiles, sparkling blue eyes, and quick wits. The house had been full of good Irish humor.

Though she still suffered from some degree of upset stomach each morning, the powerful grip it initially had on her seemed to be lessening. The trip was tedious in all respects, despite the fact that they spent their nights in the Pullman car. So when the big locomotive ground to a stop in Grand Central Station on Harrison Street, she could hardly wait to set her feet on the ground.

She took Davie by the hand and followed as Hiram moved quickly to procure a carriage to take them to their new home.

Upon arrival, Della had to admit that the house was impressive looking, especially its rich green color and the carving on the portico.

Inside, she admired the size of the parlor, larger than the one they'd left behind. The four bedrooms upstairs were adequate with bedsteads already in place. However, it was the kitchen she most admired. It had a modern stove and running water. No more pumping water; she could simply turn on the tap. The outside washroom had electricity and Hiram promised a modern washing machine.

The wind blew every afternoon while Della and the maid Hiram had hired helped unpack the trunks. The linens and bedding, dishes and silverware, along with other belongings she couldn't bear to leave behind had been packed in trunks and wooden boxes for shipment. New furnishings arrived every day, all of which kept Della busy assigning places for it.

However, she insisted the work of settling the house pause long enough to make a cake to celebrate Davie's fifth birthday on October 1st. His eyes sparkled in the light of the candles she lit. She had mentioned his special day to his father before he left for work, so the boy was especially excited when he was presented with a gift wrapped in colorful paper. He wasted no time unwrapping it, and squealed with delight at the sight of more train cars and additional train tracks to add to his collection.

As a result of all the activity of getting settled in their new home, it was nearly a month before Della mentioned Hiram's promise of a visit to her family.

"It's almost 300 miles," Hiram said. "I'm not convinced it's a good idea to risk such a trip in your condition."

So close and yet so far, Della thought. "Oh, I'm feeling much better every day now. I'm really concerned about Aunt Gertrude. Her letters have been very short recently and she never mentions my brother, Richard. The last time I heard from my sister, she said he was thinking about getting married. I'm wondering what happened. If we wait much longer, it will be winter."

As if to confirm Della's forecast, a fast-moving storm arrived that evening and left a dusting of snow to cover the city.

Chapter 55

No amount of snow was going to deter Della from reminding Hiram of his promise. She even walked to the train station to obtain a copy of the schedule of trains running between Chicago and Dayton. He could hardly ignore such a reminder when he found it beside his coffee cup the next morning.

He threw up his hands. "Alright, alright. I agree, we need to make the trip before winter sets in. I'll get the tickets on Monday. But we can't stay. For now, it'll have to be a short visit. I have too much going on at work."

It was early November in Della's hometown when they stepped off the train. The trees along the streets were shedding their fall colors of red, orange and gold. The sky was gunmetal gray. Della was wearing the new winter coat Hiram had bought for her. Since relocating to Chicago warmer clothing was required for the whole family. But none of that was on Della's mind as the carriage Hiram had engaged turned onto Carson Avenue. Her heart was thumping and she leaned forward, glancing at the familiar neighborhood homes as they drove past them.

"There it is!" She pointed to a house in the middle of the block. Hiram guided the vehicle over to stop at the curb in front.

Her back instantly stiffened as she gazed at the building, hardly believing what she saw. The shutters, once a deep blue, were faded and paint-chipped in spots. One of the window screens hung loose. The box elder bushes by the front porch steps were like two dead sentinels. For a split second, she thought she'd made a mistake.

She glanced at her husband, wondering his reaction. As if he took no notice, he opened the carriage door and stepped out. She didn't wait for him to come around to open the passenger side, but left the carriage and stood a moment staring at the house. How could her brothers let this happen to their home?

Though the condition of the house was unsettling, she hurried around the vehicle toward the porch. With Hiram and the boy right behind her, she lifted her skirt to climb the concrete steps to the entrance.

Knowing the door was never locked, Della didn't hesitate to open it and step inside. She glanced around the parlor. The furnishings looked the same as when she'd left.

"Hello! Anybody home?" she called out. Hearing a noise in the kitchen, she moved in that direction.

Her Aunt Gertrude appeared in the kitchen doorway. Looking like an old crone, she gripped a cane and squinted as she shuffled toward them. She peered at Della as if she were a stranger. When the realization came, the old woman's face creased and tears filled her eyes.

"You've come home! Praise God!" she exclaimed, her free hand flying to her heart. "I'd nearly given up. What day is this? Oh my, but it's a joy to see you." Then turning, she hurried to the bottom of the stairway to the second floor.

"Lon! Come down. Della's come home." She fished a handkerchief out of her apron pocket and wiped an eye as Della introduced her husband.

A moment later, Lon appeared at the top of the stairs, hair disheveled and red-eyed. He gave his nose a swipe and descended to the parlor.

"Please, make yourselves comfortable." Aunt Gertrude said, motioning with her cane. "I'll make some coffee and telephone Etta."

Della settled onto the brown divan. She patted the cushion next to her and motioned to Davie, while Hiram seated himself in a nearby matching chair.

"Did you get my letter?" Della asked, looking at her brother. "Where's Richard?"

Lon ran his fingers through his hair and moved over to occupy another cushioned chair. "Oh, he married the Olsen girl last June and moved to Minnesota. He's hoping to find work there."

Though crippled as she was with arthritis, Aunt Gertrude managed to bring in a tray with Grandma McCrea's coffee cups and flowered coffee urn. She set it on the library table. The old lady filled the cups and served everyone, then eased down into the rocking chair.

Della took a sip and noted that it didn't taste fresh, concluding that her aunt must have simply heated the morning's brew. "Where's Lizzie?" Della asked. "I thought she was looking for a school position around here."

"No," Lon answered. "When she recovered from the pneumonia, she went back to her teaching job over in Indiana."

Della took another sip. The room felt rather chilly. It made her wonder if they were conserving coal.

The front door opened, letting in a gust of cold air. Etta entered along with her three young sons and carrying baby Ruth in her arms.

Della quickly set her cup aside and rose to embrace her sister, then leaned back to look at the baby. "Oh, Etta. She's a beauty, and she has your blue eyes." She gently stroked the baby's cheek, then she turned to her nephews. "My goodness.

Look at you boys. You've all grown a foot, and so handsome." She ruffled the youngest one's blond hair.

Hiram rose from the chair he'd been sitting in, and Della turned to introduce him and his son to her sister.

Etta told her boys to sit on the hearth and be quiet. They were dressed in rough overalls and stared intently at Davie whose clothing was more in line with what a city boy would wear.

Della resumed her seat and during the following hours of conversation, she described the train trip across the country and commented about how glad she was to see the fall colors again after living on a dry mountainside.

When she asked her brother about his job prospects, he shrugged. "It's past harvest time. No work now till spring."

"I wish Lizzie were here," Aunt Gertrude chimed in.

Etta related the sad state of the year's harvest, that granary had had to lay off workers and the fact that they would need to borrow from the bank in order to plant in the spring.

"I was beginning to think we'd never see you again," Aunt Gertrude said. "Do you suppose we can all get together for Thanksgiving?"

Della glanced at Hiram and then out the window. It was starting to snow. "It will depend on the weather, I suppose." She put her cup on the tray.

Hiram also noted the falling snow. "I'm sorry," he said. "But it will be dark soon. We must return the carriage to the livery. We'd better leave."

"We're taking the night train," Della explained.

Aunt Gertrude's jaw sagged. "You mean you're not here to stay?"

"I'm afraid not, Auntie," Della said. "We have a home in Chicago."

After a several moments of protests, apologies and hugs all around, Della, Hiram and Davie walked out into a cold wind. Della pulled her coat tight around her and let her gaze fall on the pavement. This wasn't the home she remembered, the one she'd been longing for over the last two years. It seemed old and shabby. The warm and loving atmosphere was gone. It appeared that life was an everyday struggle now.

"Mr. Bennett, I am so embarrassed," she said as they walked back to the carriage. "My family seems to have fallen on hard times." She pulled a handkerchief from her purse, ready to wipe her nose. "I don't know what to think. So much has changed since my parents and I left Ohio, far more than family letters revealed."

Hiram took her arm and patted her hand. "If your brother is willing to move to Chicago, I could find employment for him. The economy is expanding. There are plenty of jobs there." He reached to open the carriage door for her. "And your aunt could come and live with us. The house is certainly big enough."

It was a surprising offer, but one so typical of him. All during the ride back to the hotel, she pondered the path her life had taken. Hiram was a good man and though she'd never conceived of marrying someone as old as him, she had to admit that he was a good husband, far better than she'd expected. He had a generous heart and his son was a treasure. She looked up at her husband and smiled. It was going to be alright. She had her own family now and fair prospects of a better future, something that a year earlier had seemed impossible. As all these thoughts settled in her mind, her attention was drawn to the stirring of a new life in her body.

The End